A LONG WAY BACK

J. Everett Prewitt

A Northland Publishing Company Book
Copyright © 2015 by J. Everett Prewitt

For information, address:
Northland Publishing Company
11811 Shaker Boulevard
Cleveland, Ohio 44120

Library of Congress Control Number: 2016907511
ISBN-978-0-9761927-5-6
ISBN-0-9761927-5-6

This book is dedicated to

my parents

Margaret Ann Prewitt

1914-2010

and

Selmer E. Prewitt

1908-2004

ACKNOWLEDGEMENTS

This book would not have been possible without the input of a number of people. I would especially like to thank my writer's group: Sarah Wiseley Croley, John Kavouras, and Barbara Hacha, author, who were instrumental in helping me develop this story. I want to thank my muse, Sandra Upton-Houston. Vietnam combat veterans Norman Mays, Major, USA (ret), Ernie Jones, Captain, USA (ret) and Julius Nichols, Captain, USA (reserves)— my lifelong friends and fellow Glenville High School alumni who contributed significantly in helping this novel take shape. I also want to thank my good friends Richard Baker, Sergeant, USMC (ret) and James Copeland, Sergeant, USA (ret), also Vietnam combat veterans, who shared their experiences so I could tell this story.

I want to give special acknowledgment to Wallace Terry, (deceased), journalist and author of *Bloods*, who shared many of his experiences when he visited with me during a portion of his time in Vietnam. And to my sister, my daughter, and my son, who have been my biggest fans and a continuous source of inspiration.

Adapt or perish, now as ever, is nature's inexorable imperative.

—H. G. Wells

I am not afraid of an army of lions led by a sheep;
I am afraid of an army of sheep led by a lion.

—Alexander the Great

CAST OF CHARACTERS

Anthony Andrews: The reporter who doggedly pursues the story while forced to confront the shock of combat, a deteriorating family life, and a group of soldiers unwilling to relive the nightmares of war.

Sergeant Willie Stinson: The reluctant leader who has spent his whole life swimming upstream. This venture is no different, having to combat the enemy with an inexperienced force and the war weariness that comes from fighting too many battles.

Sanford "Rabid" Fletcher: Second-in-command. A former gang leader who rails against any authority and becomes a disruptive force while his fellow soldiers are trying to survive.

Myron "Professor" Turner: Instrumental in saving his fellow soldier's lives because of his ability to foresee events.

Leroy "Tank" Casper: A leader and stabilizing force. Although third-in-command, he rallies the troops to keep pushing during the most dangerous times and when they are at their lowest.

Raphael "Lucky" Holland: Joined the Army to become strong. Mission accomplished unless drugs become a burden his recently acquired manhood can't overcome.

Marcus Glover: His quick temper almost gets him killed, but he maintains strength under the worst of conditions.

Xavier Warfield: A fastidious dresser who becomes a good friend, and a better warrior.

Clarence "Country" Bankston: Playful but lethal when he has to employ his combat skills to save his fellow soldiers.

Erving "Preacher" Robinson: A soldier molded by religion; transformed by war.

PART I

CHAPTER 1

The two words swept through the mess hall like a northeastern wind blowing across Southeast Asia: "They're here!"

It was mid-afternoon, July 1, 1969, in Cu Chi, Vietnam, and the sun was unrelenting. The swirl of dust from the Chinook helicopter created a surreal red and brown mist that coated sweating bodies like a new skin.

As Anthony Andrews gathered with the hushed crowd to watch seven weary-looking soldiers disembark and collect their gear, his eyes narrowed. All seven were black.

But what Anthony noticed more than their color, the torn and ripped uniforms, or the grime covering every inch of their bodies was their eyes: fluttering, darting, haunted. Most of the men looked thin and undernourished. One walked with a limp, one was carried in a poncho, and another, who helped the soldier in the poncho, cursed under his breath.

Anthony pulled out his Yashica camera and took pictures.

"Where are they coming from?" he asked a private first class who stood next to him, mesmerized, his hands poised as if to clap and his eyes tearing.

"Somewhere around War Zone C."

Anthony, unsure where War Zone C was, looked at the soldier whose eyes remained fixated on the men. "What happened there?"

The private never took his eyes off the men as he replied in the softest of voices, "From what I hear, hell happened there."

A military police jeep came to carry the two wounded soldiers. The others, with no one giving a command, gathered themselves, straightened, moved their obviously bone-tired, filthy bodies into formation, and began to march into camp when three more jeeps with MPs came and picked them up, too.

"The 25th Infantry Division in Cu Chi provides the reactionary units combating the Viet Cong insurgency," Anthony had read in a briefing manual when he first arrived.

Those men must have returned from one of those missions, Anthony thought as he turned to locate Major Leonard Rainey Bertram, headquarter battalion's executive officer. As a black reporter assigned to write about the black soldier in Vietnam, he was sure there had to be a story behind the return of those seven men. It was certainly the type the *Washington Post* was looking for, and without a doubt, something Anthony wanted to be the first to tell.

Major Bertram, Anthony's liaison, was standing beside his desk when Anthony found him. Anthony found it odd that in the few days he'd been in Cu Chi, he'd never seen Bertram sit at the desk.

Cu Chi was Bertram's second tour, having commanded a rifle company in the 25th in 1966. At six feet, two inches, the major was a few inches taller than Anthony. With a square jaw that appeared to be permanently clenched, he projected a commanding presence. But as Anthony approached, he watched Bertram's eyes widen as he ducked at the sound of a mortar falling some half-mile away before regaining his composure to greet Anthony.

Anthony ignored Bertram's reaction and his reddened face as he shook the major's hand. "Major. The men who just arrived? Who are they? Where did they come from?"

Bertram glanced down then beyond Anthony. "I'm not sure. We just received word of their return. I'll let you know more when I find out."

"I'd appreciate it, because I'd like to interview them."

Bertram nodded as if he had anticipated the request. "I do know they will have to be debriefed before they can talk."

"How long will that take?" Anthony asked.

Bertram shrugged. "Who knows? Could be days, could be weeks."

Anthony looked at the major a few seconds, head tilted to the side. "Really, Major? Is that standard procedure?" Anthony asked, then hesitated. Although this was the first time he'd been denied immediate access to any soldier, he didn't want to anger his primary source after only a few days in country. Yet, he had a job to do.

"It is in this case." The major pulled papers from a pile on his desk and bent over to sign them.

Anthony straightened up. "Okay." He pulled out a pad, his pen poised to write. "Can I at least get their names?"

"Not yet."

Anthony looked up quizzically, then turned to leave. "Major?" Anthony said as he stopped at the Quonset hut door.

"Yes?"

"The sooner the better for me, okay?"

Bertram nodded.

Anthony wondered if the reason the major never looked him in the eye during their conversation was because of Bertram's embarrassment from his reaction to the mortar round—or because he knew more than he was telling.

It became apparent after a week had passed, it was the latter. Anthony never got the interview, nor did any of the other correspondents, including the Army's *Stars and Stripes* reporter. And he still had no names.

Upset and curious at being closed out, Anthony tried to piece the men's story together from whispers and mutters in the mess hall and barracks.

"Only ones left..."

"Two weeks in the field..."

"Ambush..."

"Lost..."

"Reported MIA..."

"Reported KIA..."

But no one would talk to him directly.

"Sorry, Mr. Andrews—orders."

"It's classified, Mr. Andrews."

"Word from the top," one sergeant related in a whisper, "is anyone caught giving out information on those men will face an immediate court martial."

"Can they do that?" Anthony asked.

The sergeant shrugged. "Who wants to be the first to find out?"

CHAPTER 2

Anthony Andrews had arrived in Saigon on June 25, 1969. The acrid sewer smell and the stifling blast-furnace heat assaulted his nose and body as soon as he stepped off the plane. But the anxiety of visiting a country at war trumped all his senses.

Duong Thu Huong, a man whose head barely reached the height of the omnipresent motorbikes zipping along the uneven streets throughout the city, met Anthony at the airport. In a jeep that rattled and shook even in neutral, Thu Huong drove Anthony to a storefront office off Tu Do Street, where Anthony filled out forms to obtain his South Vietnamese and American press ID cards.

Already wary, Anthony recoiled from a Vietnamese man rushing from a store he and Thu Huong passed. He scolded himself for over-reacting as the man hurried in the opposite direction. As he looked around, though, it seemed tension shrouded everyone like an article of clothing.

Before being driven to the air base, Thu Huong had recommended a restaurant where Anthony ate *Bún riêu*, a soup made of thin rice noodles topped with crab and shrimp paste. Appreciation for the food and the country, Anthony mused as they bumped along a dirt road, would be an acquired taste.

The aged, gray, dented prop plane that was to be Anthony's transport to Cu Chi was similar to the crop dusters he'd seen in rural Ar-

7

kansas, except larger. The door was so small, though, he bumped his head when entering. Three soldiers boarded with Anthony, but their presence provided no comfort.

It was the second time that day Anthony had worried about his safety, and with valid reason. Besides the constant grinding noise after it took off, the plane shuddered from crosswinds and bounced in the air like a paper glider.

None of the passengers talked during the choppy ride as they looked down on the geometric designs created by the rice paddies and the strange, round, moving objects Anthony later learned were straw hats the Vietnamese wore while planting.

The landing was as shaky as the take-off. Once off the plane, Anthony vowed to look for alternative transportation if he had to fly again.

It was after settling into his hootch, a metal hut-like structure with a screened door and concrete floor, that Anthony was first introduced to Major Bertram, who briefed him on the base and the 25th Infantry Division's mission. Following the meeting, Anthony walked the base, familiarizing himself with his new home and refining how he'd approach his assignment.

The 25th Infantry base camp was comparable to a small city with red dirt roads, wood boardwalks, metal and wood Quonset huts, barracks, and hootches. Helicopters seemed to be in constant motion. On the ground, Frank Sinatra's "On a Clear Day" played through the loudspeakers.

Deep in deliberation, Anthony almost bumped into Arne Nielson, a blond-haired, slightly overweight veteran war correspondent from Eden Prairie, Minnesota, who worked for *Newsweek* magazine.

"I remember you," Nielson said, smiling. "The ethics seminar."

"I'm surprised, seeing as how you drank Chicago dry that night," Anthony responded.

Nielson laughed. "But for some reason, my drinking never interferes with my memory. I also remember more than one woman at the seminar being smitten by your Nat King Cole looks."

Although he'd heard it before, it was times like these Anthony was most grateful his dark skin hid his blushing. But what kept him humbled was his father's admonition when Anthony was admiring himself in the mirror at sixteen. *You ain't going nowhere in this world just because you think you're pretty.*

"Can I buy you one, Anthony?" Nielson asked, patting Anthony on the shoulder.

"How long have you been here?" Anthony inquired as the two settled into an empty table at the officer's club.

"Two months now. *Newsweek* wanted me back to compare what's going on now with what happened in '65."

"Two tours. Wow. Where were you before this?"

Nielson pointed east. "Next door. Prince Sihanouk is experiencing unrest in Cambodia partially because of his stance against communism, which pissed off Hanoi. Just when the shit is going to hit the fan, they pull me out. But, hey," Nielson raised his hands, "I'm just a reporter. What about you, Anthony? What's your angle?"

"The *Post* asked me to write about the positive experiences of the black soldier."

"Your executive editor," Nielson said, nodding.

"How'd you guess?"

"No guess, man. Ben Bradlee's been a supporter of the war from the beginning. Anyway, those would make good stories." Nielson swirled his glass before taking a sip of Jack Daniels, then downed a Miller beer chaser. "I suggest you look at the new versus the old recruits as a side story."

"Why's that?"

"When I was here in '65," Nielson answered, "the black soldiers were just…soldiering. There's been an attitude change with these new troops. The first black soldiers were career professionals and took care of the Army's business without question. A lot of these new recruits are draftees who were involved in the Civil Rights Movement. They challenge anything they consider racist over here when it comes to assignments, decorations, promotions, you name it." Nielson laughed. "A few have created black-only barracks and won't let any white guys in."

"Really?" Anthony said, remembering seeing two black soldiers raise their fisted right hands in a black power salute when returning to his hootch the previous day.

"Actually," Nielson said more seriously, "it's already hit the fan here."

"How so?" Anthony asked, watching as Nielson finished another shot.

"So you don't know about the riot."

"No."

Nielson looked at his watch. "I've got an interview with General Williamson and his staff in a few minutes. We'll talk tomorrow."

CHAPTER 3

That morning, Anthony wrote his first letter to his wife, Carla:

July 2, 1969

Hey Baby,

I'm here. Arrived around 0400 hours (4 a.m.). Sorry I had to leave you and Mali so soon. Things have been moving so fast for us—first the move from Cleveland to D.C., learning to report the Washington Post *way, and now this assignment. Believe me, when I get back, I will make it up to both of you. I already miss you two more than you can imagine. When I call to let you know I'll be arriving, please pull out your black sheer lace negligee and give Mali a sleeping pill. (Just kidding about the sleeping pill.)*

This place is so different from what I expected—from the food to the air to the general atmosphere and attitude. It will take some getting used to. The heat is suffocating—it rains almost every day, and the Vietnamese food is...let's say, different from anything I've ever eaten. I'll be dining with the officers, so I should get something close to American food during the rest of my stay.

My hootch is a wood hut with a tin roof set on a concrete floor. A good wind could blow this thing into the sea, but for now it's home. One thing for sure, the price is right over here. Bought a case of RC Cola for $2.40.

I'm at the headquarters of the 25th Infantry Division, and it's already getting interesting. Hadn't been here more than a few days when I see these seven black soldiers getting off a helicopter. They looked as if they'd seen the devil. What's interesting is nobody will talk about it. You know me, though, I'll find the story.

Just heard "Keep On Pushing" by the Impressions coming out of one of the barracks. As a matter of fact, they've been playing it repeatedly. I imagine those seven men would consider the song appropriate.

Got to go, babe. I promise to write as often as I can.

Love you,

Anthony

***

About 2 A.M., Anthony lurched up, hearing the sirens and the shouts almost simultaneously: *Incoming!* He jumped from his bunk, fumbling for pants and shirt as the clamor of boots hitting the dirt outside his hootch was drowned out by the whistle then the whomp of the first mortar round.

The ground shuddered from the impact as Anthony burst out of the door. But as soon as he crossed the road, he cursed, remembering he had left his flak jacket and helmet.

The next round sounded closer. Anthony took off at a full sprint. Two more mortars fell even nearer as he dove headfirst into the concrete bunker, nearly hitting his forehead at the entrance.

"You okay, man?"

Anthony looked up to see a muscular black soldier smiling down at him. The man, wearing three elephant hair bracelets Anthony had noticed on a few of the other black soldiers, gave Anthony a hand and offered him a smoke as they leaned against the concrete wall.

Anthony waved off the cigarette and laughed nervously, his heart pounding as loud as the mortar rounds. "Yeah. I guess," he said above the whir of helicopters and the commotion of troops manning their posts.

The soldier chuckled and stuck out his hand. "Terrence Means."

"Anthony Andrews."

"Welcome to Vietnam."

As he looked around at the other soldiers in varied attire, Anthony didn't feel as stupid about forgetting his protective gear.

"Anyone ever get a Purple Heart for banging their head on a bunker entrance?" he asked.

The men chuckled quietly.

***

The shells dropped for the next ten minutes, and then an all-clear siren wailed in the stillness of the night. Anthony walked the area looking for any damage, but seeing none, returned to his hootch and lay down, tensing at every sound until reveille, the bugle call to wake, sounded.

"Three killed, two wounded," Bertram told Anthony that morning.

A shudder sliced through Anthony. "Where?" he asked as he gathered himself.

Bertram grimaced. "Company B, 1st Battalion. The guerillas walked those rounds right toward headquarters. Missed HQ by thirty yards, but got a direct hit on the barracks."

Back at his hootch, Anthony lay on his bunk, staring at the ceiling, trying to reconcile the mortar attack with the dead and wounded men. He wondered how Bertram had fared the previous night. Anthony understood how mortars could have evoked Bertram's previous reaction and hoped he wouldn't suffer a similar fate.

CHAPTER 4

Listen, a couple of days ago I saw seven black men in filthy uniforms getting off a chopper, looking wasted. Do you guys know anything? I couldn't interview them, and Bertram gave me nothing," Anthony asked as he sat with Nielson, Alrek Olson from the Swedish newspaper *Aftonbladet,* and Vince Molinari of *ABC News.*

The three shook their heads.

"It sounds strange they didn't let you talk to them," Molinari said.

"That is strange. They say why?" Olson asked.

"They had to be debriefed, is all Bertram would say," Anthony responded. "And he was evasive about when they'd be available."

"We'll do some digging and let you know what we find," Olson volunteered.

"Cool. Thanks. So tell me about the riot."

Anthony wanted to get it from Nielson and the other two before confronting the major. If Bertram's response to the uprising was anything like his response concerning the seven men, Anthony doubted he'd get the full story.

Nielson dropped two cubes of ice in his glass before taking a sip. "It appears one of the black soldiers at headquarters took a truck to town, unauthorized. A white soldier reported him, and the black soldier jumped the white soldier for telling.

"Colonel Moreland A. Bolt, the battalion commander, had the MPs arrest the black soldier and put him in lockup for taking the truck and for the assault. The other black soldiers in his company found out and confronted Captain Fitzgerald, the company commander, since the arrest was based solely on the white soldier's testimony. They demanded his release within four hours, or they would storm the jail. Black soldiers from other support companies sent representatives saying they'd go, too."

Anthony remembered catching a glimpse of Colonel Bolt when he first met with Major Bertram. The colonel was a large man with a flat, red face. With the addition of a beard and a pillow, mothers would place their children in his lap.

Vince Molinari crossed his arms. "Picture one-hundred-fifty mad black soldiers storming a stockade; then picture the Army's response."

"So what happened?" Anthony asked as he stood to pace, expecting the worst.

"The colonel let the soldier go," Nielson answered.

Anthony turned toward him. "Just like that?"

"Not quite. They still planned on trying him, but they wanted to avoid any unnecessary confrontation. Anyway, the white soldiers got mad because this guy is free, and..." Nielson said, raising his hands, "there was an altercation between a few of the black and white soldiers the next day, with their primary weapons being fists and metal bunk adapters. Soldiers from both sides joined, and it escalated."

"And...?"

"The MPs finally broke it up. They arrested who they thought were the instigators and sent them to the Long Binh Jail."

"When did this happen?" Anthony asked Nielson.

"June twelfth?"

Olson and Molinari nodded.

Anthony thanked the three reporters as they departed, wondering if the full story of the riot would be as elusive as the story of "The Seven," a name he decided to give the men from the Chinook.

***

Anthony finished his first story for the *Post* based on interviews he'd conducted with a few of the soldiers, including a black master sergeant. They confirmed Nielson's assessment about the differences between the old and the new soldiers. The title of the article, "Bad Blood," was named after the militant black soldiers who named themselves Bloods.

Having been in Vietnam for a little more than a week, Anthony had only the black soldiers' point of view on why they rebelled against military authority. The master sergeant labeled the men undisciplined. But was it that the older soldiers accepted the mistreatment? And why would army culture be any different from what was happening back home? It wasn't plausible so many soldiers were mad at nothing.

"You need to go on a patrol," Nielson advised Anthony at lunch.

"Why?" Anthony asked.

"A few reasons: One, you can't write in depth about a war if you haven't experienced it. I'm talking about being there in the mix. Two, it gives you more credibility with the soldiers you are trying to identify with. Three, there's a different feeling in the jungle. There's genuine camaraderie. You'll get a better sense of this war after you've been out there."

Nielson gave Anthony a half-smile. "When you're in your foxhole trying to stay alive and you have to rely on your fellow soldier to make it happen, you two are married. Not like the racial problems back on base where soldiers have too much time on their hands."

Anthony leaned forward. "So has every correspondent gone out?"

"Everyone I know. I've been on three."

Even though Anthony had enough to write about on base, he agreed with Nielson that going into the field would give him a broader perspective, more stories, and open more doors. "I'm game. I'll ask Bertram today."

"You'll be a different person when you return. I guarantee."

CHAPTER 5

Anthony hadn't had time to read Carla's letter the previous night. He unfolded it, having twenty minutes before he was to see Captain Bertram.

July 10, 1969

Honey,

I'm glad you made it there safely. Mali and I miss you so much. I won't give her a sleeping pill, but she will be at someone's sleepover the first night you are back. And regarding the negligee, I've sent you a picture. DO NOT SHOW THIS TO ANYONE, NOT EVEN WHAT-EVER BEST FRIEND YOU MIGHT HAVE MADE OVER THERE.

Anthony, please be careful. I've read where journalists have been killed in Vietnam. Do not get adventurous or think you need to test your manhood. You can do that when you get home.

Be safe.

I love you.

Carla

P.S. I know what 0400 means. You don't have to interpret for me.

He gazed at the half-naked lady in the picture, looking unlike any university professor he'd ever met: hazel eyed with a slim but shapely build. Her closely cropped hair framed a burnt-brown face that had the blunt but striking features of Eartha Kitt, and the attitude to match.

Anthony kissed the picture and carefully slid it into a pocket in his suitcase.

CHAPTER 6

That's an order, Captain," Bertram bellowed, slamming the phone down.

Anthony listened as Bertram and whomever he was talking with engaged in an intense argument.

"Look, I don't want to cause any problems," Anthony said.

"There will be none," Bertram responded stiffly. "Report to the landing strip near the 12th Evac at 0600 hours tomorrow. You know where it is?"

"I've got a base map. I'll find it."

***

The captain, whom Anthony assumed Bertram had been talking to, approached Anthony briskly, ignoring any formality. "You the war correspondent?"

"Yes. Captain Valentine?" Anthony asked, holding out his hand, brightening at the sight of a black officer.

The captain turned abruptly and motioned Anthony to follow. A stocky, red-haired sergeant approached them. Valentine mentioned something to the sergeant then disappeared among his men.

"Anthony," the sergeant said, holding out his hand. "I'm Sergeant Harry Wrenford. I'm your mother on this mission.

"We're going to an area near War Zone C, northwest of Tay Ninh province. Enemy movement was spotted near a village. We're to check it out."

Anthony's eyebrows rose when he heard the destination. "Oh?"

"Stick by me when we get off," Wrenford hollered over the heavy hammering of the Huey troop-transport helicopter taking off. "You might have to scramble depending on the circumstances. Follow me and do what I do, okay?" the sergeant asked, checking Anthony's gear.

"Sure. No problem there," Anthony replied, licking his lips.

Two door gunners in flak jackets never glanced at the men boarding as they prepared their mounted guns pointing out of each side of the Huey. As the helicopter gained speed, it skirted the top of the trees so close Anthony feared one of the skids might catch a branch. He took a deep breath, wondering if he would regret this decision. An image flashed through his mind of Carla, glaring, with her hands on her hips, before he willed it out of his head.

Anthony managed a half grimace as he thought back to the near-death incident he'd experienced in a confrontation with the Klan in Arkansas. The encounter had taught him a valuable lesson, though: The greatest danger often births the greatest story.

***

When the first Huey helicopter swept into the landing zone, Anthony watched from above as the men hit the ground running south.

As his Huey bumped to a landing, Anthony jumped and followed Sergeant Wrenford as he and Lieutenant Dillard Maynard jogged to the area where the first soldiers had gathered.

Maynard, the commander of 3rd Platoon, seemed to be in charge, giving orders to the officers of the 1st and 2nd Platoons. Anthony looked for Captain Valentine, but he and the remaining helicopters never set down.

Anthony wanted to question Wrenford on Valentine's whereabouts, but the sergeant was busy preparing the troops to move out. Who was he to question a maneuver? Valentine and the rest of the battalion would probably meet with them further on.

Wrenford motioned to Anthony to follow him near the front of 3rd Platoon, the lead platoon, as the troops moved out through a patch of what Private Norman Whitaker described to Anthony as "wait a minute" vines. Even though Anthony had become used to the heat, the vines tugging at him every step of the way, the red ants, and the swarming mosquitoes were enough to make him second guess himself again.

They had traveled northwest for close to twenty minutes and had crossed a narrow stream when Wrenford stopped abruptly and peered into the denseness to their left. The look on Wrenford's face caused the hairs on Anthony's neck to stand up.

Wrenford extended his arm at a forty-five-degree angle then lowered it to his side. As the troops hit the ground, looking for cover, Anthony crouched behind a tree surrounded by knee-high brush. Wrenford slid into a depression in the ground and raised his rifle slowly—a second before all hell broke loose.

CHAPTER 7

A smattering of rifle shots turned into an all-out battle in seconds. The shocking uproar of small arms, machine guns, rockets, and mortars was deafening; it started toward the front of the column, then quickly surrounded the platoon as men dropped from the onslaught. "Down!" Wrenford yelled as he pushed Anthony farther to the ground. "And stay down!"

Anthony winced as he slid to a prone position. The butterflies he'd felt on the helicopter had turned into dragons that tore away at his inside.

Even more horrific than the dreadful roar of the weapons were the soul-wrenching screams of men who were hit. Wrenford had left him, but he could hear the sergeant and lieutenant yelling orders. Anthony peeked around the tree in time to see Private Whitaker fall back against the tree before slipping to the ground, blood gushing from a hole in his neck. Anthony rolled over and pulled Whitaker out of the line of fire to save him from further injury, but one glance told him the effort was futile.

The whistle of mortar rounds made Anthony recoil as shards of metal gouged the surrounding trees fifty feet away. When he glanced toward the location of the shell's impact, the dissipating smoke revealed an enemy soldier in a green uniform, rifle in hand, running through the dense brush, parallel to the rear of the platoon, forty yards away.

Anthony cringed as several more joined the Vietnamese soldier. He looked around to warn someone, but no one was within hearing distance. Anthony turned back, horrified to see them make an abrupt turn toward him.

Could they see him? Anthony looked back for help again before grabbing Whitaker's weapon. Partially hidden by the brush and vines, he crawled to the other side of the tree and raised the weapon in his quivering hands.

The men were within thirty yards when Anthony rose and fired the first burst. The rounds were low, kicking up brush and dirt in front of them. The attackers stopped and simultaneously returned fire. Anthony ducked as bullets flew past him or hit the thick Banyan tree with a thunking sound.

He peeked from behind the tree trunk, watching as the men turned to run to their left, and fired another burst. One of the Viet Cong grabbed his throat, his mouth spraying blood. A second VC ran into the stricken fighter as blood appeared on the back of that enemy soldier's shirt. The two crumbled to the ground together; the rest disappeared into the high brush.

Three American soldiers raced to Anthony's side as he pointed in the direction of the fleeing enemy. Four more soldiers approached, and they gave chase.

***

"Second Platoon is flanked!" Anthony heard the private scream into the radio telephone. Bullets, sounding like a swarm of mad wasps, kicked up red dirt around the operator as he dashed to better cover.

As he held Whitaker's weapon, ready to fire again, Anthony watched a medic scurry past him toward screams of "Medic!"

It felt as if hours had passed. Anthony's mind was numb. The sounds of battle shifted to the south as the crackle of weapons firing one burst after another became even louder. Shortly after, a different sound penetrated the air. The hiss of artillery rounds followed later by rockets from Huey Cobra helicopters was joined by thuds and reverberations of shells and bullets battering the ground and anything in their path, upheaving dirt, shrubs, and sod.

As they carried the wounded and dead past Anthony to an open area, he recoiled at the sight of a soldier with a single bullet hole in his forehead, another with half a foot missing, and one with a wound so horrific his intestines were spilling through a loosened gauze bandage.

He fumbled in his bag for his camera, cursing his trembling hands as a medevac helicopter plunged in to gather the severely wounded and then the dead.

The volume of firing crescendoed again before tailing off to sporadic small arms fire. Wrenford approached with two of his men. "You okay?"

Anthony exhaled. His hands hurt from gripping the weapon so hard. How long had he held his breath? "Yeah, Sarge."

"Good. You done good. They were trying to hit us from the rear. You helped stop 'em," Wrenford said, patting Anthony's shoulder before moving on.

***

"The enemy's been routed," Maynard called in to headquarters. "First platoon pursued the remainder to an open area. The Cobras did the rest."

Maynard paused, listening. "I'm not aware, sir." The lieutenant paused again, "Yes, sir. I will."

Wrenford and Maynard glanced at each other, then gave clean-up orders to their men.

Anthony stood by the two men, waiting to hear more, but except for an occasional head shake by Maynard, Anthony could only guess their concern had something to do with Valentine missing in action.

CHAPTER 8

Anthony jumped from his bunk, startled by the rattling of the flimsy wood door to his hootch. He had just drifted into a restless sleep.

"Yeah?" he croaked.

"It's me, man. Nielson. You okay?"

"Yeah," Anthony responded, trying to clear his throat.

"It's close to 2000 hours. You need to get out. You need to eat."

Anthony rubbed his eyes. "Give me a few."

"I'll meet you at the club. I'll tell 'em to keep something warm for you."

"Thanks."

Anthony sat back down and took a deep breath. Sighing, he struggled up and tried to shave with trembling hands before noticing the dried blood on his palms. He stopped, threw the razor in the sink, pummeled his hands with soap, and watched the reddened water wash down the drain.

He pulled Carla's picture out of the suitcase and looked at it for a few minutes, before taking a deep breath and stepping into the dark.

***

"Wow, man," Nielson stated with one hand on Anthony's shoulder and the other holding a full glass of Jack Daniels. "I wish I could have been there."

Anthony glared at Nielson but said nothing. The numbness of combat had rendered him speechless.

"You okay, though?" Nielson asked, looking at Anthony closely as Nielson wolfed down a sandwich of scrambled eggs and bacon.

Anthony nodded.

"Fifteen dead, eighteen wounded on a fuckin' sweep for a squad of VC. Damn!" Nielson took a drink. "If what I hear from my source is correct, G-2s got some explaining to do."

"G-2?" Anthony asked.

"Division Intelligence," Nielson answered scowling. "Valentine's company was supposed to be looking for the suspicious activity of twelve to fifteen Cong sighted in one of the villages. Instead, they run into a buzz saw—part of a North Vietnamese battalion. Everybody's trying to figure out how they got there." Nielson looked at Anthony's plate. "You gonna eat that ham?"

***

Bertram glanced at Anthony twice, then nodded as Anthony sat near Bertram's desk. Anthony, lips pursed, nodded back.

"I hear you did a little soldiering."

Anthony licked his lips and nodded again.

Bertram moved beside Anthony and placed a hand on his shoulder. "Sorry about that, Anthony. I didn't plan on you bustin' your cherry on your first outing, but this was a serious screw-up all the way around."

"How so, Major?"

"Here's what I can tell you," Bertram said, pacing beside his desk. "There weren't supposed to be so many Charlies in the area, especially not regular forces." Bertram paused, rubbing his chin. "And for some reason, the commanding officer..."

"Valentine?"

"...wasn't anywhere to be found." Bertram pounded his desk once. "Unless he has a damn good explanation..."

Anthony hung his head. The first black officer he met, and he was in trouble. "I don't suppose he would be available for an interview?" Anthony asked.

Bertram shook his head.

CHAPTER 9

July 18, 1969

Dear Carla,

I'm sorry I haven't written more. I've been busy trying to get information on the seven men I mentioned. Things have been hectic in other ways here, too, but I'm okay.

I will see you soon, baby.

***

"Your story "Bad Blood" was rejected, Anthony," Marie Simmons, a *Post* editor, relayed on the headquarters' phone.

"But it's one of the major stories over here."

"I'm sure, Anthony. We want the positive accounts, though. You went on a patrol, right?"

"Yeah."

"Weren't there any hero stories?"

"Shit, Marie. They were all heroes."

Marie laughed.

"What?"

"It's the first time I've ever heard you curse."

"First time for everything," Anthony muttered under his breath.

"Write the hero stories then, Anthony."

Anthony had anticipated the *Post*'s response. It was a check to see how far they'd let him go. Now that he knew, he'd write the stories they wanted, and he'd write the stories *he* wanted for another time, another publication.

***

The day would be another busy one. Anthony had tried to push aside memories of the battle by staying occupied. Hopefully, lining up a series of interviews would help.

After showering, he returned to his hootch to find a folded piece of paper under his door.

Anthony,

I'll be in the field with the 1ˢᵗ Cav. I found some interesting information for you. Should be back in a few days. We'll talk then.

Nielson

Anthony smiled, refolded the paper, and slipped it into his shirt pocket.

While Anthony continued to interview, he took every opportunity to gather more information on The Seven, the riot, and Captain Valentine.

"Tell me about the riot," Anthony asked Terrence Means, SP4 from Brooklyn—Anthony's bunker mate during the mortar attack and his last interviewee that day.

Means, a member of the Black Panthers, was a five-foot-eleven bodybuilder and one of the more militant soldiers at Cu Chi. His reputation preceded him since Anthony had learned of Means from others he'd interviewed. Because he was constantly challenging authority, Means was always one step removed from being thrown in the stockade. Means also had a following of like-minded soldiers who weren't shy about confrontation.

Means frowned. "June twelfth? I was in Vung Tau." He scratched his jaw. "I'm sorry I missed it, but it wasn't no riot; it was a brawl."

"What's the difference?"

"A riot is like a rebellion, a revolt. A riot makes it sound as if just the black soldiers were involved in violence when, in fact, they were only protecting themselves."

"How many?" Anthony asked.

Means called over one of his friends, Private Ernie Daniels, a wiry, six-foot-tall soldier with a short afro, to corroborate his estimate. "Close to forty of us and maybe a hundred of them at the end?"

Daniels nodded.

"Forty?" Anthony asked.

Daniels snorted. "Yeah. Five of them jumped one of us, and it blew up. Before you knew it, it was on."

Anthony scribbled a few notes before stopping and staring at Means and Daniels. "June twelfth? When did those seven soldiers go on patrol?"

Daniels frowned. "It had to be right after. Maybe seven to eight days later."

Anthony cocked his head as he wrote. "Any connection between the seven men sent out and the ri...brawl?"

Means looked at Daniels, then at Anthony and sniffed. "You don't know, do you?"

Anthony waited.

Means looked around, motioned Anthony into a vacant barrack, and asked Daniels to stand watch.

"Instead of the stockade, Colonel Bolt came up with another form of punishment."

"Which was?"

"Those guys, the seven soldiers, were not only in the fight. They were part of the so-called riot leaders."

"So how did they end up in the field?"

"There were fifteen total—all black."

"Out of forty?"

"Yeah. Bolt told them, 'Since you guys love to fight, I'm going to give you the opportunity.' "

"Who were they with?"

"What company?" Means asked.

"Yeah."

"Man, they came from all over, but most from headquarters."

"Headquarters?"

"Yeah. Non-combat troops."

"Seven came back. What happened to the other eight?"

"Nobody knows. From what I understand, nobody expected any of them to come back. Maybe the eight bought it like the other seven were supposed to."

Means pushed Anthony out of the door when Daniels signaled someone was coming. "We'll talk later," Means whispered as they exited.

"You got names?" Anthony whispered back.

"Later," Means answered as he walked briskly in the opposite direction.

July 26, 1969

Dear Anthony,

What's wrong? I know something is. Your letters have never been so brief. Are you really okay? You didn't mention the picture I sent you. You haven't mentioned Mali. You haven't told me you missed me—none of that.

Your dad said to say hi, and your mother worries whether you have the right clothes and are eating enough.

A LONG WAY BACK

Let me know you are okay.

Please be okay, honey.

I LOVE YOU!

Carla

CHAPTER 10

As Anthony headed toward headquarters to pry additional information from Bertram, he overheard a captain tell a lieutenant, "A journalist caught one last night," as they walked the wooden plank path ahead of him.

Anthony stopped the two officers. "I'm sorry for intruding. Do you know who it was?"

"I'm not sure. Just that he was on patrol yesterday."

"Damn!" Anthony said under his breath as he half walked, half ran to Bertram's office. He found the major behind a hut talking to two other officers.

"Major?"

"Anthony. You heard?"

"Not the whole story. Was it..."

Bertram nodded.

Anthony's stomach churned. He bent over as he felt his breakfast rise. "What happened?"

"There was a firefight. Nielson disobeyed orders and got in the middle of it, taking pictures. Took one in the chest."

"Jesus."

"They medevaced him out immediately, but he died en route. I'm sorry. I know you guys were friends."

Anthony ran his hands over his eyes. "Yeah."

"If you want to write his family after the official notification, I'll get you the information."

"Thanks."

Bertram tapped Anthony's arm. "Look, Anthony. You've been through a lot since you got here. Why don't you take a few days off, go to Saigon, and relax? It'll do you good. I'll get someone in the adjutant's office to arrange transportation."

***

Major Bertram was wrong. Saigon did Anthony no good. The Caravelle Hotel with its Italian marble, bulletproof glass, state-of-the-art air-conditioning system, and a Berliet private generator did nothing to calm his nerves.

The Caravelle was the center of the universe for the international media covering the war. It was in the middle of Saigon, in Lam Son Square, offering an oasis in an otherwise chaotic city.

From Anthony's window, he could see the spires of the Saigon Cathedral, the U.S. Embassy, and the Opera House. The Saigon River was a few blocks away. On the street, residents, looking like a swarm of Japanese beetles, glided around on rickshaws or buzzed around on motor scooters.

Even the popular Saigon Bar on top of the hotel didn't help. Early evening of the first day, Anthony and fellow foreign correspondents stood on the roof, having drinks and watching the air strikes across the river. The planes were so close a decent telephoto lens could pick up their markings.

He wondered if any of *these* correspondents had been in a firefight or on patrol. He doubted it, judging from the boisterous laughter and cheers at the rockets and bombs as if they were at a Fourth of July picnic.

"Having fun?" Adele Mason, the cute, flirty correspondent from the *San Francisco Chronicle,* asked.

"Not really," Anthony answered, preparing to leave the bar, never to return.

"Ohhhh. Why not?"

"Not my kind of party."

"No?" she purred, running her hand along Anthony's arm. "What is your kind of party?"

"A slumber party."

Adele smiled coyly and moved closer. "I'm game, Anthony."

"Alone," Anthony countered as he pulled his arm away, finished the last of his drink, and took the stairs to his floor. He stopped at the first landing and looked up, before shaking his head and continuing to his room.

Early that night was the first dream: One, two, ten, twenty, and then so many soldiers in green he couldn't count, rushing toward him, shooting, screaming...

The next day, Anthony walked the streets to get his head straight. He returned to his room late morning, ordered room service, and drank and slept the remainder of his R&R away.

CHAPTER 11

Back on base, Anthony trudged on, continuing his search for answers, but he was thwarted at every turn. If no one was talking before, soldiers were tight-lipped even among themselves concerning The Seven and the fight. The seven soldiers, plus Captain Valentine, seemed to have disappeared.

"Means is in the stockade," Daniels whispered while passing Anthony on the way to his post.

"What happened?"

"You."

"What?" Anthony sighed. So it was true. Anyone talking about the seven men was subject to punishment. Why would the Army go to that extreme? Anthony felt guilty getting Means in trouble, and it was clearer than ever, if he was to find what happened, it wouldn't be in Cu Chi.

The *Post* loved his stories of men like Sergeant Ronald Mansfield, a sniper from Dayton, Ohio, who took out two Viet Cong snipers plus a North Vietnamese major in one outing, or Sergeant Fredrick Sommerville from Brooklyn, New York, who rallied 2nd Platoon after his lieutenant was wounded to help turn back the recent battle outside Tay Ninh. Then there was Spec 4 Milan Richardson from Elba, Alabama, who after his M-60 jammed, engaged in hand-to-hand combat after the Viet Cong had breached the wire in one area of the Dau Tieng base camp perimeter, killing two and wounding two others with a .45 and a trenching tool before being wounded himself.

Since it was nearing the end of August and Bertram had provided no further insight into Anthony's queries, he prepared to return to D.C., having almost completed his two-month stint. In the remaining days, he hung out with the enlisted men, drank Jack Daniels, and slept.

***

Anthony received another letter from Carla in the afternoon.

August 30, 1969

Anthony,

Now I'm really worried. Your last letter said you were okay, again, like you were still trying to convince me you were. That letter was not you, Anthony. What's going on over there? At least I know you are alive. Were you hurt? What happened? And when will you be home?

Love you,

Carla

***

When Anthony awoke the next day, hung over, in an empty bunk in the enlisted men's barracks, he knew it was time to leave. Was the liquor how Nielson had coped?

Anthony's last days on base were uneventful, except for the send-off the black soldiers gave him for telling their stories. The soldiers surrounding him gave him the black power salute as he boarded a jeep taking him to the airstrip.

"Be safe, man. We'll try to stay in touch," Daniels said.

Even though his articles were well received by the newspaper, Anthony felt his mission was incomplete. On the plane back to the States, the events that transpired during his stay ran over and over in his mind. He thought of those soldiers who fell to enemy fire trying to do the best job they could. He thought about the dragons of dread and fear a soldier carries to the field of combat, harnessed by dedication, discipline, and resolve.

Because of their example, Anthony knew he wasn't finished. As much as he wanted to put Vietnam behind him, his experience was etched in his soul as he imagined it was for each soldier. And that was why there was still work to be done, even if it meant dredging up the horrible memories.

Anthony would answer the questions left at Cu Chi. He'd seen hell, and he had witnessed it in the eyes of The Seven. And because of that, he felt a bond he imagined connected everyone who experienced war—a shared horror of lost lives, torn souls, and uncertain futures. It was his duty, his obligation to find those men and tell their stories.

CHAPTER 12

Anthony didn't understand his nervousness as the plane landed at Cleveland Hopkins Airport. But when his wife and daughter met him as he passed through the door to the concourse— greeting him like some war hero— they hugged and kissed Anthony's anxieties away.

On the way back to the house, Carla made small talk but kept glancing at him. Mali kept up a constant chatter. Anthony was relieved just to listen as he leaned back and savored their presence.

"I baked salmon for supper. Is it still your favorite dish?"

"You know it, honey," Anthony responded, sliding his hand along her thigh.

Carla peeked in the rearview mirror at their 6-year-old daughter, who was gazing out the window, before putting her hand over his.

"Mali's got a sleepover tonight," Carla said squeezing his hand.

"Momma made me," Mali muttered with her lips stuck out.

"You get to see Daddy for the rest of your life, baby. He needs to rest tonight, though. Okay?"

"If you say so."

***

Anthony stood closely behind Carla, his hands on her hips as they both watched Mali leave with Dale and Marlene Cofield. As soon as the door closed, Carla turned and threw herself at Anthony. Wrapping her arms around his back, she kissed his face repeatedly before opening her mouth and receiving his tongue.

Anthony ran his hands along Carla's back and then her legs, lifting her dress, caressing and then squeezing. He loved the small whining sounds she made when she became excited.

She unbuttoned his shirt and tongued his chest. He unsnapped her bra and marveled briefly at her before reciprocating while unzipping her skirt.

The two crumpled to the carpet as they continued to stroke, kiss, and explore. Her whimpers accompanied by his heavy breathing increased in rapidity and volume as she shifted her hips and pulled Anthony on top.

"Oh my," Carla blurted continuously, shuddering as her eyes rolled back while Anthony released all the love and desire he had stored for two months into her.

***

Exhausted from their nonstop lovemaking, Carla finally found the strength to get up. She stood, still flushed with exertion and exhilaration, looking at her sleeping husband, her forehead wrinkled in concern.

It wasn't that he was such a beast, more hungry for her than he'd ever been; it wasn't his bellowing as he peaked, releasing some pent-up emotion stored deep inside him; it was his eyes.

Even when he laughed, his eyes didn't. It wasn't until they made love that they came alive.

CHAPTER 13

Close to a month had passed since he'd returned from Vietnam, and Anthony was no further ahead in his investigation than he had been before he left. He had begun to run and work out again to calm the "devil," as his aunt described it. He spent ten to twelve hours a day investigating and writing for the *Post* and himself. Six of those hours he tried to sleep, but sleep was elusive.

Although the work hours were grueling, the stillness was the hardest. That's when the nightmares of Tay Ninh slipped into his thoughts. The Vietnamese charging toward him in their green uniforms, the bullets flying, the screams of the wounded and dying, the black body bags, and the fear that any moment could have been his last remained buried in his psyche.

It had been tough returning home, answering questions when he didn't want to talk at all. His mind was a jumble of thoughts; his emotions continually collided. Carla was his only constant. He couldn't get enough of her in bed.

But it only took a week for the devil to surface.

"Honey, where's the oatmeal?" Anthony asked.

"Oh, I moved it. It's in the lower cabinet on the left hand side."

"Why did you move it?"

"Hmm?"

"It was good where it was," Anthony said.

47

"I didn't like it there. So I rearranged the cabinets a bit."

"Rearranged? Why?"

"Anthony. What's the big deal?"

"I think you should have consulted me."

"What? First, you weren't here. Second, it's no big deal. No, let me rephrase that. First, it's no big deal. Second, you weren't here."

Anthony could feel the blood rushing to his face. "First, it is a big deal. Second, it is a big deal," he snapped as he pulled cartons of food from the lower-left cabinet and threw them on the floor before putting the oatmeal box in its original place.

"Anthony?" Carla spluttered as he stormed out the door.

I was wrong, Anthony thought as he walked around the block. *I've got to do better. But how? The outburst came from nowhere. It was like a mental ambush. As if something was attacking him from the inside. How could he stop an assault when he didn't know the enemy?*

"I'm sorry, Carla," Anthony said after returning home, going to the kitchen, picking up the cartons, and replacing them in the cupboard. "I just need some time to get my head together."

"Okay, Anthony. But I hope it's soon. I'm worried about you. Your temper is getting worse. We've had at least one argument a day, and this is the fourth time you've had these outbursts, about nothing."

Nothing? Anthony tensed. There it was again. He took a deep breath and walked away feeling proud he had quelled the rage—that time.

But in spite of his ongoing efforts, the anger that welled up without warning continued to plague him in the months ahead.

"I said I'd paint the garage, why do you keep bugging me about it?"

"Anthony, here you go again. What's wrong with you?"

"I don't like being nagged."

"I merely stated it'd be nice to have the garage painted this weekend since the weatherman predicted rain next week."

Anthony hit the dinette table with his hand, cracking the wood top, then threw one of the kitchen chairs against the refrigerator. "When I get to it!"

Despite holding her hands over her ears, Mali, who had been sitting in the living room, jumped at the crash of breaking wood and ran upstairs to hide in her bedroom closet.

"What is your problem?" Carla asked before running up the stairs to comfort Mali.

Anthony couldn't answer. He could hear Carla consoling their child. He wanted to do the same, wrap his arms around both of them and protect them, but he couldn't be the comforter and the threat.

What he most admired about Carla most was what he now feared—her calm, cool, decisive approach to a problem. "You need to see someone, Anthony."

"I'll be okay. I just need time."

"No. You need counseling."

"I can do this on my own."

Carla paused, sighed, folded her arms and frowned at Anthony. "Well, then, you figure it out **on your own**. But I will not subject our child to these continuous eruptions, this irrational behavior. We've talked for more than two months about this, but nothing's changed. And I don't see it changing anytime soon.

Tomorrow Mali and I will visit my parents. I'm not sure when we'll be back. If you can't control yourself now, Anthony, who says it won't get worse and you do something you will regret the rest of your life?"

"I—"

Carla held up one hand, "There's no more discussion."

Once her mind was made up, Anthony knew no amount of pleading would make her stay.

***

Saturday morning, ten days after Carla left, Anthony was tying his shoes for a five-mile run, when the doorbell rang. The mail carrier handed him a mangled package that was too large to fit in the mail chute. There were enough stamps to have been sent from China or… Vietnam. Curious, Anthony looked for a return address, but there was none.

He pulled out the papers and laid them on his desk. Each paper had the heading 25th Infantry Division Roster. There were numbered pages with names, rank, serial number, unit, and hometown. There was no note or any other document disclosing the purpose of the papers.

Anthony sifted through the sheets, trying to understand their importance. He examined them again, looking for a clue, and then stared into space. What was the sender trying to tell him? Balling up a blank sheet of paper and throwing it against the wall, he left the roster on his desk and went for his run.

The *Post* was abuzz Tuesday morning with editors scrambling to put together the most complete story of the Moratorium to End the War scheduled for October 15 and the March on Washington planned for november 15.

"They've got no business protesting this war," Leonard Shanklar, a *Washington Post* reporter asserted.

"What?" Anthony asked, turning so quickly he almost knocked over his coffee.

"They're nothing but hippies afraid to serve."

"George McGovern is a hippie?"

Denise, a paralegal at the *Post*, stopped typing to watch Anthony and Leonard Shanklar.

"Most of them are and should be thrown in jail."

Anthony cocked his head. "Because they protest, they should be jailed?"

"Look," Shanklar argued. "You were over there, Anthony. You see what the troops are going through, fighting for our freedom, yet they come back to the United States and are screamed and spit at—

people calling them baby killers and all that nonsense."

Anthony stood and walked from around his desk toward Shanklar. "I support the troops, but I don't support this bogus war. That's what they are protesting."

"People calling the soldiers baby killers?" Shanklar asked.

"The real baby killers are the political hacks who put these young men and women in harm's way," Anthony retorted.

"Well, I'm sorry, Anthony, but I believe the president and his generals know more than we ever will about this conflict. If Vietnam falls, so will other Asian countries. I mean, my God, North Vietnam is a Peking satellite, and China is a danger to our way of life. If we have to combat communism wherever it arises, then we should. It just happens that now it's in Vietnam."

"I can't believe you, a reporter, said that," Anthony exclaimed, his voice rising with every word. "First, China and Vietnam don't even get along—haven't for centuries. The only reason China helps North Vietnam at all is because it hates us more. This is an internal war. Do you really believe Vietnam is so much a threat to the United States it justifies getting thousands of young Americans killed?" Anthony asked, hitting a divider that fell toward Denise's desk.

"And now, instead of ending the war, there's talk of invading Cambodia?" Anthony continued, spitting out each word, unaware as Denise caught the falling divider.

Shanklar stepped back from the verbal assault. The only sound in the press room where the eight people had gathered was a typewriter in a cubicle down the hallway.

Anthony took a deep breath, went back to his desk, and shoved the stack of papers on his desk into a drawer. "They've got every reason to protest, and they have every right not to get jailed doing it," he said as he walked out.

***

"You okay, Anthony?" Bill Walden, Anthony's section editor, asked later that day.

"Yeah, Bill. I'm okay."

Walden leaned back and rested his chin in his hand. "You've been a bit edgy since you've been back." He paused. "And the scene with Leonard…That's not like you."

"I know, Bill, and I apologize. He just pushed the wrong button."

Walden laughed. "It's not unusual for Leonard. Look, Anthony, I served in Korea. I know what war can do. I've talked with management, and they've agreed to give you a well-deserved vacation. We should have thought of it earlier, and I take full responsibility for not suggesting it. How's it sound, Anthony?"

"How long?"

"How's six weeks? And we won't count it as a vacation."

Anthony hesitated before answering. "Um. That's fine. Thanks, Bill."

***

Still jittery from his encounter with Shanklar, Anthony had mixed emotions about his "vacation." What was he thinking, becoming so angry with somebody because they had another point of view? That wasn't him.

Before driving off, Anthony bowed his head, recalling Arne Nielson's words in Cu Chi, "You'll be a different person when you return. I guarantee."

On the drive home, he stopped at a liquor store and bought two fifths of Jack Daniels. *Okay, Arne, we're going to try it your way.*

CHAPTER 14

Anthony awoke from a blurry sleep. His head hurt, and his tongue felt as if he had dragged it along the Chesapeake Bay beach. He stumbled to the bathroom, then to the kitchen, fixed coffee, and sank into a chair.

What day was it? He tried to remember what happened the previous night—where he'd been, what he'd done—but his mind was blank. Gradually his memory returned as he gazed at a half-empty liquor bottle. He'd drunk and then gone to a bar. How'd he get home in the condition he vaguely remembered being in?

Anthony went to the attached garage and looked at his car—no scratches, no dents. That was good. He went back to the kitchen, finished his coffee, and went to shower.

As relieved as he was about the car, it shocked him to see his discolored face and a small knot above his right eye in the mirror. Wincing as he touched one of the bruises, he noticed the cuts on his right hand and gained more memory. There was a fight. Was it about the war? He scratched his head as he struggled to recall. No, there was a woman. A woman? He stared at the mirror.

The cold shower helped clear his head even more as the woman's face came into focus—pretty, dark-skinned, tall. Then he remembered a guy—big, buffalo-mean, grabbing him because they were talking, laughing. She had reached for his hand. That's when big man stormed over.

Anthony scratched his head again. He remembered being hit, then the guy falling, grabbing for something to hold onto, and he remembered being pulled off him.

Then she reached for his hand again.

A shiver ran through Anthony as he mined his memory for more details. He stumbled to his bedroom, breathing a sigh of relief as he looked at the empty bed. Anthony slumped on it, then lay down, deciding to rest a while longer and gather his thoughts.

"Hi. You're up," the woman said, entering the bedroom from the second bathroom.

Anthony's body snapped as if a mortar shell had landed two feet away.

"I hope you don't mind," she said, smoothing Carla's bathrobe.

Anthony stared, trying to comprehend. "What? Where?" His eyes darted from her to the bed. "Who are you?"

She smiled. "Constance. You forgot?"

Anthony sat speechless.

"Are you ready to finish what we started last night?" she cooed, bathrobe open.

Anthony recoiled. "What? Did we...?"

She giggled. "Not yet, honey. I tried everything, but you were so out of it," she snickered.

Anthony straightened, took her arm, and steered her toward her clothes piled on the hassock. "I'm sorry. This was a mistake. I was…I wasn't…."

She looked bewildered but finally smiled. "Hey, hey. Look, I understand," she said, removing the robe. "I'm disappointed, but I'm surprised you let me in to begin with. You're obviously married." She looked at the family picture on the dresser. "And she is evidently not around. You were inebriated last night, so I can respect that. But I have to say, you were kind of scary at the bar."

"What do you mean?"

"You had the look like Sonny Liston had when he fought. I've never seen it on anyone outside the ring. It took three men to pull you off him."

Anthony could only shake his head. She must have had him confused with someone else, he thought, until a pain shot from his right hand to his shoulder as he reached for the bedroom doorknob.

"I'm just happy you got Marvin off my back. He's my ex, but he acts like we're still married," she explained as Anthony walked her to her car, his eyes darting from one neighbor's house to another. "Everybody in town is afraid of him because he's an ex-boxer."

"Ex-boxer? That wasn't…"

"Marvin Hanson."

Anthony's head jerked up. "What?"

Constance laughed. "Maybe folks won't be so afraid of his ass now."

CHAPTER 15

Returning from taking a drive along the Potomac River to clear his head, Anthony clenched his fist, ignoring the pain, and stared at his swollen fingers. He passed a liquor store, slowed, unclenched his fist, and sped past it.

As he sat at the kitchen table, something moving to his left caught his eye. It was a mouse. It stopped in the middle of the kitchen floor and looked at Anthony for a moment before sauntering toward the back door. After seeing a human being a thousand times bigger, why wasn't it afraid? Maybe because it knew it was faster? That it could escape?

Anthony envied the little creature that appeared to have its life under control. And because of that, he decided to get a live trap instead of poison, because a mouse with an attitude like that deserved to live.

After coffee, Anthony dialed Charles "Chucky" Aaron White, his best friend since elementary school.

"How you holding up since Carla left, Anthony?" Chucky asked.

"I'm losing it, man," Anthony confessed.

"Losing what?" Chucky responded. "You had a fight. All couples do."

Anthony recounted the previous night.

"Whoa! Okay. So let me get this straight. You beat up this ex-boxer, then took his wife to bed?"

"Ex-wife. We didn't…"

"Now we are getting to where you are losing it. That was Constance Hanson, the former model, right?"

"Seriously, man. I'm drinking, fighting—that's not me." Anthony paused. "One minute I'm sad, then anxious; some nights I can't sleep, and when I do, the nightmares… Drinking helps for a moment, but I can't…" Anthony sighed. "I can't continue like this."

Chucky was silent for a few seconds. "You've been through a lot, my friend."

"I just got shot at, Chucky. It's not like I was in the bush for weeks or in sustained combat. It was a one-time thing. I wasn't even hit."

"I'm no psychologist, Anthony, but you were almost hung in Arkansas, you were shot at two times different times, courtesy of the Klan, and you've seen death and dying beginning at age thirteen when you watched a boy get lynched. I would guess all that could have an, uh, cumulative effect."

"I've been handling it up to now, though, Chucky."

"Maybe you've been suppressing it up to now, Anthony. From what little I've read, it doesn't go away altogether."

Anthony sat back. "Maybe you're right, but I've always been able to maintain. I'm scared it's taking over now, though."

"If you're saying you think you're crazy, I'm not sure deranged people stop to analyze themselves, Anthony. They go wild and keep stepping. You need to talk to someone besides me, though. I'm just a math professor down here. I think what you're going through might be temporary, but if not…"

"Man, I wish you were here," Anthony said.

"Don't you have any friends in D.C.?"

"I know people, but they're not friends."

"What about your second family in Cleveland? Cread Williams is a veteran. And Raymond…have you talked to them? Have you spoken to any of the Williamses since you moved from there?"

"No. I'm a little embarrassed. It's been so long."

"If they knew what you've been through, I'm sure they'd understand."

"You're right, Chucky. I should."

"Yes, you should, because you will not make many friends beating up on people."

***

After Anthony hung up, a knock on the front door snapped his attention back to the moment. Could it be Carla? She hadn't returned his calls, but maybe she had come back. But, no, she'd walk right in.

It was the mail carrier with a package similar to the one he had delivered a few days earlier. Anthony studied it. Same kind of stamps, same writing, same size envelope, he thought as he laid it on the kitchen table.

Anthony opened it to see the same papers he had received before.

He looked downward, in thought, then retrieved the other set. Anthony sat and stared at the two stacks of papers, absentmindedly riffling one stack, then the other. The first three pages began and ended with the same names.

The phone rang, and Anthony almost tripped getting to it.

"Mr. Andrews?"

"Yes?"

"Congratulations, you've just won—"

Anthony hung up before the caller finished.

He looked at the two stacks again before tossing the second one in the kitchen trash can. They apparently sent it twice to make sure he got at least one of them. Anthony sat rubbing his forehead then put the remaining stack aside. But who was sending them—and for what purpose?

***

The "vacation" allowed Anthony to finish painting the garage and tool shed. Carla would be happy. The thought of her still caused a twinge in his gut. He missed her more now than at any other time in his life. He needed her more than any other time in his life. And he sorely missed his daughter. *Jesus, what's going on with me?* Anthony thought as he went back to the kitchen and picked up the phone to call Carla for the second time that day. He stood holding the phone to his ear, waiting. Finally, his father-in-law answered.

"Hello?"

"Mr. Monroe?"

"Yes. Anthony?"

"How are you?"

"I'm good, Anthony, and you?"

"Um, okay, sir. Is Carla around?"

"Anthony, let me give you a bit of advice."

"Yes, sir."

"You've known Carla long enough to know she's going to operate on her own terms with this issue."

"Yes, sir."

"So there's no need calling twice a day hoping she will respond. What you need to do, son, is to be ready when she makes up her mind she wants to see you again."

"Yes, sir."

"That means getting yourself together, son. It's hard to influence anything on the outside until you repair what's wrong on the inside. Do you understand what I'm saying?"

"Yes."

"Good. You're a smart young man. I like you. Norma likes you. Whatever happened between you two can be fixed. However, you've got to do the fixing on your end first."

"Okay. I'm working on it, Mr. Monroe, believe me. Could you do me a favor?"

"What's that, son?"

"Tell her I love her?"

"She knows, Anthony, but I'll tell her."

"Thank you, sir," Anthony said before placing the phone in the cradle and slumping into a chair at the kitchen table. At least he knew where Carla got her wisdom.

After he'd washed the paintbrushes and discarded the cans, Anthony returned to the house, showered, put Miles Davis's album *Workin' With The Miles Davis Quintet* on the turntable, made a cup of coffee, and sat at the typewriter, downhearted. He toyed with a pencil before throwing it across the room. How could he even begin to tell the story of The Seven and the other missing soldiers if he had no names, no history, and only an unconfirmed motive for their circumstance?

Miles's song "It Never Entered My Mind" played as Anthony sat, thinking. He played it repeatedly because soothing music was what he needed right then.

* * *

Countless calls and letters to the soldiers he'd interviewed came up blank. They seemed afraid of something—even after leaving Vietnam, even after leaving the Army. Means, the weight-lifting militant at Cu Chi, had been shipped to another stockade as far as Anthony could determine, and Ernie Daniels, his friend, was nowhere to be found.

It was his fault not getting the names of the seven soldiers. That should have been a priority. Anthony frowned as he tapped a pencil on the desktop. But how could he have known there'd be a clampdown?

He slid a blank sheet of paper across the desk. To hell with it, he thought as he got up to get a glass of grape juice—he'd write the story without the names. At the refrigerator, Anthony glanced at the stack of papers on the kitchen table again. The men's names were probably there, but how would he know one from another?

Back at the typewriter, Anthony typed: *There was something eerie about the seven bedraggled soldiers who returned from War Zone C. It was odd they were all black, and it was even stranger no one would talk about their mission. According to unsubstantiated...* Anthony stopped. How could he publish an unsubstantiated story?

The jarring ring of the telephone made him spill juice on the counter.

"H-hello."

"Anthony. How are you?" Bill Walden asked.

Anthony winced. They'd fired him. "Bill? Fine."

"You getting a well-deserved rest?"

"Uh. Yeah, Bill."

"Good. Well, I wanted to be the first to congratulate you."

Anthony paused. "On?"

"You, my friend, have been nominated for the Worth Bingham Prize in the international reporting category."

"Worth Bingham? Are you kidding?"

"No. Those were great articles, Anthony, obviously written from the heart. Enjoy the rest of your vacation."

"Yes, sir."

Buoyed by Walden's call, Anthony sat at the kitchen table and began typing again. After finishing a few pages, a thought penetrated his concentration. There were pictures. He had taken photos of The Seven when they exited the helicopter. He tapped his head with one finger. Where were they?

CHAPTER 16

Every day, Anthony fought the need to drink. Some days he was more successful than others. He was at his weakest when the dreams were the most vivid. And every day he scoured the paper, drawn to any news on Vietnam. He read voraciously from any news source he could access, even while battling the anxiety caused by the memories.

A week before Anthony was to return to work, he came across an article titled "Lost Soldier," by Jeremiah Remming, in a *Muhammad Speaks* magazine. The author wrote of a PFC Soledad, a former veteran, who had written to the paper concerning Private Jeremiah Frankford, a friend stationed with the 25th who was sent on patrol and never returned. The story described Soledad's search for his friend, who had mysteriously disappeared. Anthony tore the article from the magazine and placed it in his burgeoning file of Vietnam articles and other written material he had collected.

The next morning after breakfast, he pulled the story out again. Soledad had run into the same problems as Anthony. He called Remming to leave his name and number for Soledad to call. The telephone rang two hours later.

"Mr. Andrews?" an operator inquired.

"Yes."

"There's a collect call from a Mr. Soledad in Oakland, California. Will you accept the charge?"

"Yes."

"Mr. Andrews?"

"Mr. Soledad, thanks for calling."

"Sure."

"Do you know who I am?"

"Oh yeah. I heard of you from other friends at the 25th."

"When were you there?"

"August 30, 1968, to July 1, 1969."

Anthony's grip on the phone tightened, but he didn't want to get excited only to be disappointed again.

"I was with the 2nd Battalion, 27th Infantry."

"So. How are you doing, Mr. Soledad?"

"Please. Call me Furman."

"Okay."

"So, so."

Anthony took a deep breath. "Yeah. I understand." He paused to gather himself. "Look, I wanted to talk to you regarding the article about you in *Muhammad Speaks*. Any further luck finding Frankford?"

"Naw, man. I thought he might have been discharged early and left, but his parents haven't heard from him either." Soledad took a deep breath. "That's bullshit, man. How does a soldier just disappear like that?"

"Maybe he was MIA."

"Nope. At least the Army stated he wasn't missing."

"When did he last go on patrol?"

"He shouldn't have been on patrol. He was a clerk."

"When was the last time anybody saw him?"

"June 17. He was with other headquarter guys being herded some-where nobody knows about."

Anthony's heart skipped a beat. "Look. Can I call you back? I want to check something. I'm looking for some soldiers, too."

"Sure." He rattled off his phone number. "I'm living at this shel-ter, so if you don't get me the first time, call back, okay?"

"You bet." Anthony paused. "Oh. Wait."

"Yes?"

"Did Frankford have a middle name?"

"Yeah. Kendrick."

"And where was he from?"

"Akron, Ohio."

Anthony smiled at the mention of a city near his former home. "Okay. Thanks." Anthony placed the phone in the cradle, pulled the roster from a box and looked up Jeremiah Kendrick Frankford.

Anthony sighed after he had gone through the Fs and then the Ks and the Js looking for any name that resembled the private's name—another dead end.

He sat back, staring at the wall. How could a soldier be missing like that? He flipped through the rest of the roster to the last page and a date. It read August 5, 1969. Frankford should have been there. Anthony sat a while longer. Why would he think he'd have any more luck than Frankford's best friend?

The whir of the garbage truck's tailgate down the street interrupted his thoughts. Anthony emptied the contents of the kitchen trash into the garbage can in the garage and dragged it to the street.

His neighbor, Mrs. Solomon, was waiting when he returned.

"Hi, Anthony."

"Hi, Mrs. Solomon. How are you today?" Anthony mentally kicked himself. She was the most talkative person he'd ever met. Carla usually drew the brunt of Mrs. Solomon's unending conversations. But asking her how she was doing guaranteed a discussion that could take them into the next week.

"Well, I'm glad you asked…"

Anthony made a point of looking at his watch. Minutes, hours, weeks, then dates flashed through Anthony's mind. He raised a finger as Mrs. Solomon droned on. "Could you wait a minute, ma'am?" The garbagemen had pulled in front of Anthony's house. He dashed to the front lawn to drag one of his cans back into the garage as a confounded Mrs. Solomon and the garbage crew watched.

Anthony searched through the trash to retrieve the second copy of the roster, laying it on the ground, wiping tomato paste and congealed egg whites off it, and flipping it open to the last page where it showed a date of June 1, 1969. He picked up the sheets of papers before remembering Mrs. Solomon, but she had turned to walk back to her house, muttering.

As he rushed into the house, the telephone rang. Anthony ignored it as he flipped through pages until he got to the Fs in the second roster. Frankford! Jeremiah Kendrick!

Bingo! He thought as he wrote Frankford's name, rank, unit, serial number, and city on a piece of paper. He was doubly elated to hear a familiar voice on the answering device provided by the *Washington Post.*

"This is Terrence Means. If this is Anthony Andrews the reporter, give me a call at 718—"

Anthony snatched at the phone, but it fell. He grabbed it from the floor. "Hello? Hello?"

CHAPTER 17

Anthony called the number Means had left on the tape, but it was busy. He called three more times in succession with the same results. It was 10:00 P.M. and he was exhausted. He'd call the next day.

In the middle of another tortured night, this time with mortar shells falling around him like hailstones, it came to him as he awoke, out of breath and sweating as if he'd run a marathon. Anthony leaped from the bed and pulled the two rosters together, going over each page name by name. It was dawn when he finished, but the thrill of yesterday turned into unbridled exhilaration.

There were two rosters because the names of the fifteen men who were sent on patrol were on the June 1 roster but not on the August 5 roster. They had been removed.

He pulled out the pictures he had taken and laid them next to the list of fifteen names. If only he could place the names with the faces.

The clock read 6:15. It was too early to call Means, but it'd be the first thing he did. Then he'd devise a way to track these men with the information he had.

***

"Got out two months ago," Means said to Anthony, "with an OTH."

"OTH?"

"Other-Than-Honorable Discharge."

"What's that mean?"

"It means when I look for a job and they look at my service record, they'll see I was a troublemaker," Means chuckled. "The adjutant says, though, that if I keep my nose clean for a few years, it could be upgraded to a general discharge."

"They can do that?"

Means snorted. "Well, if they can't, then it wouldn't be the first time they lied, but I'm betting they can. They can do anything they want."

"And what do they mean by 'nose clean'?"

"I imagine they were telling that to everybody who they thought knew what was going on with the fifteen men. I guess they figured one way to keep things under wraps was to give out OTHs, or the threat of an OTH, and wait. And if one of the soldiers squealed, what's the word of an OTH'er worth?"

"So that's why nobody talked to me even after they were discharged," Anthony mused aloud.

"It's one reason."

"So how much do you know, Means? Or maybe I should ask how much are you willing to share?"

"I'll tell you all I know, man. Fuck the Army. If I had been on base, I would have been on patrol with those brothers, and I'd have been in the middle of that shit."

"What about your friend Ernie Daniels?"

"Haven't heard from him."

"I want to meet with you. Have you been in contact with anyone else since you've been out?"

"Naw, man. I've been scrambling, trying to work a few odd jobs to keep a roof over my head. Put the past behind me."

"I've got names."

"All of them?" Means asked.

"I'm fairly sure."

"How?"

"I got rosters from before and after their mission. I thought you or Daniels might have had something to do with it."

"Naw. I was in the joint, and I doubt Daniels would've had access. It's doubtful he knew anybody who did. I suspect he's an OTH'er himself."

"Yeah, probably. But look. How can we get together? I want to go over these names and anything else you weren't able to tell me in Cu Chi."

"I ain't got no travelin' money, so I guess you got to come to me."

"No problem. Let's pick a date—the sooner the better."

That night, sitting at the kitchen table, Anthony heard a scratching sound in the kitchen. He looked next to the refrigerator to see his little friend wasn't as smart as he was bold. He couldn't be too harsh on the little fellow, though. Who could resist a dab of peanut butter? Anthony took the cage to the backyard, opened it, and shook the mouse out. "You got a second chance, little buddy. Use it wisely."

Anthony could only hope he'd be afforded the same opportunity.

***

Things were looking up in one respect. Anthony wanted to celebrate but thought better of it. Even though the nightmares persisted, he had gone more than a week without a drink. As close as he was to getting answers regarding the seven black soldiers, though, he was getting no closer to normalizing his own life.

Something in him, something unknown, continued to fester and boil. There were times his brain felt as if it was in a deep, dark hole that was impossible to crawl out of. Most times he felt like a different person, a person he'd have been afraid of in the past, and he felt helpless trying to return to the pre-Vietnam Anthony.

CHAPTER 18

Anthony felt the stare before he saw the man in Manny's Five Star Restaurant sizing him up. The ex-boxer looked even bigger than Anthony remembered. But for some reason, it didn't matter.

When Marvin Hanson caught Anthony's eye, he slammed money on his table, stood, and stomped toward Anthony's booth.

"What's up, brother?" Anthony asked, leaning back in the booth, playing with the straw in his orange juice.

Hanson stopped, looking Anthony over. He stood glowering for a while before nodding as if he had solved a puzzle. "You one a them badasses, ain't you?" His fists clenched and unclenched, and his voice increased in volume with each word.

"Sir," a police officer in a far corner booth broke in, "you'll have to lower your voice."

"No, brother," Anthony said quietly, leaning forward and taking a sip of juice. "I just try to take care of my business."

Hanson stared at Anthony a few more seconds. "This ain't over," and slammed out the door.

"Wow. What did you do to piss him off?" the waitress asked as she poured Anthony more water.

Anthony shrugged. "Just boys being boys."

"You know who he is, right?"

"Yeah. I know."

After finishing breakfast, Anthony paid the bill and left. At the first red light, Anthony sat for a few minutes, looking in the mirror, contemplating the stern image in front of him. He rubbed his jaw as he studied his face and cocked his head. He held out his hand. It was steady as a rock.

He looked back in the mirror. *Who are you?*

***

Means had arranged a jitney to pick Anthony up from JFK Airport. That was cool. The hotel was not. Anthony hadn't heard so much moaning in the middle of the day since the Kappas had started a porn movie marathon in college. The hotel was definitely not family oriented.

"How's the accommodation?" Means asked when Anthony arrived at his apartment.

Anthony smirked at Means's t-shirt saying, *I Know I'm Going to Heaven 'Cause I Already Been Through Hell.* "Besides asking whether I wanted to pay by the hour or the day?"

"Hey, man. I'm sorry, but it was the closest hotel to me."

Anthony laughed. "Yeah? Well, you should have told that to the pimp outside the place. He looked at me like I was competition."

"Foster is one of my boys. He mentioned you seemed cool under the circumstances."

Anthony grimaced. "Guess that's what war does to you."

Means sat on his living room couch, the only other piece of furniture besides a beat-up mismatched yellow chair, and chuckled.

"Anyway…" Anthony pulled out two copies of the list of fifteen men he'd obtained from the rosters. "You recognize any of them?"

Means looked at the names and muttered something under his breath. "Yeah. I think I know two of 'em, but I can't tell for sure. Wait. Sergeant Willie Stinson! I know his name."

"How's that?"

"Everybody knew Sarge. They tell me during the rumble them boys scattered like rabbits when he started bangin'."

Anthony took notes, then pulled out the pictures he'd taken at the Chinook. "Know any of these guys?"

Means eyes brightened. "I was never good with names, but I remember this brother, and this one," he said, jabbing at men in the photos. "That's, uh, The Preacher, The Professor, Tank…"

Anthony stopped him. "Means. I can't go by nicknames. Match the pictures to their real names," Anthony insisted as he tapped the list.

Means's shoulders slumped. "We never dealt with real names, you know?"

"Is Sergeant Stinson in the picture?"

Means squinted, concentrating. "Naw. He ain't there."

Disappointed, Anthony nodded but took note of the nicknames and the location of each nicknamed person in the picture. At least he had one name, but there had to be a few Willie Stinsons in Cleveland. Hopefully, he was still alive.

"If Ernie was here, he'd know most of 'em," Means said, breaking into Anthony's musings.

"That's my next move."

"What?"

"You want to take a ride to Pittsburgh?"

"Now?"

"Yeah."

"Why not? It's Friday," Means answered. "I got two days off and nothing else to do. Plus, I'd love to see the brother."

"Cool. I'll rent a car."

***

There were five E., Ernest, or Ernie Daniels in the Pittsburgh phone book. Anthony had checked before he'd taken off for New York. Three of the Daniels had never been in the army. One hadn't ever answered the phone. An older lady answered the last phone call.

"Ernie Daniels, please?"

There was a long pause. "He ain't here."

"Is this the home of Ernie Daniels who was in Vietnam?"

"Yeah."

Yes! Anthony mouthed. "Do you know when he'll be in?"

A longer pause. "He ain't here."

"Are you his mother?"

"Who's asking?"

"My name is Anthony Andrews, ma'am. I met Ernie in Vietnam. I'm a reporter and wanted to talk to him concerning his experiences there."

"He ain't here."

"Well, could you tell him I called?"

The silence was followed by the click of the phone.

The elation in finding Daniels overrode any concerns about Daniels's mother's reluctance to talk. Anthony was on a roll now. He had names, and he had a contact. Things were starting to fall into place. With Daniels's input, he might hook up with a few of The Seven and Sergeant Willie Stinson.

***

"So, outside of the OTH, you got nothing positive to say about the Army?" Anthony asked Means as he pulled onto Interstate 78.

"Nothin'."

"How did you join?"

"They drafted me. I tried everything I knew to get exempted, but they drug my ass in kickin' and screamin'."

"It seems like there should have been some positives. What about free education after you leave…and the ability to buy a house with nothing down?"

"You never served, did you?" Means asked.

"No. I didn't."

"None of it means shit if your ass is dead."

"I hear you," Anthony replied as the bullets hitting the tree punctured his thoughts.

"Plus, it ain't no different from the real world. Regardless of how well you perform, you ain't gonna get promoted like *they* do; you ain't gonna get the gravy jobs or the money *they* do."

"Some became officers, though."

"Let me tell you somethin', Mr. Andrews."

"Anthony. Call me Anthony."

"Let me tell you somethin', Anthony. If you made it past major, you gave up somethin'."

"I'm not sure I understand."

"Most of the black colonels and generals had to kiss somebody's ass to get there. They gave up a piece of themselves."

Anthony had nothing to counter Means's assertion, so he deferred to his point of view, even though Means the militant probably distrusted any person in authority.

"The *stractest* officer I knew was a black major—Major Kendall Jamison."

"Stractest?"

"Strategically ready and combat tough. His battalion had more victories and fewer casualties than any other battalion. His men loved him, but he didn't take no shit from the top. So in spite of his outstanding field performance, he would never even make light colonel, much less general in a million years because he didn't play their game. You dig?"

"Yeah. I hear you."

"The army ain't shit for a black man. Look at me. Look at us. All we wanted was equal treatment, and we end up OTHs or dead."

***

"We're on 'The Hill,'" Means observed as Anthony negotiated streets based on a map he had bought at a gas station.

"What's 'The Hill'?"

"That's where our people live."

Anthony laughed. "Are you hungry, Means?"

"I could eat."

"Okay. Look out for a place."

"Let's try Mame's Restaurant over there," Means said, pointing down the street.

"You sure? Quite a few dudes standing around."

Means shrugged. "You hungry or not?"

Anthony parked the car so it'd be visible from the restaurant window.

"Excuse me, brothers. Can we get through?" Means asked as he approached the group lounging at the entrance of the restaurant.

"What you need, man?" one of the men in the crowd asked.

"Food, my brother. Just food," Means responded.

A couple of the men chuckled.

"Where you from that you come here lookin' for food?" a heavy-set, pock-marked, dark-skinned man with what looked to be a perpetual scowl asked.

Means turned to the man. "You trying to tell me the food's no good here?"

Sensing hostility, Anthony turned with Means. "Or is this just a restaurant for you brothers?" Anthony asked.

The heavy-set man looked at the two, his eyes narrowed before chuckling. "We don't see many people got the balls to walk through a group of Purple Knights."

"I apologize, brother 'cause you see, we *ain't* from here. No disrespect," Means said.

The heavy-set man looked at Means and Anthony once more before turning to leave with the others following. "Enjoy your food."

The waitress spilled water on the table and nervously cleaned it up. "They must a thought you were cops. They stomped a guy last week when he didn't buy any dope."

"I believe it," Means said matter-of-factly.

"You the police?"

"No, ma'am. Me? I'm the furthest thing from it. Let me have the pork chops and grits. You are buying, right?" Means asked.

"Got you."

"How's everything?" the waitress asked about ten minutes after serving the food.

"Great!" Means exclaimed wiping his mouth with a paper napkin and pushing the plate away.

"You're going to get a stomachache eating so fast," the waitress admonished Means.

Means laughed. "I know. I've heard that before. It's a bad habit I picked up from the army."

Upon leaving, Anthony tipped the waitress double. "This is for the excellent food and the motherly advice," Anthony said smiling.

As the car pulled onto the highway, Means rolled the window down and took a deep breath. "I like how you handled yourself back there."

"I didn't do anything."

"You woulda," Means said, then paused. "And that's kinda interesting because you don't appear the type."

Anthony stared at the cars ahead of them. "Yeah?"

***

Ernie Daniels's address was an apartment on Herron Avenue. The apartment, with Harold's Southern Ribs restaurant on the first floor, wasn't hard to find. The sweet smell of smoked meat followed Anthony and Means up the stairs. Apartment 202 was at the end of the steepest steps Anthony had ever climbed. After catching his breath, he knocked on the door.

"Yes?"

Anthony recognized the voice immediately.

"Mrs. Daniels? I'm Anthony Andrews. We talked on the phone concerning Ernie."

"I told you he ain't here."

Anthony smiled. "Yes ma'am, but it's important we talk to him."

"What didn't you understand about 'he ain't here'?" She paused. "He dead."

Anthony looked at Means in disbelief. "A…I'm sorry, Mrs. Daniels. What happened? When did he die?"

There was silence on the other side of the door before Anthony heard the soft scuffle of shoes fading.

Anthony and Means stood at the door looking at each other.

"Damn," Anthony muttered as he took a deep breath and let it out slowly. "Let's see if we can find what happened."

CHAPTER 19

Ernie Daniels's obituary was in Monday's *Pittsburgh Tribune* and the current week's *New Pittsburgh Courier*. Anthony read it. "State track champion. Graduated in the top twenty percent of his class from Carnegie Mellon University in engineering. Did you know this about Ernie?" Anthony asked Means.

"Naw, man. I met him when we were in 'Nam and only for a few months. He was just a down brother to me."

"But they don't say how he died." Anthony read further. "His funeral is tomorrow. Let's go."

"Cool with me."

***

Calvary Baptist Church was full. Anthony looked around, hoping he might recognize someone who had served with Ernie or Means. He asked Means to do the same.

"See anybody?"

"No."

Anthony watched as the family came in. A stately lady who appeared to be Ernie's mother, and who looked nothing like the angry woman behind her apartment door, led the procession.

After the funeral, Anthony tried to approach Mrs. Daniels, but could not get through the throng of family and friends. He gave his business card to the funeral director. "I was in Vietnam with Ernie. I'd like to share my memory of him with his mother."

***

"It appears we hit a dead end with Ernie," Anthony said as they pulled out of the church parking lot.

"Yeah. It was a good try, though. Just a little late," Means added.

Disheartened, Anthony didn't respond.

"Did you know a Captain Valentine?" Anthony asked, as he pulled onto the highway heading back to Brooklyn.

"Yeah. He was cool for an officer."

"What do you know about him?"

"Nothing much, except the other officers didn't like him much."

"Why?"

"They say he did too much fraternizing with his men. He was similar to Major Jamison."

"You know he was missing when his company got ambushed outside of Tay Ninh?"

"Yeah. I heard it from one of my Ranger buddies who was assigned to his company."

"Ranger?"

"Yeah. I was in Ranger school."

Anthony laughed. "Means, you are full of surprises—or maybe I

86

should say contradictions. You hate the Army, but you join one of the most elite groups in the service?"

"Ain't so strange. I was protectin' myself. If I had to go to war, I wanted all the training I could get. Plus, it would come in handy when I got back to the states."

"What happened?"

"One week left to graduate and I hurt a guy real bad in a hand-to-hand combat contest. I kinda freaked out. I get like that when it's somebody I don't like. They thought I did it on purpose, so they kicked me out."

"Sounds as if there's more to the story."

Means shrugged. "You'd think I'm the kind of guy they'd want."

"Not if you're hurting your own men."

"Yeah. Probably not."

"So, what did you hear about Valentine?"

"I heard one of his former soldiers was in the fifteen who went out on patrol and never returned. Valentine volunteered to do the recon around Tay Ninh, then took a company to find the remaining men. They were supposed to court martial him for dereliction of duty, but they didn't far as I know."

Anthony turned to Means. So Valentine was connected to The Seven. "How come you didn't tell me this before?"

"We just started talkin' a few days ago, man. I forgot until you mentioned his name," Means answered. "Anyway, *you* the reporter."

"You know what happened to him?"

"Nope. Here today, gone tomorrow."

Seems to be a recurring theme, Anthony thought.

CHAPTER 20

Anthony sensed something was wrong before he even neared his house. The few neighbors on the street stared instead of waving. *Someone must have died.*

As he turned into the driveway, he saw his picture window was broken. Even the verbose Mrs. Solomon spoke slowly.

"Don't know what this world is coming to when a person can't go away and come back to peace and quiet."

"What happened, Mrs. Solomon?"

"Nobody knows. Mr. Calhoun across the street said he heard glass breaking last night and a car speeding away. He thinks it was one of them souped-up jobs from the sound of the engine. You might want to talk to him. He's the one who called the police."

"Did they come?"

"Not yet."

"Okay. Thanks, Mrs. Solomon," Anthony said as he turned the key in the lock. He walked cautiously through the kitchen checking the stove because he smelled gas. He passed through the dining room toward the living room, looking left and right until he saw the object that broke the window. It wasn't a rock. It was a broken Coke bottle with a rag nearby. The spilled liquid smelled like gasoline.

Two thoughts immediately crossed his mind. He was glad Carla and Mali weren't home, and he had to get things right before they returned.

***

"Who would do that, Anthony?" Means asked over the phone.

"It must have been this guy Hanson."

"Hanson. The only Hanson I know around there is a—"

"That's him."

"The boxer? How you end up buggin' with him?"

"We had a fight over a woman. I knocked him down. Actually, out."

"What? He trip or somethin'?"

"No. But I had been drinking. I don't remember much except he fell on the floor after I hit him, and he didn't get up."

Means chuckled. "Now who's, uh, contradictory? A quiet, soft-spoken, married reporter knocks out a former light-heavyweight boxer, previously ranked in the top ten after throwin' down a few shots and walks off with the boxer's woman. No wonder you were ready to bug in the restaurant. What happened to her?"

"Uh. Nothing. It was his ex-wife."

Means laughed. "I'm sure there's more to that story, too." Means paused. "But to tell you the truth, I doubt it was Hanson."

"Why?"

"Because throwin' a bottle, even a Molotov cocktail, through the window of somebody who just kicked your ass is a punk move. And regardless of what happened in the bar, Hanson ain't no punk."

"Well. Whoever it was, they meant to burn this place down."

"Considering the circumstances, you seem kind of cool."

Anthony pursed his lips but said nothing.

"Maybe they meant to torch it, maybe not. Was the rag burnt?"

Anthony thought a moment. "No."

"Then it was just a message." Means grunted. "Sound as if you might need a little help."

"No. I should be okay," Anthony replied.

"Let me know. I shipped enough stuff from 'Nam to start a small war."

"Isn't that against the l... I appreciate it Means, but the police should be able to handle it."

"You live in a black neighborhood?"

"Mixed."

"Then they might."

CHAPTER 21

T he police came later that day, asked a few questions, took pictures, and took the bottle fragments and rag as evidence. They performed the tasks so perfunctorily, Anthony didn't expect to hear from them again.

"Sir?"

"Yeah?" Anthony responded to the window installer as he turned from going up the stairs to the second floor.

"I don't know if this is important, but we found this piece of paper when we were sweeping up under that chair," the installer said pointing to a leather high-back chair.

"Thanks." Anthony sniffed as he unfolded the paper. It smelled like gasoline, too. There were three words. *FORGET ABOUT IT.*

It was Hanson; Anthony was sure of it. Anthony wished he could talk to him, tell him nothing had happened with his ex and nothing was going to happen. He held the piece of paper by a corner in case there were fingerprints.

***

The next morning was Anthony's first day back to work. The staff greeted him with pats on the back and "Way to go, Anthony." "Good job, man." Even Shanklar shook his hand.

In his search for The Seven, Hanson, and Means, Anthony had pushed the Worth Bingham nomination to the back of his mind.

"Awww," Anthony remarked as he noticed the flowers and card on his desk. The gestures relieved the anxiety he felt about coming back to work.

Expecting more congratulatory words, he opened the card and laughed. "Welcome back. Now get your ass to work. Bill."

***

The card refocused Anthony. He would put The Seven on hold for a while. Considering the job, Hanson, and, hopefully, the return of Carla and Mali, there was more than enough to keep him busy.

In addition, he needed to step away from Vietnam, period. The dreams were less frequent, but he hoped if he could concentrate on the tasks at hand, he'd be the better for it.

***

As he scanned through the mail upon returning home that evening, Anthony's hands trembled when he saw the envelope from Eden Prairie, Minnesota. His reaction confused him. Who did he know in Minnesota? Anthony opened the envelope slowly, and then it hit him like a left hook to the temple. Arne Nielson, the reporter for *Newsweek,* was from Minnesota.

Inside the envelope was another envelope with a letter addressed to Anthony.

October 18, 1969

Dear Mr. Andrews,

We are forwarding this to you since it had your name on it. Arne spoke fondly of you and mentioned you were working on finding someone. We hope whatever's in the envelope will help you with your search.

Sincerely,

Erik and Aniki Nielson

P.S. Thank you so much for the kind words you wrote us about our son.

Anthony hesitated before opening the enclosed letter. Would it hold the secret to The Seven or was it a Pandora's Box of bad memories that'd pull him back into the folds of the nightmares he was trying to escape?

Anthony steeled himself, took Arnie's envelope to his favorite chair in the living room, and slit it open.

Hey, man. It's hot as hell out here. Hope you are staying cool.

Anthony smiled, relieved at the greeting.

But his relief lasted as long as the first sentence.

Anthony, I know you might have heard those fifteen men were lost. They weren't lost. Be careful. Watch your back. There was a screw-up. Officers' careers are on the line. More info later.

94

Questions flew around Anthony's head like ricocheting bullets. He sat trying to sort out what those few sentences meant.

***

"It was odd, Mr. Andrews. There were no prints on any of the evidence we collected, including the note you brought in. We usually can find something, but whoever threw the bottle was careful, very careful."

Anthony thanked the officer. He was surprised they had called and even more surprised they had tried to solve the case. He'd already planned his next move. He would go to the bar where he had fought with Marvin Hanson to straighten things out. Anthony figured if Hanson knew he had no designs on his ex, he might back off.

Anthony had no intention of telling the police it was Hanson. That'd be a punk move on *his* part.

The Shanty was quiet for a Thursday night when the place served short ribs, baked potato, and coleslaw as a special. Anthony looked around, then walked over to the bar. "Has Marvin Hanson been in today?"

Joe the bartender turned. His eyes widened, and the grin on his face was so broad, Anthony could have fit a beer bottle in it sideways. He pointed at Anthony. "You the…"

"Yeah," Anthony replied, blushing.

The bartender shook his hand. "Why you lookin' for him? You wanna go another round?"

"No. I just want to talk to him. Has he been in?"

Joe giggled. "Man, he ain't been in since you decked him. I'm guessin' he a tad embarrassed."

"Well," Anthony said as he pulled out a pen and wrote his name and number on a napkin. "Tell him to call me if you see him."

"Will do, champ."

Anthony gave a half-hearted wave as he walked out the door.

Boy, Anthony thought, he was having no luck finding anyone. However, he had found Means. No. Means had found him. But he had found Ernie Daniels. Not much good came of it. But he did have the name of the seven soldiers.

The phone rang, jarring him back into the present.

"Hello?"

"This is Virginia Ector. I'm Ernie's sister. I understand you wanted to talk."

CHAPTER 22

I'm sorry for your loss."

"Thank you. It was nice of you to come to the funeral. So how did you know Ernie?" Virginia Ector asked.

"I was writing a story about black soldiers. Ernie was one of the men I interviewed."

Virginia was silent for a moment. "Do you know how he died?"

"No. I wondered…"

"Suicide."

"Sui…Why?"

"I can only guess." She paused again. "My brother was successful in everything he did—sports, school…But when he got a Dishonorable Discharge, it depressed him."

"Dishonorable? You sure it wasn't an Other-Than-Honorable?"

"No. He made it very clear he received the worst of the discharges."

"Did he say why?"

"He never said, but he had a job waiting for him at an engineering firm, Schlacter and Associates. He was to be the first minority hired until they found out he was dishonorably discharged. No one else would hire him either."

"I'm sorry."

"I wish I knew what happened in the Army for them to treat him like that."

Without knowing Virginia Ector, Anthony admired that although sad, there was no bitterness in her voice. "I'll do my best to find out for you."

"Thank you."

***

"Daniels committed suicide," Anthony related to Means over the phone.

"What?" Means asked.

"That's what his sister said."

"Wow."

"Evidently he was to get this great job when he returned home but was turned down because of his discharge status."

"That's it?"

"Far as I can tell."

"There's got to be more to it. He didn't seem that weak."

"You never know what's going on in somebody's mind," Anthony offered.

"Yeah. You got that right. But with his background he had more options."

The phone rang as soon as Anthony hung up. Two days with no calls, then two in a row. Maybe…

"Hello?"

"What you want?"

Disheartened it wasn't Carla, Anthony took a deep breath. "Mr. Hanson. Look. I want to set things straight between you and me."

"Why?"

"Well. I just wanted you to know I have no interest in your ex-wife."

Hanson laughed. "Five hundred other people do, why not you?"

"I–I have somebody."

"Why are you tellin' me this? I ain't interested in your love life, fool!"

"Somebody is. I got a Molotov cocktail thrown through my window and a note saying 'forget about it.' I figured…"

"What? You think it was me?" Hanson asked. "You some kind a cat. That's another woman's man tryin' to get to you, player."

"So. You didn't—"

"If I want to take you out, I'll be in your chest, not throwing bottles at your house. That's a sissy move."

Anthony sat back after hanging up, relieved, but confused and frustrated. Instead of making sense of the puzzle, it had just become more complex.

CHAPTER 23

For some reason, the dreams had come back with a vengeance. The screams were the kind that pierced his brain, then tore through his body, causing him to shiver for minutes after.

It made Anthony reconsider Chucky's suggestion of getting help. It might even get Carla back—but not yet. Things needed to be more settled.

Virginia Ector gave Anthony new resolve and one more reason to find out what happened to the fifteen men and the location of those who had survived. *Leave no man behind.*

He pulled out the sheet with the names and his notations and read them aloud as if a spirit would hear and reveal the information he needed.

Anthony started to take a sip of Jack Daniels to salute the men. Instead, he took the bottle and the names into the backyard and poured a few drops on the ground to honor each of them for their service.

***

"Means?"

"Yeah, Anthony."

"I got a question."

"Yes?"

"Is there any reason most of these guys came from Cleveland?"

Means laughed. "Man, Cleveland guys stuck together like the Mafia. That's why they're on your list. When the fight broke out, Ernie said they did the most damage."

"You named Rabid, Preacher, and the Professor. Do you know any more about them?"

"They were from Cleveland."

"Anything else?"

Means paused. "Naw."

"If you asked around, you think you could find out their real names?"

"Maybe. I know Rabid was a gang banger. I didn't know Preacher or Professor that well, but I'll check and get back to you."

Anthony noted Means's comments. "Thanks. I'll be in touch."

CHAPTER 24

"Mrs.—or is it Ms.—Ector?" Anthony asked over the phone.

"Mrs. How can I help you?"

"This is Anthony Andrews. Is this a good time to talk?"

"Yes, sure."

"Did Ernie talk to you about Vietnam?"

"No. When he came back, he was the quietest I'd ever seen him."

"He mentioned nothing about people he might have served with?"

"Um, no. Not that I remember, but my memory is not the greatest." Virginia Ector hesitated. "He wrote, though. He wrote a lot."

Anthony's need to know was heightened by the possibility that Ernie's letters might further divulge answers to The Seven. "Would it be possible to read those letters?"

"I don't know, Mr. Andrews. Our mother would have a fit if she knew I'd given them to anyone."

"I understand, Mrs. Ector, and I respect that. However, something terrible happened to black soldiers over there, and it was covered up as far as I can determine. I can't tell you if any of it relates to Ernie, but I know Ernie knew of the situation that got them into that mess, and anything I can find to uncover what happened to them might help another mother in her grief."

Anthony held his breath, waiting, hoping he had been considerate enough.

"Well, if you put it like that, Mr. Andrews. I guess I could share them with you, but I don't want what he wrote to be publicized. Can I trust you not to?"

Anthony exhaled quietly. "Mrs. Ector, I promise you I won't. It's important to provide answers to the families whose sons died and resolution to those still alive, nothing else."

As Anthony hung up the phone, he sat back trying not to be too optimistic. They were just letters and might disclose nothing. But Ernie was the closest without being in it. He had to have written about a situation as bizarre as The Seven. Anthony would bet on it.

***

Two days after his phone conversation with Means, the mail carrier delivered a medium-size envelope. The return name was Ector.

Anthony ripped it open and pulled out sheets of paper wrapped in a neat bundle with a cover letter.

Mr. Andrews. I'm sharing these letters with you and have the utmost confidence they will remain private. I hope there's something in them that will help you in your search.

There were close to twenty letters. Anthony unwrapped them and began skimming, looking for names, references to the brawl, anything. Most of the letters were mundane, describing the food, the base, and reassuring his sister he was not in harm's way. One letter saddened Anthony. Daniels described his relationship with Colonel

Bolt, whom he'd clerked for.

He doesn't like me for some reason, so I guess I don't like him either. One thing for sure, whatever his problem is with me won't affect what I do after the army.

Anthony bowed his head. He wished Daniels had been right.

Anthony was on the fifteenth letter when he read:

Something's wrong. Two of my good friends, Casper and Warfield, are missing. Probably has to do with the fight, but I never processed any paperwork on them, and nobody's answering any questions.

The next letter was another reassuring response to his sister. But the seventeenth letter, dated June 25 read:

Casper, Warfield, and now Sampson, Turner, James, and Glover are still missing. It's been seven days. Even if they were on some kind of mission, like somebody said, that would be crazy, because based on their military occupational specialties, most of them shouldn't be in the field at all. And if they are, it shouldn't have taken so long. I hope they aren't lost or dead. But if so, there should be a search team. I haven't heard anything like that happening. I'm really worried. These are my friends.

PART II

CHAPTER 25

June 18, 1969

At 0700 hours, under a gray overcast sky, the Chinook dropped fifteen men at the bottom of a flattened hill. To Sergeant Willie Stinson, the bunkers lined with sandbags seemed haphazardly placed; he assumed there was a purpose to their positions. A thirty-foot observation tower loomed over two larger bunkers with fifty-caliber machine guns mounted and pointed toward the north and west.

"They look like zombies," Stinson observed as he and Casper glanced at the hill's occupants. The soldiers sat around playing cards or lounging in their underwear near their bunkers, talking slowly and moving even slower. Most were unshaven and their hair unkempt. It didn't take but a few seconds to understand their listlessness as cannabis smoke wafted around the fifteen soldiers trudging up the dirt path.

A sergeant met them at the base of the hill and led them up a rock strewn path. Not one of the resident soldiers gave the visitors more than a glance, much less a greeting. The place stank of unattended open latrines and garbage. *No discipline*, Stinson surmised as he looked around. *If we are meeting officers who condone this, we are in serious trouble.*

Barbed wire and concertina coils covered the hillside. Three tents dotted the hill. Stinson figured the command post was the larger tent with sandbags stacked five feet high around it and topped by three long whip antennas.

On a wooden sign in front of the command post, *Fire Base Serenity* had been meticulously carved into a strip of wood and nailed to a wooden stake. Another sign, just as artfully done on an arrow-shaped piece of wood pointing west said *Complete Serenity 13,813 KMs.*

Two somber-looking sergeants stood in the back of the tent as the fifteen men crowded in. With no formal introductions, a Captain Ramsey began speaking. "There's been ramped-up activity by the Cong in the area. We think they're gathering for another assault on our bases near Tay Ninh. We need to know where. You are to find evidence of NVA activity and report back to us," Ramsey said, rolling and unrolling a sheaf of papers.

"Your mission is to be our eyes and ears. You will be dropped southeast of your objective. You are then to proceed northwest to a ridge indicated on a map Sergeant Stinson will be given. Report any and all activity, but you are not to engage. Any questions?"

The men looked at each other with blank faces. After a pause, Ramsey continued, "If after reaching your destination, you have seen no Cong activity, you will meet with soldiers from the 1st Cav, who will give you further instructions on getting back to base."

Without any fanfare, the men were herded aboard a Chinook, and ten minutes later, dropped into a valley. Stinson quickly led the men out of the clearing to a tangle of trees, bushes, and vines.

***

A sinking feeling flashed through Myron "Professor" Turner, a clerk in the adjutant general's office as he wiped his glasses and watched the helicopter lift and fade into the distance. Even though he was with fourteen other soldiers, it was the loneliest he'd ever felt in his life.

Turner, whose father used to call him Sammy Davis Jr. because of his looks and stature, had listened carefully to Captain Ramsey. Was it the way he talked—a slow, somber speech unlike the kind he'd heard other troops receive before they went to the bush? Or was it the way the captain never looked any of them in the eye? Maybe it was merely the voice in Turner's head saying unh-uh.

The last time Turner heard that voice, Farley Williams wanted to take him to a party in Akron. Farley had been invited by a girl he'd met at Dearing's restaurant. Turner didn't feel good about the situation and begged off, warning his friends to decline, too.

"Why, Turner?" Farley had asked.

Turner shrugged.

Farley had laughed, slapping Turner playfully on his back. "Catch you on the rebound, then."

The next day Turner was told Farley had been shot and wounded. Ralph and Frank were severely beaten. The girl who'd invited Farley wanted to make an ex-boyfriend jealous. It worked. The ex and his boys took it out on the three from Cleveland, who barely made it home.

The ex, however, had made a serious mistake. Farley Williams was a member of the Williams family, a feared and respected family in the Cleveland Glenville area. It only took Cread Williams, a cousin, to send three of the assailants to the hospital. The ex, to Turner's knowledge, was still being treated a year later.

But there was no choice this time. Turner couldn't say no. They were already in trouble because of the so-called riot. Disobeying an order now would put him back in the stockade.

He sighed as they entered the jungle. Turner knew many of the guys because they were Clevelanders, but they were mostly clerks, cooks, and drivers—support personnel. That scared him. None of them, as far as he could determine, except Sergeant Stinson and maybe Casper and Fletcher, had placed one foot in the bush their entire time in country. What he'd heard of the rest gave him no comfort, no comfort at all.

* * *

Sergeant Willie Stinson had hung his head when the captain had called his name to lead the squad. He had hoped there was at least one person in the group who outranked him. Sixty-two days and he would be a civilian. He should be sitting in the NCO club, sipping a Bud with the other short-timers, but instead, he was out here with these doofus-assed, sons-a-bitches.

He wouldn't even have been involved in the fight if the odds had been better, but the black soldiers were outnumbered three to one. At first he tried to break up the fighting, but then one of the white soldiers swung on him. Stinson had worked on his temper since he was a teen, but the tipping point was never far away.

The punch transformed him from a peacekeeper to a combatant, sucking him into a maelstrom of bodies, fists, and clubs, provoking him to throw blows so hard and so often, some of the other fighters stopped to watch in awe.

The clash lasted about ten minutes before the MPs arrived, shooting into the air, rushing in to break up the small skirmishes, and arresting those they thought had resisted. Stinson was one of those arrested.

Of all the evil he'd done in his life, he was being punished for trying to do something right?

***

Stinson gathered the soldiers in an area surrounded by chest-high brush and fifty foot trees with exposed roots as tall as the men. "Listen up," he shouted as the throbbing whir of their helicopter faded into the distance. "This is simple," he said, as he looked at the map under the plastic overlay. "We head north, following this ridge line until we cross this stream…"

"Man, somethin' ain't right," Specialist 4 Fletcher interrupted. "All we got are these M-16s and grenades. Where's our heavy weapons? We should at least have a sixty. And what about a medic?"

At six-feet-two inches even, Fletcher was taller than Stinson, but not as bulked. The scar across his forehead, half covered by a tightly wound black rag, gave him the appearance of a Barbary pirate, which was appropriate given his background.

Born in the Carver Housing Projects of Cleveland and raised by his aunt with four of her own children, Fletcher grew up angry— angry at being abandoned, angry at being poor, and angry at being hungry. The anger, partly assuaged by his membership in the Skulls, a small but vicious Cleveland gang, was only submerged completely in combat where he was given the name Rabid.

Fletcher had gained his reputation four months ago, after his company had entered a village suspected of sympathizing with the VC. He and four other GIs entered the village first, shooting indiscriminately, killing an elderly couple before their Sergeant Manor yelled cease fire.

"You are lucky if I don't court-martial your asses. Who told you to fire?"

"Shit, Sergeant Manor," Fletcher had replied. "They all gooks. What's the problem?"

In a movie, Stinson would have been Fletcher's counterpart with a constant scowl and dark, piercing eyes surrounded by an ebony-toned broad face. Where Fletcher could have been a guard for a basketball team, Stinson would have been a fullback for a football team.

"This is a recon mission, Fletcher," Stinson responded. "Didn't you hear the captain? We are not to engage."

Sergeant Stinson raised his hands as he looked at Fletcher. "We ain't got much choice about this thing, do we?" he said, looking around. "Our best bet is to follow orders and complete this mission as quickly as possible."

Stinson had doubts too. The instructions were sketchy, his men were untrained, the terrain was unknown, and the enemy? With all those variables, making it there and back could be a problem.

CHAPTER 26

Self-doubt didn't visit Willie Stinson often, even though he was an orphan who had moved around more times than a desert nomad. It never bothered him because he thought it was the plight of all strays.

Willie's forte in life was his physical ability. He was fast, strong for his age, and good at whatever sport he played. At the age of ten, Willie threw a football sixty yards. He could almost dunk at fifteen although not quite six feet tall, and Willie was faster than anyone at any school he attended, including guys on the track team.

Willie grasped early on that being good at the physical wasn't enough, however. He'd competed against bigger guys all his life. He wasn't always the strongest, but his will was.

After three fights established his reputation at Patrick Henry Jr. High School, Willie only needed to fight sparingly until he moved to another family, and then it would start again. And every time he moved, his reputation grew.

In fights or competition, Willie became like a race car shifting to whatever gear he needed to drive to victory. He never thought much about it, but occasionally there would be a fleeting notion, a wave of consciousness that for brief moments allowed him some self-analysis. Willie knew he was different because people treated him differently. He knew he was good because he always won. But the drive, that need, the burning desire to win? He figured everybody had it, except his was more intense.

But he never took it for granted.

To be the best at anything, Willie understood he had to be a student first. So during most of his waking hours, he sought ways to be better. That meant practicing, getting stronger, and watching the older boys who excelled.

He studied Melvin Johnson, who weighed 150 pounds at most, but could shoot a basketball from half-court with little or no effort by bringing it as far behind his head as possible before releasing it like a slingshot.

He even snuck into a ballet studio on Euclid Avenue to try to understand the importance of balance because he'd overheard one of the basketball coaches telling his team about the agility of ballerinas. And most importantly, he learned to recognize an opponent's weakness and how to exploit it.

"You too intense, man. You need to lighten up. It's just a game," Leroy, one of his teammates, told Willie once when they were playing basketball at Pattison Park.

Willie scowled at Leroy. "If you ain't playing to win, then why are you playing at all?"

But as he grew older, Willie attributed at least part of his drive to his past. Abandoned at five by a father he'd seen but never knew and a mother who died the same year, Willie's life was in the control of strangers. By the age of eight, Willie had been with two different families. In each case, he guessed he'd done something wrong. If the family didn't want him, why should anybody else? All he had was himself. Nobody wanted a castaway.

It wasn't as if he acted up, at least no more than he heard other kids did. He never talked back and did whatever chores his foster parents asked, but for different reasons it was necessary to move on. Nobody ever told him why.

At first he thought this was the natural order of things, each house a way station until he grew old enough to take care of himself. Because he made few friends and never connected with his foster parents, moving around didn't seem strange to him until he moved to Thornewood Avenue in the Glenville area with the Stinsons at the age of fourteen. The house was the best he'd lived in, and the street was the quietest he'd lived on. He even made a friend—kind of.

That's when he met Raymond Williams, and that's when his world changed because Raymond was Willie's equal in those things Willie valued most. Raymond was as fast, could throw as far, could play baseball and basketball as well, and Raymond could fight.

Willie discovered the latter when they fought over a foul in a basketball game. When Willie cried, frustrated he wasn't winning, it was the most embarrassing moment of his life. That was the first time self-doubt crept into his mind.

CHAPTER 27

For Sergeant Willie Stinson, uncertainty raised its ugly head again in the jungle. But it took Fletcher to ratchet it up even more as the men gathered around Stinson.

"How in the hell are we supposed to follow this piece of paper? Where are the coordinates, the landmarks, names of nearby villages, rivers, roads? What do we accomplish with this?" Fletcher asked, poking at the plastic-encased map. Four mountains, two ridges, a valley, two streams, a lot of trees and a north arrow. Are you kidding me? It looks like some five-year-old drew this up."

Even though he and Fletcher had similar backgrounds, Fletcher was no Raymond. There were no doubts about Fletcher, just the mission, so Stinson felt no need to compete. He had seen guys like Fletcher before. They self-destructed if they didn't see the light, and he doubted Fletcher ever would.

"To get from here to here," Stinson asserted, stabbing at two places on the map.

Although Stinson understood Fletcher's concerns, Stinson cared less about the mission than the fact he'd been put in charge. He hadn't joined the army to lead. And he was more surprised than anyone when he'd received a battlefield promotion on LZ Abbey for "bravery." But in reality, he fought so fiercely at the landing zone because he had no option. Charlie had penetrated their line. Stinson had run from one breach to another, firing and killing enough of them for his company

115

to regroup.

"Chaos births heroes," Captain Alexander had proclaimed when HQ notified Stinson of his promotion.

They also told Stinson he might be recommended for the Silver Star, but after the clash between the black and white soldiers, he'd be lucky to keep his stripes.

Before the fight, he had been a rebel like Fletcher. The army still meant nothing to him, though. So *his* mission was simple. Get his ass back to base, in one piece, as quickly as possible.

Stinson scratched his chest as he looked at the map again. It *was* skimpy on info, but his greatest problem would be the men. If they did encounter the enemy, he and these men would be toast. To protect himself, Stinson would have to perform field training on the move to ready them for combat.

"Lack of preparedness breeds surprise, and surprise breeds panic." Stinson marveled at how much he remembered from Sergeant Appling, who had adopted him after LZ Abbey.

As he glanced around, Stinson recalled signing up one and a half years ago. At the age of twenty-four, he was already older than the eighteen-and nineteen-year-olds who joined with him.

These kids were no different from most. They had probably never even heard a weapon go off before joining. While most of them were living at home being fed by their mommas, making few decisions and having even fewer responsibilities, he had already been shot at.

Two besides Stinson had been in battle, and one was already questioning their task. He needed everybody to be on the same page if they were going to return walking instead of being tagged and transported back in a black body bag.

After stripping most of them of unneeded items, like a majority of the pots and pans whose clanking could be heard ten miles away, checking their ammo supply, adjusting their rucksacks, and having them tape their dog tags together, Stinson called his two veterans, both Specialist 4s, aside. "Fletcher, Casper. "Look. I will need your help on this if we are going to complete this assignment like soldiers. Can you do that?"

"Yeah, Sarge," Casper said immediately.

Fletcher shrugged.

CHAPTER 28

To Stinson, the jungle was like some large, multicolored creature. In spite of the exquisite green, red, yellow, and purple plants and flowers, the stately trees with their exposed and winding roots, and the cheerful sounds of birds and small animals, there was a menacing darkness that seemed to lurk behind its mask of innocence and tranquility.

It was the stench of decay that had impacted Stinson on his first patrol. Living things had died there. And the winding vines that draped from tree to tree appeared like the tentacles of some alien life form. But it was the inhabitants not seen and the sounds not heard that were the most chilling: the slithering reptiles, the deadly diseases, and the two- and four-legged predators that lay in wait for their next victim, adding to the stink only the perished could create.

The rain started as soon as the men began negotiating the vines and brush. It began as a few light drops; then the sky unloaded. Sheets of water fell, drenching everyone in seconds. The temperature was so hot, a steam-like mist rose from the muddying dirt. Stinson could only grimace as he slapped at hordes of mosquitoes and killed leeches and red ants falling like raindrops. The heat, the rain—nothing was right about this.

"W—we need to rest," Holland said as the rain subsided.

"We've just been humping for two hours," Stinson responded. "This ain't no picnic, Holland; we rest when we get to—"

The splat of bullet meeting flesh was followed a millisecond later by the crack of a rifle. One of the men's eyes widened before he stumbled and then fell.

"Take cover!" Stinson yelled as Warfield dragged the soldier's body behind a tree.

Instead of dropping and facing the attack, two of the men ran. "Get back here!" Stinson yelled as Casper took off, too. "Damn," Stinson swore as he positioned the remaining men while trying to determine the direction of the shot. "Where'd he get hit?" Stinson whispered, peering from behind the thick trunk of a palm tree.

"The chest," Warfield answered.

"You know how to seal the wound?"

"I'll do it," Fletcher offered.

"Do it, then," Stinson said as he motioned the men farther into the jungle to wait and watch.

Stinson bit his bottom lip and took a deep breath. Two months earlier, ten of his company had died in an attack that began like this in Trang Bang. The first bullet had missed his head by inches, killing the medic behind him before all hell broke loose.

He leaned against a tree for a second, gathering himself, hoping desperately this would not be a full-scale battle because they were nowhere near ready for it. And neither was he.

CHAPTER 29

It was Ly Trung Trac who first spotted the Americans. She was grateful Colonel Han had chosen her and her men to help protect a twenty-kilometer stretch covering the supply trails from the north. She was also thankful for the opportunity to be in charge of a combat unit. Trung had known war since she was twelve, when the Viet Minh defeated the French at Dien Bien Phu in 1954.

At five feet, four inches, she was slightly taller than the average Vietnamese girl, with hair that flowed to her waist, and the thin, willowy body desired by Vietnamese men. At fourteen, she was courted by men in three villages, but her father rejected them because they weren't worthy in his eyes. But Trung, in turn, rejected her father's wishes, and chose to become a *Phu Nu Cong Hoa*, a woman warrior, and fight the Americans instead of assuming the role of a subservient housewife, who, like her mother and aunties, worked the rice paddies, cooked, cleaned, and gave their husbands many babies.

She had started as a courier and a guide for the guerillas but rose quickly through the ranks after she grabbed a fallen weapon and shot two ARVN soldiers when her cadre was ambushed. Now she had risen to a command position, a rare honor. Trung vowed not to dishonor the opportunity or her name, which had also been given to a famous and historic female Vietnamese fighter.

At least thirty-eight of Trung's comrades had been killed within the past three months, primarily from ambushes and claymore mines set along the trails by American soldiers. Trung vowed to make sure not one other comrade would die under her watch. But before they had settled in, she was commanded to move north to attack a group of American soldiers who had just landed when Trung stumbled upon the men three hundred yards away.

Her forty-three men included ten veterans. The rest were fourteen- to eighteen-year-old boys with minimal training. Some were motivated by idealism, driven to join by the exhortations of their leaders, and others by the urgings of their families. With her training and guidance, though, all would be hardened soldiers within six months.

At first she thought the black soldiers were one of the assault patrols, but their reaction to Quan Doc's one shot caused her to reconsider. She snorted as she watched three of the men run in fear. It was contrary to anything she had ever known or heard about the black soldiers, and it confused her.

Were they lost? No. Not this far in. Plus, she had heard the *máy bay chuồn* that had flown them in. No one came to this area without a purpose.

Quan raised his Soviet Mosin-Nagant bolt-action rifle for another shot, but Trac stopped him. There were fifteen of them, lightly armed and poorly trained. It would be easy to wipe them out with the forty-three men under her command.

Trung squatted, scratched her underarm, and spat. She was intrigued. As long as she had been in battle, she had never encountered a group like this. It was a puzzle to her, but once she solved it, they would die like the rest of the invaders.

121

CHAPTER 30

Two of the men turned and raised their rifles at a noise to the rear.

"It's Casper," one of the soldiers whispered, "with the two runners."

Stinson turned to see Leroy Casper with two rifles strapped to his back herding Clarence Bankston and Darius Ward at gunpoint. During the brawl at Cu Chi, Casper had reminded Stinson of a larger version of himself. Casper had fought through five attackers to get to his buddies. Bodies fell so fast, it seemed as if a runaway truck had plowed through the crowd.

"What you want to do with 'em, Sarge?"

Stinson glared at the men. "Nothing, right now. Give 'em back their weapons. I'm feeling like we're going to need everybody we can get—and soon." Stinson remembered the two cousins from Mississippi from the mess hall. They were loud, boisterous, and irritating—and from their action today, gutless. "If they run again," Stinson proclaimed, "any of you have my permission to shoot their asses."

"Sar—" Ward tried to say.

Stinson raised his hand. "You've got nothing to say to me, and I got only one thing to say to you. You pull that shit again, you are dead."

***

One by one, Stinson made the men pull back to continue. He pointed to Bankston and Ward. "Make a stretcher to carry him."

"How, Sarge?" Ward asked.

"Two large branches, a poncho…Show them, Fletcher," Stinson said, exasperated he even needed to explain.

Stinson handed Casper his field glasses. "Stay behind for a few minutes and see if anyone is following us."

***

He could feel their stares. The men looked to see how Stinson was handling the wounded soldier's continuous moaning interspersed with low gurgling sounds that could wear on a priest. But there was nothing he could do about it. They would have to get used to it, as he was trying to.

Why him? Stinson thought. Stinson couldn't remember his name, but had seen him a few times. He was one of the more popular soldiers on base—quiet, thoughtful, and observant.

But this was war, and death was random. All you could do was your best. Fate decided the rest.

One of them being shot meant somebody out there was intent on taking them out. Even if it was a lone sniper, unless his men eliminated him first, the odds no one else would be wounded or killed were low.

Stinson sighed to himself. Even though surrounded by the men, he felt as lonely as a boater with no paddle drifting farther and farther away from the safety of the shore. It wasn't until they had covered a few more kilometers and Casper had reported no movement that Stinson exhaled, yet an uneasiness lingered.

In retrospect, enlisting in the army had been a terrible move. As unhealthy as it had been in Cleveland, almost being killed for a misunderstanding, at least he was at home instead of some foreign country. Stinson shuddered as the memory of Ho Bo Woods, Dau Tieng, and LZ Abbey battles surfaced again.

During the Dau Tieng battle, when it looked the worst, Sergeant Appling had asked him, "If you ain't ever in over your head, how do you know how tall you are?" Appling was a man of few words, but when he spoke, generals listened. He was one of the few with rank Stinson admired and the only reason he hadn't gone AWOL.

Stinson grunted and pushed his shoulders forward. His life had been nothing but challenges. His response to Appling had been two words: "Tall enough. "

But now with all the death he had caused and witnessed, and all the suffering he had seen, he wondered whether he truly was tall enough.

***

It was another hour on the trail before Ward tapped Stinson. "He's gone," he informed Stinson as Ward wiped the sweat pouring from his forehead.

The men turned to look at Stinson. Wrenford sniffed, trying to hold back tears. It became contagious. Holland cried outright. Soon the whole squad was either sniffing or bawling. Stinson scowled at the men but said nothing as he knelt to check for a pulse. He then put the lens of his field glasses under the soldier's nose to confirm. He rubbed his jaw before turning. "We need to bury his body where nobody but us can find it," Stinson commented, marking their location on the map.

Something tugged at Stinson as he scanned the troops. They were like lost children. Stinson retrieved the soldier's dog tags. *Rest in peace, Chancellor James.* He stuffed the dog tags in his pocket. Bankston and Glover dug a hole while the rest gathered next to a six-foot-high, concrete-hard anthill. "Aren't we going to pray before we bury him?" Robinson asked.

"If you want."

Mitchell Sampson laughed. "Pray?"

"Yes. Pray," Robinson replied, turning to Sampson. "You don't believe in prayer, in God?"

"If there is one, he ain't in Vietnam," Sampson retorted.

"God is everywhere."

"Yeah. How come so many people dying over here? How come he dead?" Sampson blurted, pointing to James.

"It's God's will."

"Bullshit! That was Charlie's will."

"Give the man some respect, Sampson," Frankford interjected.

"Respect? Well, then he should respect I'm a...a Buddhist."

Warfield snorted. "You ain't no Buddhist."

"How you know?" Sampson replied.

"I ain't seen you meditate, chant, or ring bells."

"Maybe not. But as far as he's concerned, I am," Sampson countered, pointing to Robinson.

"Could care less," Sampson muttered as he turned away.

"Couldn't," Turner responded.

"What?" Sampson asked.

"Couldn't care less," Turner responded.

"You say it your way. I'll say it mine," Sampson snapped back.

To Stinson, the argument was accomplishing the opposite of what he needed to achieve. They would not last past the first firefight if they didn't understand the importance of unity. So what would Sergeant Appling say? Stinson wondered as the men stood silently after the exchange between the two.

"Look, this may not be the worst of it. Understand that. What happened to James could happen to any one of us. But if we focus, if we work together, we can deal with whatever's thrown at us.

"There's an enemy out there. They know more about us than we do about them. But we have some control over this situation if each one of us thinks of ourselves as a family, as a unit, as brothers, as one," he huffed, glancing at the two runaways. "Each to protect and each to be protected. We are all connected. What one of us does affects the others. If we have to fight, we have to learn to fight together, as men, and for ourselves. We are not fighting for the 25th, the Army, or the United States of America. We are fighting for each other. We *can* accomplish this mission and get *back* to base safely, but only if we stick together and work together. You understand?"

"Yeah," some mumbled as others looked down.

Stinson had surprised himself. It was no Dr. Martin Luther King, Jr. speech, and it was the most he had ever said to anyone in his life. But hopefully, it served its purpose.

***

"Call base and tell them we have one KIA from an enemy sniper," Stinson said to Robinson, who was also Stinson's radio telephone operator.

"Not working, Sarge," Robinson reported after a few minutes working the dials.

"What do you mean not working? Try again."

"I get nothing."

Stinson slid next to the soldier to whisper, "Did you maintenance check it at the base?"

"They gave it to me right before we boarded, Sarge. They told me it was fine and that it was preset."

Stinson tapped one finger against his lip. "You got more than one battery?"

"Yes."

"Change it."

***

Holland listened to the exchange, and a fear welled up in him that caused his knees to shake. Some thought he was tough because he came from "down the way," like Fletcher. But people didn't realize just because somebody was from the ghetto didn't mean he was a bad dude.

He wasn't a fighter. Being picked on so much was the main reason he joined the army. He thought it would toughen him up and teach him skills. But when he was assigned to headquarters as a cook and heard the horror stories of those serving on the front line, he was grateful to peel potatoes and make stew. Now this, he thought as he stuck his hands in his pockets and pursed his lips. The VC would be worse than anybody messing with him back home.

He should have ignored Glover when he yelled, "Come on!" when the fight started. Responding to those two words could mean his life.

CHAPTER 31

Trung smiled as the large American soldier stared into the jungle, trying to detect movement. She would give them a half-hour start. She could wait. They wouldn't be hard to trail. Her men and the Americans seemed to be going in the same direction anyway. It was possible these men would lead them to the soldiers the colonel had ordered her to attack.

It was *Bac Ho*—Uncle Ho—who had lectured her on the virtues of patience, and she'd been an avid student.

"If you sharpen an iron rod long enough, in the end you get a needle, my daughter, " he'd said in a voice barely louder than a whisper before she departed to wage war on the aggressors.

***

Stinson pulled Robinson aside when they took a break. "How's that radio?" he whispered.

"Nothing."

"No radio," Fletcher muttered having overheard the conversation. "What happens if we hit a shit storm? We got no support. Nothing."

Stinson clenched his teeth, trying to ignore Fletcher as he deliberated. No radio, and not sure who was out there and what awaited them once they reached their destination. The situation was getting worse instead of better.

Taking off on his own crossed his mind briefly. He didn't need this. He hadn't done anything wrong. The guys under his so-called command were dead weight. Stinson laughed at himself, shaking his head slightly. So how tall was he thinking like that? It was just another challenge in a torrent of difficulties he'd had in his life. What the hell was new?

Staying meant being in charge, so he needed to be at least one step ahead of the situation. A misstep could get him killed. He had little to go on except the map, the captain's instructions, his prior experience, and Sergeant Appling's wisdom. Stinson sighed. That would have to do.

"I don't get a good feeling about Fletcher, Sarge," Warfield said to Stinson as they crossed a shallow stream.

"Why's that?"

"He's questioning your every move. Blames you for James's death. Said if you had been paying attention, it wouldn't have happened."

Stinson bristled. "What do you think, Warfield?"

"Unavoidable as far as I can determine, Sarge. I'm with you."

"Fight, Sarge," Bankston reported.

"What?" Stinson rushed to the rear to find Casper holding Somner and Robinson holding Matthews. "What's going on?"

"A family thing," Casper explained. "Somner was bragging about banging this chick. She turned out to be Matthew's half-sister."

Stinson glared at the two men. "Didn't you guys just fight together at the base?" Stinson waited. "Didn't you?"

Neither man answered.

"Did you see how we overcame when we stood together?" Stinson pounded his fist into his hand. "Didn't you just see a bullet rip through James's chest?" Stinson turned and took one step before pivoting and grabbing each of the men by their shirts. "Didn't anything I said earlier get through to you?" Stinson pushed them away. Somner fell and started to get up, but Stinson pointed at him to stay down.

"Here's what's important out here: survival. I will not repeat myself, gentlemen. How we conduct ourselves could be a matter of life or death. Nothing else matters. Understand?" Stinson hissed as he glared briefly at Fletcher.

"Yeah, Sarge," each of the men mumbled.

***

Besides the fact Stinson was in charge, there was something else Fletcher didn't like about him. Fletcher had always sensed weakness in others. And as strong and in charge as Stinson tried to appear, there was something fragile about him—something that might break if pushed hard enough.

When Fletcher had taken out Ray Ray, the former leader of the Skulls, it was because he had found his weakness. The gang, under Fletcher's leadership, had grown like the weeds around the vacant houses in his territory. They sustained themselves from the protection money they got from the pimps, drug dealers, and numbers runners.

There was some resistance until a few of them turned up missing.

The message had spread quickly. Pay or take a trip. Fletcher felt he could read a person within a few minutes of conversation. It never took him long to find out who would give it up and who would have to be dealt with, who was weak and who thought they were strong enough to defy him.

The blusterers—the ones who pretended they were stronger than they were—got stomped on. Stinson was a blusterer.

***

The rain began again. Stinson cursed under his breath. He hated rain, but only since Vietnam. The monsoon season was the worst. On the last patrol, it felt like the sky had sought him out to pee on him, constantly, steadily, for days on end, drenching him, rotting clothes, rotting everything.

"This is crap," Sampson complained as they trudged through the downpour.

"Could care less, Sampson," Somner mimicked.

The men looked miserable. Stinson understood. Most of them were hardly prepared to set up camp in a public park, much less negotiate an unforgiving jungle that continuously tested their will.

Because of the sniper, Stinson anticipated a battle. He prayed there would be none. But what he wished most was that these troops wouldn't have to experience another death or the horror of taking a life and the darkness that comes with it—a darkness that seeps into a person's body and slowly poisons the spirit.

It had started outside Tay Ninh: his first firefight, his first kill, then Ho Bo Woods, LZ Abbey, and Dau Tieng. It began moving, oozing through him slowly, like a snake, slithering through his gut as it would have slid through the exposed tree roots surrounding them, finding warmth in his breast, then wrapping around his soul, squeezing, sapping his strength, sapping his spirit, sapping his will.

He had tried to ignore it, but as death and destruction mounted, it took over. And now, as he prepared to begin another journey, he was resigned that the snake would be his constant companion.

Stinson sighed as he looked around. Who could he trust to stand strong if they had to fight? He went over what he knew of the men: three clerks, a cook, a colonel's driver, the two runners, the two fighters and a next-in-command who was a hot-headed, anti-authority, pain in the ass.

"Damn."

CHAPTER 32

They'd humped ten more kilometers through the jungle without incident before Franklin, acting like he was a performing mime, threw down his weapon and gear, slapping, dancing, and jiggling before stripping off his shirt, pants, and boots.

"Red ants," Stinson chuckled as he slapped the tiny, fierce creatures off Franklin. The others came to his aid, shaking out his clothes and boots. Stinson smiled at Franklin. All during his ordeal, he never uttered a sound.

Stinson pointed to a green football-shaped group of leaves. "That's their nest for future reference."

The men proceeded another kilometer before dark began to descend. Stinson was tired to the core, but cautiously relieved. They were one-third the way there.

Stinson walked the perimeter, stopping at a foxhole. "It's not deep enough, Glover."

"How deep, Sarge?"

"Up to your armpits."

Stinson shook his head as he watched the men settle in. So much to teach.

Somner approached Stinson carrying a machete. "Look. Sarge. Found it behind that tree."

"It's rusted, but it may come in handy." Stinson replied. "Keep it."

Except for Casper and Fletcher, the soldiers jumped at every sound. Their eyes darted back and forth at any motion, and they huddled together whenever they could, like cattle sensing wolves nearby.

Holland played with his knife. Glover sat against a log, frowning. Bankston and Ward cleaned their weapons and then offered to clean the others'. Warfield cleaned his boots. There was no need to remind them of noise discipline. Each of the men spoke in whispers.

After downing a can of cold ham and lima beans soaked in hot sauce, Stinson began training, hoping to take their attention away from a fear of the unknown. Teaching the men basic combat and ambush drills was essential. He felt it.

"Prepare, prepare, prepare," his sergeant had advised him when he was given a squad. "There is never enough preparation when you might have to fight for your life."

To Stinson's surprise, the men were avid listeners. Maybe his speech was working—or maybe it was James's death.

After training, the men huddled again.

"So where you from, Sarge?" Casper asked.

"Cleveland."

"Yeah, but what part?"

"Off Fifty-fifth."

"East Tech?"

"Yeah."

"You play ball?" Robinson asked.

"Didn't like coaches." Stinson looked around. "How many we got from Cleveland?" he asked.

Nine raised their hands. "Any other East Tech Scarabs?"

"I went to Tech for a year," Casper answered.

"Play ball?"

"Football. Boxed, too."

Stinson laughed. "I figured that the way you were knocking heads during the fight."

"I-I'm Tech," Holland answered.

Stinson cursed under his breath. "Where'd you live, Holland?"

"H–Haltnorth, Sarge. What about you?"

A sinking sensation hit Stinson as he stared past Holland into the jungle. "Outhwaite."

"W–wow. R–right around the corner," Holland said as he stared at Stinson. "M–maybe we know some of the same people."

Damn. He knows, Stinson thought. "Maybe," he answered.

Holland? What were the odds?

***

Holland stared at Stinson's back all afternoon. His mother had written that his father had died in a blown robbery attempt two and a half years ago. His partner was Willie Stinson. She related what some of his friends had said and concluded Stinson hadn't done his part, thus causing his father's death.

It wasn't as if Holland and his father were tight. He only saw him a few times a year, and he was usually high on something. But now he was dead, and the man responsible was within twenty yards. He could easily put a bullet in Stinson's back as his mother would have wanted, but he would wait. There would be other opportunities.

***

"Sarge, we were having this discussion earlier," Casper said. "If you were given twenty-five thousand dollars, what would you buy first? Sampson would have the biggest party anyone had ever seen. Franklin would buy a decked-out Cadillac or a nice foreign car. Robinson would donate to the church. Holland would purchase a large house in a quiet neighborhood for him and his mom."

"What about Casper?" Stinson asked.

"He hadn't decided yet," Robinson responded.

"Turner?"

"Me neither."

"Fletcher?"

Somner glanced at Fletcher gazing into the jungle and dipped his head in Fletcher's direction. "Dope, so he could sell it and quadruple his money."

"Seems to me, with that type of money, you'd start a legitimate business and sleep at night," Stinson said.

"You would think," Casper added.

"What about you, Sarge?" Robinson asked.

"Me? I would buy peace of mind."

"What store sells that?" Warfield asked sarcastically.

"None I know of," Stinson replied. "But if any of you hear where, please let me know, and I'll buy a little for each of you, too." *Because you will probably need it before this is all over*, Stinson thought. "Try to get some sleep. We're up at 0600."

It was easy posting sentries the rest of the night because nobody slept. Whoever the sniper was had gotten their complete attention. He hoped the only enemy going forward would be the jungle, but in the back of his mind, he doubted it.

***

Xavier Warfield had sniffed at the conversation that night and had offered nothing. He had been one step from being locked up but was given an alternative: jail or the army. He never thought he'd have to shoot somebody, but it was self-defense. Only the judge didn't think so.

When somebody tries to rob you, shoots at you and splits, what's wrong with finding them and putting them away instead?

Warfield had gotten a job at Ford Motors and was getting ready to move into an apartment with his boy Glover when Corvell Rollins tried to rob him. Corvell didn't know Warfield recognized him, but they had played ball against each other when he attended Glenville and Corvell attended East High.

Maybe he shouldn't have gone to the party alone. Maybe he shouldn't have rolled dice with strangers. Maybe he should have left after he hit them up for a buck twenty-five, but he didn't.

He could still feel the cold metal against his neck when someone demanded, "Give it up."

Warfield sniffed again. Give it up? He had turned and grabbed the gun, kicking the robber in his knee, but the gun fell and Warfield took off running. There were three shots fired before he turned the corner on Forty-second and Central Avenue. It took one glance for Warfield to recognize the green suede jacket and matching cap. And it took two days to find the owner.

Warfield could have left it alone; after all, he still had the money. But it was the principle. One shot and Corvell was down on his front porch. Seven minutes and the police had him cuffed. It was probably the fastest response time in the history of the Cleveland police. And because of his principles Warfield ended up in purgatory.

At least Corvell survived. If he hadn't, there would have been no choice between jail and the army.

Warfield looked around at his fellow soldiers. Even after the Corvell incident, he hadn't learned. When the fight broke out, it was almost out of instinct that he jumped in as soon as Glover hollered, "Let's go." Besides having always responded to Glover's appeal, when he saw some guys he knew like Robinson and Casper, in the fray, he had to. Those were his brothers.

Warfield sighed. He should be spray painting car doors right now instead of wondering whether he would survive. But he would. If nothing else, he was a survivor.

***

Marcus Glover didn't engage in the conversations either. He was still pissed about being drafted and about being in the jungle instead of filing papers. When he received the draft notice, he had done something really stupid: he'd gotten into a fight—a horrible, unnecessary fight over a girl—and then in Cu Chi, another fight, not as horrible, but just as unnecessary.

He wasn't even dating Sandra, a former cheerleader for Glenville High, but he fought over her anyway.

For some reason, Oscar Adams, a fellow Glenvillite, had a way of getting on his nerves. Glover couldn't explain it and never understood why others didn't feel the same way. That made it even more personal.

Maybe he did want Sandra, but Oscar getting under his skin outweighed any hidden feelings he might have had for her. He hadn't thought about it much –since he was already going with somebody— but that day at Riley's pool room, Oscar made a snide remark to his friend Larry.

"I got to watch Glover," Oscar said loud enough for Glover to hear.

"Why?" Larry asked.

"He's after my woman."

"Aw…" Larry started to counter.

Maybe it was an accumulation of things past, maybe it was Glover's irritation at a punk's insecurities, or maybe it was the draft notice sitting on his dresser at home that made him respond as he did.

"How you know I haven't had her?" Glover asked, putting his pool stick in the rack.

Regardless of the circumstances, the place, or the two individuals involved, a fight was not only inevitable, it was necessary to cleanse the air that had become polluted with that one sentence. Just like the fight on base—one dirty word, defiling the air that had to be disinfected.

Oscar swung, reluctantly, and Glover countered with all the evilness, spite, and hatred that filled his soul. It was a nasty, one-sided fight Glover immediately regretted.

"Your temper is going to get you in trouble," Warfield had said matter-of-factly when he heard about the fight.

Glover couldn't disagree.

Even today, in this stink hole of a country where he might lose his life, the regret of the fight in Cleveland endured.

***

That morning, Stinson turned his boots upside down and banged them against a tree.

"Why'd you do that, Sarge?"

"In case something snuck in them at night. All of you should do the same."

The sound of boots hitting the trunk of a tree sounded like a distorted recording of the "Anvil Chorus."

"Whoa!" Ward cried as a rat fell out of one of his boots and scampered through the men into the bush.

**

As they trudged through a field of saw grass that tore at their pants, Turner adjusted his glasses and tugged at Stinson's shirt. "We're not in Vietnam."

"What?" Fletcher asked, having overheard.

"This isn't Vietnam," Turner repeated.

"Dumbass." Fletcher punched Turner in the back of the head with his palm, almost knocking Turner's glasses off. The others laughed.

The punch was hard enough to make Turner stumble. He narrowed his eyes as he adjusted his glasses while he tightened his right hand around his weapon, but he said nothing.

"Where the hell are we if not Vietnam?" Stinson asked Turner, not noticing Fletcher had hit him.

Turner didn't answer. He couldn't. Turner didn't know how he knew. He just knew. It was a voice that came from nowhere. He called them epiphanies. And as fast as they came, they left, leaving Turner with a thought, but no reference, no explanation.

"Where?" Fletcher teased. "Where are we, Professor?"

The men chuckled steadily, as his friends back home had. No one believed him then. No one would believe him now. So he trudged on, still gripping his weapon firmly, praying Fletcher wouldn't hit him again. This group would have enough trouble without him causing more by icing Fletcher.

Sampson, the point man, raised his hand. Sergeant Stinson came to the front and surveyed the open field of unharvested rice. "Keep moving, but stay alert," Stinson ordered.

After a minute, Sampson held his hand up again. Stinson motioned the men to halt.

"A village at two hundred yards," Sampson whispered, pointing ahead.

"Any activity?" Stinson asked.

"Can't see any."

Stinson moved the men along a treeline within fifty yards of the huts and observed for close to fifteen minutes. "Fletcher, Glover, Warfield, circle the area, close in, and see if anybody lives there."

"They don't. Otherwise, we would have seen something by now," Fletcher countered dryly.

"We wouldn't see an ambush, though, would we? Stay alert."

"Nothing. The place is empty, like I said," Fletcher quipped, twenty minutes later.

Stinson ignored the dig. "Good. Let's take a closer look. See when anyone was last there. Single line. Watch for booby traps."

Stinson went through each of the huts. They were the typical bamboo frame interlaced with palm fronds with a layer of rice straw thatch on top. The floors were earthen. Everything was covered with dust. There were clusters of bamboo, metal, and wood, rusted cooking utensils, filthy blankets, dirty clothes, and a stench from decaying cooked food. Whoever had lived there had been gone for a while and seemed to have left in a hurry.

There was no evidence of a battle, so why would they leave a village that looked to be fairly old and established? Why would they leave a place where their ancestors were probably buried?

"What's with this flag, Sarge?" Ward asked. "I thought the Vietnamese flag was red with a yellow star?" The flag, hanging in the front room of the hut, was blue with a red stripe and a temple with three pyramid-like towers. "I saw one in a couple of the other huts, too," Ward added

"How the hell do I know, Ward. Could just be wall decoration. There's nothing here," Stinson answered, marking his map, relieved a flag was the only question he had to deal with, because more important questions were looming. He could only hope he would have the answers when their time came.

CHAPTER 33

I see something, Sarge."

Casper had climbed halfway up a large banyan tree to check their surroundings when he spotted movement.

"What?"

Casper pointed to the dense, seven-foot-tall elephant grass to the left of them. Stinson halted the men and looked in that direction. "What is it?"

"I can't tell, but there's something or somebody out there."

Stinson took Casper's place and pulled out his field glasses. "Yeah. There," Stinson pointed as the grass shifted slightly.

Stinson motioned his men to get down. If it was what he thought, the nightmare was about to begin. Stinson scratched his neck. Maybe it was the wind? He looked at the tree leaves. They were still. Could it be locals? But if so, they would have shown themselves instead of running the risk of being shot.

Turner adjusted his glasses. "It's not what we think it is," he whispered.

No one paid him any attention.

"What you think, Sarge?" Casper asked quietly.

Stinson shrugged. "I don't know yet, but I'll assume the worst. Let's move out and see if they follow. If they do, we got to pick a better place to fight."

"Take these," Stinson instructed Casper as he tossed him the field glasses. "Keep tracking them."

"Okay, Sarge."

Stinson motioned the men to gather their gear. "Frankford, take point."

"They gainin' fast, Sarge," Casper whispered urgently as Frankford moved to the front of the troops.

Stinson ran his hand over his mouth. Something wasn't right. After hiding from him for more than a day, they show themselves like this? They had to know he could see them coming. Maybe they *didn't* know or didn't care, seeing how some of his soldiers had panicked from one sniper shot.

Stinson climbed back up the tree to watch the grass sway, then stop, then sway again, as whomever it was edged closer. Maybe it was a trap, he thought as he glanced around.

The waving grass now indicated they were less than three hundred yards away. Stinson sighed as he thought to himself. *Only one thing to do.* He motioned his soldiers to take cover and prepare for battle.

***

Stinson tried to calm the tenseness by making sure his men focused on position and preparation. But in the back of his mind, one word kept surfacing: *split.* This would be the perfect time. If there was going to be a massacre, why stay? But he brushed the thought aside as he looked at the men. Without him, they would die for sure.

"Where's Holland?" he asked, after taking a count.

"Holland went to pee a while ago, Sarge."

"What? Where?" Stinson kicked himself for his neglect. He'd ordered the men to move out without taking a head count.

Wrenford pointed to a huge fig tree to the left of their position.

"They are within two hundred yards, Sarge," Casper reported a few seconds later. "And they are turning toward the fig tree."

"Hold your fire until I tell you," he instructed.

Stinson could hardly see from the sweat drenching his face and burning his eyes as he dashed through the elephant grass and brush. "Holland? Holland?" he whispered as he approached. When Stinson broke into a small clearing around the tree and spotted Holland leaning against it, smoking a joint. He became so infuriated, Stinson snatched the back of Holland's collar without uttering a word.

Holland started to scream before Stinson slammed his hand over his mouth. Someone who probably heard Holland's muffled scream crashed through the high grass a few yards away. Stinson braced, knowing there was no time to retreat. The sound of boots pounding the ground behind him caused his stomach to drop. He and Holland were surrounded.

Stinson turned toward the clamor in the grass, weapon raised, as the grass tore open, accompanied by an earth shattering roar. Stinson fell backward as the crack of two rifles firing almost simultaneously caused the attacker to scream in agony and crash to the ground.

"J-Jesus!" was all a wide-eyed Holland could shriek as he scrambled backward on his knees.

The heavy thumping sound of men running resumed as Stinson's men emerged from the jungle behind him.

***

"It had to be starving. You can see all its ribs," Frankford marveled as the soldiers gathered around.

"It's still big," Casper added.

"It would've been bigger if it could've gotten hold of dumbass." Fletcher laughed, glancing at a trembling Holland.

"Who fired the shots?" a relieved Stinson asked, staring in awe at the two holes in the tiger's forehead.

"We did," Bankston answered, standing with Ward.

Stinson, hands on hips, turned toward the two men.

"We weren't running yesterday, Sarge," Ward explained, anticipating Stinson's question. "We were looking for higher ground to take out the sniper."

Stinson remained speechless.

"Me and Clarence won the marksmanship award at Fort Benning, so first sergeant taught us a little about sniping."

The laugh, a mixture of relief and wonder, came somewhere deep inside Stinson. The men laughed with him as he patted the two on the back.

As quickly as his laughter began, it stopped. Stinson turned away clenching and unclenching his fists, knowing if they hadn't fired, he and Holland would be dead, because he had frozen. He gathered himself and turned back toward Ward and Bankston. "I guess I owe you an apology, then. Even though you didn't follow orders," Stinson said glaring at the two.

"Sarge?" Bankston and Ward asked together.

"I said don't shoot until I give the order."

"Uh…" Bankston said.

Stinson looked around. "But I'm glad you did. And the rest of you, coming to the rescue? Y'all gonna be soldiers yet."

Casper nodded. "Wanted to make sure you were going be okay, Sarge."

Even though a mixture of emotions battered Stinson, he smiled inwardly, looking at the tiger again before turning to Turner. "Did you know?"

"I knew what it wasn't."

"How?"

Turner shrugged.

Stinson shook his head slowly and looked at Turner for a while longer before gathering the men to move on.

***

"You okay?" Stinson asked Holland. "Y-yeah. Thanks."

"I assume that's the last time you run off for a smoke."

"Y-yeah."

"Where's the rest of it?"

Holland produced a plastic bag.

Stinson tossed it into the bushes.

As the men lined up to move out, Stinson couldn't help but recall his last time with Holland's father, Frankie. They had cased a house for a stick-up. If Frankie had done what he was supposed to, they could have taken down at least five thousand dollars in that poker game, and Stinson would still be in Cleveland, but stupidity evidently ran in the Holland family. Instead of waiting until the gamblers had sat down at the card table, Frankie Holland went barreling into the house before Stinson could get to the basement window to cover him. At forty-two, Frankie was supposed to be the pro.

Stupid! Knowing the players, drug dealers, gangsters, and pimps were all packing, they needed to have all been in the basement sitting at or around the table when Stinson and Frankie Holland hit them. Frankie was shot five times by a man called Slinky who came down the stairs behind him.

Frankie died running down the driveway.

Frankie's friends were after Stinson because they thought he'd bailed on his partner, and now he ended up saving Frankie's son's ass?

***

Holland watched Stinson as he gave orders to the men. He lowered his head in thought, picked up his gear, and joined the column. "O-oh, well," he murmured as he fell into line. How do you kill someone who'd just saved your life?

CHAPTER 34

Trung would have killed the tiger if it had come within another twenty yards, but it would have alerted the Americans she and her soldiers were nearby. She watched with relief as the gaunt beast stalked off and veered toward a large fig tree.

The grass obstructed her view, but she could tell by the movement of the blades the tiger had spotted prey. Was it man or animal? Could it be the soldiers? They were in its path.

Trung smiled. She felt a kinship with the animal, a fellow hunter. Maybe it would do her work for her.

She watched the grass sway again as the tiger stopped, moved slowly, stopped, then took off in a burst of speed toward the soldiers. One of her soldiers muttered something that made Trung laugh softly with the men around her. It was an old village saying: "The meat has been brought to the tiger."

Trung sank lower on her haunches, waiting for the tormented screams of the victims. Seconds later, Trung's head jerked at the un-expected crack of two rifles, a roar of pain, then complete silence.

***

After the black soldiers left, Trung and her men converged on the area. She stared at the dead animal, rubbed her jaw, and then spat. Two shots, two hits. These were the same group of soldiers where two of their men had run after one shot was fired?

She refused to acknowledge a thought lurking in the back of her mind, that the tiger lying at her feet might be an omen. Because as far as she was concerned, her destiny and the destiny of the men she tracked had already been written.

CHAPTER 35

By the middle of the second day, the men were more accustomed to the heat, humidity, and the minuscule inhabitants of the jungle. No one complained, and even Holland, who was given the name Lucky by the group, had been silent since the attack. After training that afternoon, Stinson walked among the men. Robinson, Turner, Warfield, and Glover slept. Sampson wrote, and Frankford laughed quietly with Casper and Holland. Fletcher sat by himself. Bankston and Ward cleaned their weapons.

A few still jumped at the smallest of noises, but not as high, Stinson thought, laughing to himself. It didn't rain that day, and Stinson was grateful. The heat allowed the men to dry their clothes, especially their socks. A soldier could be rendered helpless with swollen and blistered feet.

Back on the march, the men trudged along silently, trying to conserve their energy under the burning sun. Casper brought up the rear and remained vigilant, watching for anyone who might be following. As the men entered an open field, Glover alerted Stinson to another village a half-mile away. Smoke rising from a few of the huts and the harvested fields indicated the village was occupied.

"What should we do, Sarge?" Glover asked.

"We'll go around," Stinson answered as he marked his map.

"Why?" Fletcher asked. "We can get water and food."

"We are here to observe, not engage, Fletcher. Anyway, we have no idea whether they're friendly or not."

Fletcher snorted. "I guess I'm not as scared as you. I'd take the chance. We the ones with the guns."

"You don't know what they got. We go around," Stinson said, glaring at Fletcher before motioning Glover in another direction.

***

While resting at the edge of a creek, Stinson summoned the men. "This is a good place to talk about ambushes again."

"Why would we need to know that, Sarge, if we are not to engage?" Robinson asked.

"It's a valid question, Robinson. Hopefully, you won't need it, but just because we're on recon doesn't mean certain circumstances won't call for it.

"Suppose you get in a situation where you have to engage because a fight is inevitable? If you can, you want to set the terms of engagement—how, where, and when the battle happens. An ambush is a way of taking control."

Stinson walked among the men, silent for a while before he continued. "In spite of all I teach y'all, I want you to remember what's most important. The outcome of any fight is more about will than skill. Regardless of your abilities, you have to want to win, want to live. You got to buy into that thought. It's what's going to get you through this shit. It's what's going to get you back home."

Stinson stared at each of the men, making sure they understood and absorbed the message. He knew the few days of training wouldn't prepare them for most confrontations, but if they believed, if they thought they could win, they would be more than halfway there. At least mentally, they would be where he wanted them to be.

Fletcher picked his teeth with a stick, ignoring Stinson and the others.

***

Casper glared at Fletcher, trying to understand his resistance to Stinson. He had figured early on Fletcher had probably been a bully when he was younger. Bullies hated authority; and Casper hated bullies. He had always been big and strong for his age, but he never felt he had to bully. And every time one of them raised their evil head, Casper was there to knock it down.

Sarge didn't have to worry about him. He had his back even if Fletcher didn't.

Besides challenging Sarge at every turn, there was something else he didn't like about Fletcher. Maybe it was his look, which resembled a beady-eyed rat.

He'd learned from watching guys like Sarge. Whatever the situation, there was little that could stop their progress. It was almost as if they were destined to be okay. Casper felt Sarge was one of those. How come Fletcher couldn't see it?

As the squad moved out and Casper ducked under a limb, Fletcher tackled him. Casper raised his fist to punch Fletcher as Somner swung his machete at a twenty-two-inch snake with a green head and yellowish body.

Casper rolled out from under Fletcher and stared at it.

"Looked poisonous," Fletcher said, picking up his rifle and turning the decapitated snake over.

"Uh, thanks."

"No problem. But you owe me."

"Owe you?" Casper asked. "We are going to owe each other before this is over, so don't look for any favors."

CHAPTER 36

The morning of the third day, a wave of exhilaration swept over Stinson as he looked at the map, then his compass. The cloud of dark thoughts that had shadowed him the first two days had dissipated. And even though they had not reached their objective, Stinson felt more confident. The ridge where they would rendezvous would be visible soon, and barring any surprises, their mission would be accomplished.

The men were shaping up; he had two sharpshooters, and they were only hours from contact and the trip back to base. He wasn't so elated, though, that he didn't continue to look behind him. What had Sergeant Appling told him? Be optimistic, but be careful.

The men had changed in the past two days, but so had Stinson. Armond Gains, his probation officer, had said Stinson had problems dealing with structure. Gains had recommended the Army because it instilled discipline, and it would keep him from going to jail since he had violated probation twice. Stinson had followed Gains's advice, not because of the discipline and not because the military would keep him out of jail, but because he needed to get out of town after the stick-up catastrophe.

He hated leaving his wife, Darlene, and their child, Jerome, but his stint in the army would allow things to blow over. Then he'd return and hopefully lead a normal life.

Stinson smiled. Gains should see him now.

***

The mood at lunch was a little more relaxed.

Casper told the sad story of a new second lieutenant who had set up an ambush at night, declared the area a free-fire zone, then walked in front to see if everybody was situated. It was the lieutenant's first and last ambush.

"A free-fire zone?" Turner asked.

"You supposed to know everything, Professor." Fletcher laughed, walking toward the group and pointing at Turner with his hand cocked like a pistol.

"Once you establish a free-fire zone, anything that moves into the area gets blasted," Casper explained.

"Yeah, well we don't have to worry about stupid moves from Sarge. He's been right on since we left base camp," Frankford asserted.

The men murmured in agreement.

"Yeah, Sarge. I'm glad you got caught up in the fight," Casper chimed in.

"What?" Stinson asked scowling at Casper.

"Well. You know what I mean."

Stinson grunted and looked at his watch. "Okay. You had your fifteen minutes. Back to training. It ain't over yet."

CHAPTER 37

Trung's eyes narrowed and her nostrils flared as she listened to the runner who had brought her the news. The Americans she had originally been ordered to pursue were three kilometers from her. They had killed four more of her comrades the previous night in an ambush along the trail she was assigned to protect. Trung had been so captivated by the black soldiers she had lost sight of her primary mission.

If she'd stayed focused, the invaders would be dead by now. At the pace they were moving, they would make contact with the other enemy force by early evening. She couldn't wait. There were twenty of them, heavily armed and dangerous, but she owned the element of surprise, and with ten more comrades meeting her in the afternoon, the numbers were on her side.

***

As Stinson and his men emerged from the jungle, the ridge rose out of the ground like some majestic temple. It almost glowed with a reddish and golden hue as the sun's rays hit its vertical creases at varied angles. It appeared to be about 5,000 feet at its peak, with one ledge about 3,000 feet from the ground.

The lower portion of the ridge was thick with vines, brush, and trees. As they got closer, it appeared climbing the side would allow them to ascend to the leveled area cutting across its front. However, access was deceptive, because at about forty feet from the ledge lip, which jutted out slightly one-third of the way up, the slope became almost vertical.

Across from their objective was a broad hill, approximately five hundred feet high at its apex, which was easily accessible.

Stinson looked at the map. The ridge and the hill were marked.

"See anything, Frankford?" Stinson asked as Frankford reappeared from scouting the area for the 1st Cav soldiers they were to meet.

"Nothing, Sarge."

Stinson looked around. "We should see something soon."

After another half hour of circling the area, Stinson announced, "This is the place." He looked at the map, then looked around. "I guess we set up a perimeter and wait."

"It would be nice to have a radio now," Ward mused.

Robinson looked guilty, although Stinson and Casper had tried every conceivable method of getting it to work. "Yeah, that would be very helpful," Stinson answered.

"No wonder they call it a Prick-25," Casper said, using the name RTOs fondly called their AN/PRC-25 radios.

***

Where were the soldiers they were to meet? After two hours of waiting, Stinson had sent four men on another half-mile wide circumference to search for their counterparts. There was no evidence the 1st Cav soldiers or anyone else had been within the area they covered.

Turner took his glasses off and wiped them. "We should be on high ground if we have to wait," he murmured to himself, but loud enough for those closest to hear him.

Stinson, angry for not thinking of it himself, gave Turner the same look he had given him after Turner had cautioned them about the tiger. Stinson looked around at the ridge on one side and the hill on the other and said, "Frankford, Warfield. See if there's a way to get to the ledge on the ridge."

"For what?" Fletcher asked.

"We'll be safer there," Stinson answered.

Fletcher frowned. "But we might miss our contact."

"If we can see the ridge from here, we can see this location from there."

Fletcher shook his head. "So you listening to the space cadet now?"

Turner's face reddened, but he said nothing.

"I'm listening to common sense. We are defenseless down here. Up there, we can see better and we are safer."

"I just want to get out of here, man. We ain't got no means of contact, so our only way out is hooking up with the other unit. We miss them and we'll be jammed. This map don't show how to get home," Fletcher stated, jabbing at the plastic and paper. "I'm for staying put."

Stinson's eyes narrowed as he glowered at Fletcher. "Who put you in charge?"

"All I'm sayin'…"

"If there's a way to get to the ridge, it's where we go. This ain't no democracy."

"Yeah? Well, you don't know every damned thing. Otherwise, you wouldn't be here," Fletcher argued, jabbing Stinson in his chest.

Although something about Fletcher had pissed off Stinson ever since they'd met, the jabbing finger was the trigger. The dormant anger that had built up over the last two days spilled out. Before he could stop himself, Stinson swung at Fletcher. It surprised Fletcher the blusterer would even throw a punch, but he still managed to duck as the blow glanced off the side of his head. He charged Stinson and both fell to the ground. Stinson twisted his body at the last moment throwing Fletcher beneath him. As he raised his hand to throw another punch, Casper caught it.

"Sarge," was all Casper said as he pulled Stinson off Fletcher.

The two snorted like Toro Bravo bulls as they glared at each other; then Stinson turned and commanded, "Frankford, Warfield, move out."

The low growl and scuffling feet caused Stinson to turn to see Fletcher charging at him with a bayonet knife. Stinson bent low to take the onslaught before Casper knocked Fletcher down with the butt of his M-16.

"This ain't over," a groggy Fletcher hollered as two other soldiers held him down. "This ain't even over."

"Keep it up, Fletcher, and one of us will die out here. You better believe, though, it ain't going to be me," Stinson said as he took Fletcher's knife and rifle. "You can bet on that."

***

"We found it, Sarge. About five hundred yards back, there's a trail leading up," Warfield reported.

"How far did you go up?"

"Almost all the way. There's some flat ground halfway up, then it gets a little steeper with some vines and brush, but it's, ah, negotiable."

"Okay, then. That's where we're going. Let's move."

"Not me," Fletcher said, arms folded.

"Me either," Matthews and Somner added.

"You disobeying a direct order?" Stinson asked.

"We'll take our chances right here and wait for the Cavs to come where they *know* where we are," Fletcher said.

A flushed Stinson stomped over to Fletcher.

"What you gonna do, hit me again, or you gonna shoot me this time?" Fletcher asked as he raised his fists.

Stinson had always been the insubordinate, so Fletcher's disobedience flustered him. His first thought was to finish kicking Fletcher's ass, but although it would be gratifying, it would serve no purpose.

"No, I'll deal with you when we get back to Cu Chi." Stinson looked at the sun beginning its descent. "I don't have time now."

"Let's go," Stinson commanded as he turned his back on the three, leaving Fletcher's rifle and knife at the bottom of the trail.

CHAPTER 38

Stinson stepped to the front of his men. Foliage on the rising trail indicated it hadn't been used in a while, if ever, which meant there would be no surprises. And except near the top where the men had to chop through some vine overgrowth, the ascent was relatively easy.

They made good enough time to survey the ground from their new position before the sun set. The three-hundred-foot wide, eighty-foot long ledge was fairly flat but sloped slightly downward toward the rear wall. To look over, a person would have to move within ten feet of the edge. The only vegetation there was two- to three-foot bushes. Stinson looked around and nodded at Turner. "I think this will work."

"Yes, sir," Turner responded, gratified somebody had finally listened to him, but disappointed Fletcher wasn't there to hear it.

Within seconds, a crushing, foreboding thought seared Turner's brain. He shuddered and glanced at Stinson. It was a dark thought, but with a herculean effort, he pushed it out of his mind.

"We can see miles away from over here," Stinson observed as he and Casper looked down to their left from the lip.

"And we can see Fletcher, Matthews, and Somner, too," Casper responded, looking down to his right at the shrunken figures.

"Warfield, I'll still need someone to stand guard. Switch off with Holland in two hours, then Frankford, Turner, Glover. If you guys hear or see anything, wake me."

***

The dream started out fine. Stinson held his wife and their child in one arm and his rifle in the other when Darlene and Jerome began to fade into a grayish mist. He called her name, but she didn't answer. Stinson stood waiting until a barely discernible noise in the haze grew to a deafening drone. He raised his rifle as thousands of VC charged at him from where his wife and son had disappeared.

The clatter of gunfire startled him awake. Confused and sweating, he wiped his face and shook his head to clear the fog. The noises were real. Although the salvo was more than a mile away, he could see an occasional weapon flash and hear the faint screams either of men giving orders or men crying for help. All of his soldiers gathered at the edge. Within five minutes, the shots became sporadic and the voices silent.

Stinson wondered if those were the men they were to meet. If so, why were they so far away? And assuming it was an ambush, were they the ambushers or the ambushed?

It was another four hours before sunrise and too soon to see anything. He assumed Fletcher and the other two men had heard it, too, and wondered what they were thinking. He looked down in their direction but saw no one.

Stinson looked at Turner. "Anything come to mind?"

"No, Sarge."

The firing stopped.

Stinson took a deep breath. "I guess we wait."

The rest of the night was like the first. Nobody slept. Everyone faced the direction of the battle, peering into the darkness—not as nervous as before, but wary.

At dawn, a sinking sensation hit Stinson as he peered into the jungle with his field glasses, trying to detect any movement. Still no contact. If the men engaged in gunfire were the soldiers Stinson's squad was to meet up with, those men were probably in trouble, which meant he and his men were, too.

Stinson turned away, trying to plot the next move. Minutes passed as the men waited. It had been twenty hours since they were to have rendezvoused with the 1st Cav. How were they going to get out if they had no idea where they were?

He pulled the map to look again.

"There's movement, Sarge."

"Where?"

"Men running."

"I see."

"Toward us."

"I see. I see." Stinson caught glimpses of men moving fast through the jungle, heading toward Fletcher's area. They'd have to cross a rice paddy to make it.

"Take firing positions. Don't shoot unless I say so."

Stinson sat on his haunches, staring through the field glasses before exhaling. "They look like ours, but be alert."

"More movement, Sarge," Casper noted, pointing about six hundred yards behind the running men. "Dressed in brown and black."

"Charlie!" Frankford whispered.

"Ward, Bankston. Take positions on the left. Watch the chasers," Stinson instructed.

The men in front approached the rice paddy. Stinson counted twelve. He needed to warn Fletcher and the other two that friendlies were nearby.

Stinson peered over the edge of the ridge but couldn't pinpoint Fletcher's location. "Fletcher!" he shouted. "Fletcher!"

The men crossed the rice paddy and headed back into the jungle toward the rendezvous area. Thirty seconds later, two shots were fired, then three more.

"Damn!" Stinson muttered as he paced.

CHAPTER 39

Trung was elated. Eight enemies killed in the ambush and only one of her men wounded. Twelve more Americans would be dead soon. She'd sent twenty men to pursue them. What the American soldiers didn't know was ten more were waiting on a hill across from the ridge if they tried to head south. Another ten were waiting among the trees if they tried to run east, the only two directions they could go.

It appeared they had run south. If so, she would hear another gun battle signaling the end of those soldiers. Then she would take care of the black ones.

Trung squatted with her men and waited.

***

Stinson looked down again. Neither Fletcher and the others, or the ones being chased, were visible. The men in black stopped at the edge of the rice paddy as if waiting for a signal. They were VC. Should he wait for them to get closer or take out as many as he could?

They were four hundred yards away. "Bankston. Ward. Shoot the ones you can see. Everybody else get down. I don't want them to see how many we are."

Three shots rang out from the ridge. "One, two, three," the two called to each other. Stinson peered out from behind a rock as two soldiers clad in black went down and then one more before the rest faded into the jungle.

Just then, the hill across from them erupted with gunfire as the ridge wall behind the men spit red stone shrapnel.

"Return fire!" Stinson commanded, pointing at the hill, hoping Fletcher and the other two were out of harm's way.

Except for Bankston and Ward, the rest of the men fired wildly at the hill. "One," Ward counted as he fired his third shot.

"Two, three," Bankston answered.

"Four, five," Ward continued as firing from the hill slowed.

"Cease fire," Stinson ordered as he peered at the hill through his field glasses. He saw two bodies clad in black sprawled next to a tree, but no movement.

Frankford pointed as one of the sprawled bodies moved. Both Bankston and Ward fired simultaneously as the body slumped to the ground. Stinson looked at the edge of the rice paddy where the other VC had stopped. He saw no one. He looked at his men and wondered if any of them had noticed he'd been unable to fire his weapon, again.

***

Trung sensed the chase hadn't gone well. The last weapons fired were American. But they didn't belong to the soldiers they'd ambushed. It was the black soldiers. Out of the din of gunfire, she'd heard the same rifles that had killed the tiger. Among the noise of battle, it was the sound of their rifles and the steady, unrushed firing that gave them away.

She balled her fist in rage. She would remember those sounds when the Americans were surrounded and begging for their lives.

***

"We need to get off this ridge," Stinson said to Casper. "There's only one way up and one way down. I'm not sure how many Charlies are out there, but if they find the entrance, they could keep us holed up here until we run out of ammo."

Casper looked at the jungle below. "I agree with you, Sarge."

Stinson glanced at Turner. Turner nodded, too. It wasn't an epiphany this time. It just made good sense.

***

"Sarge?"

Stinson didn't like the sound of Sampson's voice.

"Sarge?"

Stinson rushed past the men moving down from the ridge, almost tripping over Somner's sprawled body, his hand still clutching his weapon.

A burning sensation like a tracer round shot through his chest. "What happened?"

"He was laying there when I got here," Sampson explained.

"You see anybody else?" Stinson asked, stripping Somner of his dog tag, ammo, grenades, canteen, and rifle.

"No."

"He must have tried to join us." The burning inside Stinson intensified, fearing Fletcher and Matthews had met the same fate.

CHAPTER 40

There was no activity on the ridge. Trung figured they would come off it. Her heart pumped furiously as she ran with her men to catch the black soldiers before they descended.

She didn't hesitate as they reached the edge of the rice paddy and began to run across—a mistake she would never have made if she hadn't been so eager. The soldiers who'd fled from her trap fired on them. Her soldiers veered to the right and to the left as two fell.

***

The gunfire near the rice paddy told Stinson what he needed to know. They were coming his way. Based on the amount of gunfire, Stinson figured the Americans being chased were the ones shooting.

It took a second before he decided. "How many grenades we got? The men raised one or two fingers. Follow me," he directed as he sprinted through the jungle.

Stinson's thoughts were clear. If they came up the opposite side of the hill, they'd hook up with the runners and take out the remaining VC. There couldn't be more than four or five enemies left. And if they seized the hill, they would have an advantage over the VC charging south.

It was obvious the other Americans were on their own. By this time, there should have been air support, artillery, something. The ambushed soldiers must not have had radio contact either.

The foot of the hill was four hundred yards away. Stinson heard the grunts and puffing behind him as they sprinted down a path he had spotted from the ridge. When they got within 100 yards, he led them off the path, moving as fast as possible through the trees, bushes, and vines parallel to it.

The firing had stopped. Stinson could only guess what was next. He stayed at a point twenty yards ahead of his men as they approached. He motioned them to spread out and be prepared as they advanced. Thirty yards from the base of the hill, Stinson and his men stopped, looking and listening. They remained that way for two minutes before they moved forward.

Blood trails, an abandoned M1 carbine, a rubber sandal, footprints, and grooves in the ground where a body had been dragged away gave Stinson a moment of relief. "Turner!" he whispered.

"Yeah, Sarge?"

"What you think?"

"I…I don't. Nothing, Sarge."

"Okay. No problem. Just checking."

The foot of the hill was twenty yards away. Stinson stopped every other step. There were enough shrubs and trees to cover an enemy, and it only took one VC, one bullet, to change things.

Stinson motioned for the men to get down. "Ward, Bankston, cover me as best you can," he instructed the two as he continued to crawl forward.

It didn't sound as if the gunfire was that close, but he felt a hammerlike punch in his left shoulder and leg. A boiling-oil-like pain followed. He rolled behind a tree as the firing continued.

"Sarge is hit," Stinson heard someone say as he lay listening to another salvo of fire and the explosion of grenades. Then the hill was silent. Stinson's mind told him he could carry on. His body told him different. Casper pulled Stinson behind a tree at the bottom of the hill where Warfield cleaned and dressed the wounds.

"We need to get to the top," Stinson whispered.

"We are, Sarge."

"We…"

"There were five Charlies left," Casper reported. "We got them; we got the hill."

"Good." Stinson tried to stand but fell. "Make sure they…where's Fletcher and Matthews? Where are the other Americans?"

"Don't know, Sarge, but I know you need to stay down," Casper said.

"You the sergeant now?" Stinson shot back.

"No, Sarge," Casper responded, "but you are too weak to stand."

Stinson glared at Casper and stood. "Make sure the men are in place. The rest of the VC will be coming soon. I'll cover this area."

"You want someone with you?"

"No," Stinson said, waving Casper off as he took a position behind a tree, collapsing, before regaining his balance, then looking around to see if anyone saw it.

CHAPTER 41

Trung reassembled her men, upset she hadn't been able to get to the black soldiers before they left the ridge. But now everybody was together. She couldn't have wished for a better gift.

By the time the sun had risen to its greatest height, so would her status as a fighter.

***

In battle, silence is as scary as noise, Stinson thought, trying to keep his mind off the burning pain in his leg and shoulder. A sound to the left startled him as he jerked his head around. Men were running. Stinson pulled out a grenade, pointed one of his weapons toward the noise, and lay prone, waiting.

Bursting through the jungle in front of him were eight men—eight Americans. Stinson had never been so happy to see white faces in his life.

He started to signal them when gunfire erupted. Two fell, then two more as the others took cover. There was protective fire from his men on the hill before the silence, broken seconds later by the thrashing of men running through the jungle in the distance. There was more gunfire in the direction the men had run, then silence again. Stinson pounded the dirt with his fist, wondering if any had survived.

Suddenly, another burst of gunfire commenced from the top of the hill. Screams of pain preceded more firing before it slacked off with intermittent shooting, then increased in volume and intensity again. Stinson rolled over as someone approached him from the rear.

"Sarge?" Frankford whispered.

"Yeah."

"We've got to get out of here. There are too many of 'em," he gasped. "And we're running out of ammo."

"Where are they?"

"On the other side. They tried to come around the east side of the hill, chasing some American soldiers, but we beat them back."

"You get any of their weapons and ammo?"

"Yeah. Three AKs and a couple of bandoliers."

"Everybody okay?"

Frankford shook his head. "Sampson."

Stinson sighed. Sampson was another one of the good ones. In spite of his outburst with Robinson, it was too soon in his life to find whether God existed or not. He looked around, trying to gather his thoughts. "Okay. Tell the men to come past me and move south."

Stinson took a deep breath. How many more were going to die before it was over?

CHAPTER 42

Trung had underestimated the black soldiers. They had proven to be fighters. Moving to the ridge was smart. Getting off the ridge was even smarter. Now they would try to hold the hill, but it would only delay the inevitable. The men had been in the jungle for four days. They had to be tired, hungry, and running out of ammunition.

Trung ordered two of her men to recon the hill with caution. She'd already lost twelve. They took twenty minutes to return. The hill, they reported, was vacated. Where'd they go so fast?

***

Casper bent to pick up Stinson as the men trotted past him.

"Leave me. I'll slow you down."

"No way, Sarge," Casper replied, grunting as he heaved Stinson onto his back. Stinson winced, not at the pain, but at the thought he might be the cause of his men being killed. He looked around after Casper had run about thirty yards, pushed himself off Casper's back and rolled into a bank covered by bushes. "Get the fuck out of here," he demanded a bewildered Casper. "Go. I know what I'm doing. Tell the men if any of them try to come back for me, I will shoot them."

"This here," he hissed at Casper, waving to the surrounding area, "is now a free-fire zone." Stinson drew his right hand palm down across his throat.

Casper was so startled by the fierceness in Stinson's raspy voice, he could only stare. Then he ran, looking back once more.

Stinson held up his hand, his fingers spread, then brought them together in a fist.

Casper nodded and did the same before disappearing into the jungle.

***

As he settled into the brush behind a fallen tree, Stinson's mind wandered as he thought of the series of circumstances that had gotten him to a place where there was but one conclusion. There were no more choices.

He should have been angry, but he wasn't. Stinson shrugged as calm descended upon him like a warm blanket. Death wasn't as terrifying when you accepted its inevitability.

Stinson looked around, at last appreciating what the place could be without men with guns. He marveled at the majesty of the trees; the beauty of the red, yellow, and purple flowers; and the varied greens of the grass and bushes. Where they were foreboding to him in the past, their lushness now brought a sense of serenity.

Satisfied he'd at least come to terms with a jungle that had caused so much agony and grief, he grimaced in pain as he pulled out his grenades and pointed the two rifles. The hands that shook minutes ago were now steady as he awaited the approaching footsteps. The snake within never stirred.

CHAPTER 43

Exhausted from their mad dash for safety, the nine men slowed to a walk when they realized no one was following them. As they were running, they heard the gunfire and grenades, then silence.

"Where's Sarge?" Warfield asked Casper.

"He pushed off me, rolled into the bushes, and told me if we tried to come get him he would shoot us," Casper said, still attempting to catch his breath.

"What?" Robinson asked, stopping. "You left him?"

"He didn't give me a choice!"

Robinson looked at the other men who had bunched together listening.

"S-sounds like Sarge," Holland said.

The others nodded in agreement. Robinson stared at Casper as if trying to read his mind. Tears welled up, then he sobbed. Others wiped their eyes as they reached an open field and double-timed across.

A crashing sound in the jungle to their right caused the men to hit the ground and raise their weapons. The soldiers braced until Warfield who had taken the point position whispered, "They're ours!"

Fletcher and Matthews burst through the foliage almost tripping over Warfield. Fletcher raised his weapon until he saw Warfield's face. "Jesus Christ! I almost took you out."

"Yeah? Well, I almost took you out, too. Where were you guys?" Glover asked.

"We didn't know who was running toward us back there, so we fired a few shots then split. A few seconds later, a battle began. We didn't look back."

Casper glared at Fletcher. "Those were our soldiers you were shooting at."

Fletcher bristled. "How you know?"

"Because we saw everything from the ridge, the ridge you were supposed to be on."

Fletcher spit on the ground but said nothing.

"You hit anybody?"

Fletcher remained silent.

Warfield scraped the ground with his boot. "They were probably our contact. I doubt if any made it, even if you all missed."

"We'd better go, then," Fletcher said.

"Yeah," Casper agreed as the men began jogging again, trying to put as much distance as they could between themselves and the enemy.

***

So many thoughts jumbled around in Turner's head as he ran. But the strongest of them was the one that lingered from the ridge—the

183

one he'd tried to ignore. The one that said he would not see Sergeant Stinson again.

CHAPTER 44

Frustrated they couldn't find the wounded soldier who'd allowed the others to escape, Trung waved her men to track the ones who'd run, then stopped. It would be dark soon, and she'd become more cautious about her new quarry. The tracks would be as fresh in the morning. She would chase them down then.

That night it poured rain. Trung folded her arms and glared at the sky, wondering how much more luck those soldiers would receive. Without tracks, she could only guess where they were and where they would be picked up.

An old proverb, "Do not praise the day before sunset," passed through her mind, as did a sliver of doubt before Trung grunted dismissively. There would be just two outcomes: Either luck would run out for the soldiers, or they would win out. Only exceptionally good fortune would allow them to do the latter.

***

The men glanced at each other when Fletcher directed them to move out. They complied, because as a Spec 4 with the most time in service and time in grade, he had the higher rank. They continued to move quickly, glancing back every other second. Just before the sun descended behind the trees, Robinson spotted an abandoned pagoda.

The building had been destroyed except for its stone floor, moss-covered columns, and stone roof over the entranceway. A rear wall and one side wall had collapsed. The remaining wall leaned precariously inward. Stone debris and winding vines covered the stone floor. A tree had taken root in one of the rear rooms. The spire, previously on the roof, now lay at the side of the building.

Robinson thought about Sampson as he walked through the disarray with Warfield as they secured the area. If Sampson had been a Buddhist, he would have been upset at all the destruction. "It's cool," Robinson reported.

The rain came as soon as the men settled.

"We got lucky," Glover observed, looking around.

"Yeah. It's all we need. Rain soaked and lost," Warfield responded.

"There should be a village nearby," Fletcher said.

"Sarge said to avoid the villages," Warfield replied.

"But Sarge ain't here. We'll bed here tonight and strike out first thing in the morning," Fletcher said, sneering at the men, "and if we see an occupied village, we enter it. Any questions?"

It was another sleepless night for all but a few. The men who kept watch were assured of the company of their fellow soldiers because none accepted the fact they'd escaped completely.

By morning the rain had stopped. "If we keep going east, we're bound to run into more of our soldiers," Casper said to Fletcher.

Fletcher frowned. "It's strange, though. We've heard nothing. No artillery, no planes, no helicopters."

A few of the men glanced at Turner, who'd been quiet since

Fletcher took over.

Around noon, Turner removed his glasses and wiped his brow as the sun bore down, trying to conjure some revelation but was unsuccessful. He'd not experienced any since the ridge. Nothing to tell him whether Sarge was dead or alive, and nothing to tell him what would happen next.

"There's the abandoned village we passed coming in," Glover stated, pointing through the vines at the edge of a rice paddy bed. "Looks as if it's still empty."

The men approached cautiously as Sarge would have instructed, checking to make sure the huts were in fact still empty. As Warfield checked the second-to-the-last hut, a scurry of feet in the darkened room startled him so badly he almost dropped his weapon. As someone small tried to run past him, he grabbed an arm, pulling the person back.

The men, hearing the scuffle, ran to Warfield's aid as he dragged the young boy out of the hut. It was evident by his torn and dirty clothes he was on his own. Warfield held the boy by his collar, watching him squirm, his smallish forehead furrowed with fear and his mouth screwed into a scowl. At about four-feet-seven and maybe seventy pounds, he couldn't have been but nine or ten; with Asians, though, looks were deceiving.

"Waste his ass," Fletcher ordered, raising his weapon.

"No," Casper said, pushing Fletcher's rifle down. "He doesn't even have a weapon."

"Don't matter. He's VC," Fletcher said, raising his rifle again.

The boy shouted, "Me no VC. VC number ten." And he spit in the dirt. The boy pointed to the huts. "No family. VC kill."

He pulled down one of the wall hangings with the three pyramids they'd seen earlier. The boy pointed at it, and then at himself, saying, "Khmer, Khmer."

Everybody looked at Turner.

Turner looked at the boy's facial characteristics, noting the darker skin, the flat nose, and the thicker lips that reinforced his first notion. "We aren't in Vietnam," he said.

"It's the second time you've said that," Casper said.

Fletcher snorted. "You gonna believe this lame?" he asked, looking at Turner as if he was about to hit him.

"Khmer are Cambodian," Wrenford said. He turned to the kid and pointed to the ground. "Cambodia?"

The kid nodded. "Khmer, Cambodia."

"W-what the hell?" Holland asked as he collapsed on a broken wooden bench.

"Nah," Robinson said. "Can't be."

Warfield said. "If it's true, we're screwed."

"I don't believe him," Robinson declared, glaring at the boy. "He could be VC."

"If he's VC, where's his weapon?" Wrenford asked.

"Somebody check the huts for a weapon," Casper said.

"Nothing," Glover and Bankston reported after going through each hut, turning over anything that might conceal one.

"What's your name?" Casper asked.

"Me Da."

Wrenford stared at the flag. "You know, I heard my major talking about the Khmer Rouge in Cambodia."

Fletcher glared at Da. "That don't mean we in Cambodia even if he is Cambodian, which I doubt."

"Why would anybody send us to Cambodia?" Glover asked.

"They would if they wanted to get rid of our asses," Bankston concluded.

"Where Vietnam?" Robinson asked the kid.

"You kill beaucoup VC?"

Bankston scanned the jungle beyond the village. "Yeah, if they don't kill us first."

Da pointed east. "I show you Vietnam."

"It could be a trap," Fletcher said.

Casper grunted. "I'll take my chances. We don't know this area. We don't know where we are or how long it will take to get back. I'm for going with the boy."

The others nodded, except for Fletcher, who scowled at Casper.

Turner looked at Casper and Fletcher, then at the ground. No Sarge, no unity, and only a Cambodian kid to lead the way. It would be extremely fortunate if any of them made it back alive.

CHAPTER 45

Despite orders to return to camp for new instructions and a new mission, Trung continued to search for the black soldiers. It was personal. Until they appeared, she'd been successful in every previous encounter. There'd be no rest until their story had ended.

It took one day to find their trail and half a day to close in. Trung took her men on a route that would intersect with the soldiers by midafternoon if she'd read the signs correctly.

***

Da led the eleven soldiers through jungles of eight-feet-tall elephant grass, that made them bunch up so they could see each other. Casper didn't like it. They needed to be at least five meters apart. One grenade or booby trap and half of them would be dead.

Hours passed as the soldiers proceeded around two terraced hills before wading across a chest-high, mud-filled stream. The men held their weapons above their heads as they crossed, bobbing against the current.

After reaching the other side, they rested and removed the leeches that had attached themselves while they were in the water.

"Phew," Robinson said as he pushed a fingernail down next to the oral sucker on Casper's neck and pushed it away as Casper had taught him.

"You act as if you never seen a leech before," Casper said.

"Yeah, but once I get stateside, I don't plan on seeing another in this or my next lifetime."

Afterward, the men crossed through rice fields punctuated with palm trees. Da pulled shoots from the palm tree, and berries and weeds for the men to eat.

Glover looked at Da when he first offered the food. "What are we supposed to do with this?"

"Eat, man. Unless you got a steak hidden in your shirt," Frankford said.

"How far?" Warfield asked Da.

Not understanding, but sensing the question, Da pointed to a mountain range.

If we can get there fast enough, Warfield thought, *we might stay alive for another day.*

***

It started slowly with Glover. First he experienced a slight cramp. He tried walking it off, and it worked for a while.

"You okay, Glover?" Warfield asked, watching him walking bent over.

Glover nodded. "It's nothing. Probably from eating cold C's."

"All right. Just checking."

Glover walked on, watching as the men in front fought their way through more vines and bushes. The urge came so quickly, he almost vomited on himself before heaving the contents of his stomach at the foot of a tree, leaning on it for support.

Warfield and Robinson caught up with Glover just as he stumbled sideways, pulled his pants down and finished what his vomiting hadn't.

"You been using your tabs?" Robinson asked.

"Ran out," a weakened Glover said.

Robinson reached for his to share when the barrage of bullets began. The first burst of gunfire caught Matthews at the front of the column. Blood spurted from his neck as he fell gurgling, grabbing at it before another shot pierced his cheek, silencing him. Frankford screamed as bullets took out his legs. He tried to crawl to cover, but another four shots punctured his back, with a final shot entering his ear.

While the American soldiers buried themselves in the ground, returning fire, Ward had taken a position in a tree, firing a cadenced burst and downing three VC when it seemed every enemy rifle returned fire at him. Four bullets hit Ward instantaneously. The cracking sound was his neck breaking as he fell backward.

"Retreat!" Fletcher hollered.

"No! Charge! Charge!" Casper shouted.

"Like Sarge trained us," Turner yelled.

Without hesitation, the American soldiers rose and moved forward, unleashing a hail of bullets in short bursts. For no apparent reason, the black clad attackers retreated. Three Viet Cong gathered around one of their wounded and dragged their comrade to the rear. The remaining VC faded into the jungle as silently as they'd appeared.

The men looked at each other, perplexed, as they backed up, waiting for another attack. Da called from across an open area behind the fighting; he was waving, motioning them to follow. "Let's go," Casper whispered, grabbing a weapon from a dead Vietnamese. The men double-timed, stumbling and falling as Bankston watched their rear. They took a defensive position behind a hedgerow waiting for the attackers to follow, but they didn't.

***

Warfield looked wistfully at the mountain range Da had pointed to earlier. He shuddered as he tried to shake the flood of grief that swept over him, making him stop to gather his strength. He glanced back in the direction of the ambush and exhaled. Would any of them make it to the mountains or would those mountains be the last any of them would ever see?

CHAPTER 46

Trung was hit twice. It was the sound of the same weapon that had killed the tiger and had cut down her men. She tried to move forward but fell. Three of her men dragged her farther into the bush with the others running parallel to them. "Leave me. Keep fighting," she commanded. "Kill them!" she yelled before she fainted.

More concerned about their leader, the attackers retreated to protect her from further harm. If their esteemed leader died, it was very likely they would, too, at the hands of their own.

***

"You're bleeding," Casper said, looking at Holland's leg.

"Flesh wound," Holland said, expressionless. "Anybody got something to clean this with?"

Casper looked at Holland as if he were a stranger and smiled. Holland hadn't cried out, whined, or even fallen after he'd been shot—and he hadn't stuttered.

"We got to get the bodies," Robinson said as they moved toward a grouping of trees and a shallow stream.

"We should," Casper said, looking around counting heads. "But they'll probably be waiting for us. Who got hit?"

"Ward caught it," Warfield said.

"So did Matthews," Robinson said. "And Frankford."

Casper waited for the crying, but there was only a look of numbness among the men. It was as if a film had developed over their eyes, screening any emotional display. They'd become the zombies they'd seen at Fire Base Serenity.

Casper understood. He'd reached that point months ago. Sampson's utterance wasn't the first time he'd heard the term "Could care less." It had been a mantra the troops he'd fought with had adopted on his last mission. His only apprehension now was a question he felt sure was on everybody's mind: Would any of them ever see Cu Chi again?

"Where's Fletcher?" Robinson asked, jerking Casper's mind back from his thoughts.

A sound to their right caused all the men to raise their rifles.

"Hold your fire," a hoarse voice said, as Fletcher exited from a thatch of trees.

"Where were you?" Casper asked.

"I was chasin' one of 'em, but they got away," Fletcher said, puffing as he caught up.

Casper and the seven other men frowned as they looked skeptically at Fletcher.

"We've got to bury them," Robinson said.

The men agreed.

Casper tapped Bankston and Wrenford. "We'll get them. Cover us."

The three men approached the dead soldiers cautiously while the others pointed their weapons into the jungle where the VC had retreated. Bankston and Wrenford carried the men back to the hedgerow and removed their dog tags. Robinson said a quick prayer before burying them in a makeshift grave. The grim-faced soldiers glanced at the graves a few times before following Da toward the mountains.

***

Da led them to a worn trail. They'd started along the path when Turner blurted, "We should stay off trails."

Warfield, helping a weakened Glover as they half walked, half ran, said, "Turner's right."

The others looked at Turner as he looked back.

"They'll be following us. It's easy to follow us on the trail."

"We stay on the trail," Fletcher said. "I'm tired of you trying to take charge. We'll move faster, plus they retreated. Ain't nobody after us now."

"They're picking us off one by one," Robinson said. "We got to do something different."

"Like what?" Fletcher said, glaring at Robinson.

"We got to do something. No matter how fast we move and no matter in what direction, they find us," Warfield added.

"We keep running," Fletcher said. "You got a short memory. Remember how many were on the hill?"

"Not as many as before," Robinson answered. "We got some. Sarge probably took out more of 'em, but not all of 'em."

"Sarge? Fuck Sarge. He's dead now. Ain't shit Sarge can do for you now," Fletcher blurted, shoving Robinson against a tree.

"Ain't nothin' to do but run, and that's what we gonna do. If you slow, tired, or just a weepy-assed bitch, you die."

Turner was silent for a moment after Fletcher spoke, then said one word: "Ambush."

The men turned to Turner.

"What?" Bankston asked. "How?"

"Why?" Robinson asked.

"Like Sarge taught us," Turner responded as he adjusted his glasses. "They think we're runners. They believe we're scared. They wouldn't expect it. We take control."

Fletcher spun toward Turner. "How would you, a damn clerk, know anything? You been suckin' at Sarge's tit the whole time we been out here. I ought to kick your ass for even thinking you know what you talking about," Fletcher said, raising his hand to swing at Turner.

Turner didn't move. Casper stepped in as Turner stared at Fletcher.

"Yeah. You bad now? You think you a man now? Starin' at me like you gonna do somethin'."

"We should vote," Turner said, still staring at Fletcher.

Fletcher's face darkened, and spittle appeared on his bottom lip as he hissed, stepping toward Turner, but glancing at Casper, "Didn't you understand what Sarge said before? This ain't no democracy. I'm in charge now."

"What you have in mind, Turner?" Casper asked.

"What? You listenin' to him over me?" Fletcher asked as he turned to look at Casper.

"I want to hear what he has to say, too," Warfield said.

The others nodded in agreement.

"Well fuck me. We got a mutiny here. I'm going to write all y'all's asses up when we get back," Fletcher said, jabbing his fingers at the group which gathered around Turner.

"You will be the one who will be written up. I'm going to tell them how you left the rest of us against direct orders," Casper said, his head moving up and down as he walked toward Fletcher. "And I'm going to tell about you shooting at our soldiers back there. I'm about tired of you, Fletcher. You ain't no leader. Ever since we've been out here, all you've done is complain, disobey orders, and look out for yourself. Now you want to lead us? Forget it. We're going the rest of the way by committee. We'll let the captain deal with you when we return."

Fletcher scowled at Casper, then glanced at his weapon leaning against a tree.

Casper's head began to bob again. "I wish you would." He turned to Turner. "What'd you have in mind?"

Rifles raised as Da came from behind the tree.

"You got to be more careful, Da. We can't lose you, too," Warfield said, glancing at the mountains again.

***

Leaving Glover hidden in a thick clump of hedges, the men went back on the trail, deliberately leaving footprints as they moved southeast. After they'd traveled about a kilometer, they doubled back through the jungle.

"This ain't gonna work," Fletcher said.

Nobody paid him any attention.

"Ain't gonna work. We need to *di di mau*—get our asses out of here," Fletcher muttered.

"You going to shut up, or am I going to shut you up?" Casper whispered, standing face to face with Fletcher.

Fletcher's eyes bulged, and a vein throbbed in his throat. His face darkened as he clenched his rifle. "Don't nobody talk to me like that. Nobody!"

Robinson stepped between the two. "We're all going to die if we don't take care of business."

Casper and Fletcher continued to glare at each other before the rest of the men joined Robinson.

"Come on Casper, Fletcher," Bankston said, pulling Casper to him. Casper glared at Fletcher, then turned with Bankston and the rest.

"Where's Glover?" Warfield asked, poking the bushes where they'd left him.

"Glover!" the men whispered, spreading out to search for him.

"I told you this was a bad idea," Fletcher said.

"Over here," Holland said, pointing to torn foliage and fresh drag marks on the ground. "Another tiger?"

"Man," Turner said, pointing at the footprints on each side of the furrows in the ground, partially hidden by the two-foot-high bushes.

"This ain't good," Warfield said, looking around.

The men held their rifle at ready and formed a circle, trying to see into the areas darkened by the gigantic trees.

"We need to get to him before they kill him," Casper said.

"If he ain't already dead," Fletcher grumbled to himself.

Led by Casper, the soldiers crept single file following the drag marks.

Holland stopped and looked around at the ground "They're gone."

"They picked him up," Casper said. "The footprints are deeper here." He pointed farther ahead. "We need to split up, forty yards apart and parallel."

"What we need to do is *di di mau*," Fletcher repeated. "They could be waiting for us knowing we'd come looking."

"I doubt it," Casper said. "They probably think we abandoned him because he was sick. They wouldn't believe we would come back after all the running we've been doing."

The men nodded in agreement and split into two groups.

***

Warfield's team heard it first: a muffled scream that could have been human or animal, sending chills through Warfield's body. They stopped. Another scream, not as loud, but just as unnerving, echoed through the jungle. Robinson charged toward it, but Warfield grabbed his arm, put his finger to his mouth, and led as they moved stealthily toward the cries.

Warfield recoiled at the sight as he peeked through the foliage. Glover hung above the ground, his hands tied to a tree limb. The VC had covered his mouth with a soiled yellow cloth. He was bleeding from the chest. Bankston and Holland came up beside Warfield as one of the four Viet Cong raised his knife to Glover's chest.

Glover's muted scream and the crack of a rifle coincided as the guerilla fell to the ground. The other three VC ran for weapons lying against a tree. Bankston, Holland, and Warfield shot two before they reached them. The remaining captor made it to the edge of the tree line before Bankston's bullet found his back.

The two guerillas moaned. One tried to crawl into the bushes, but could only move inches at a time. The other lay against a tree watching with widened eyes. "They can't be more than sixteen years old,"

Bankston said to the others.

Holland shot them. "Don't matter."

Warfield laid Glover on the ground and looked carefully at the cuts. "They're just flesh wounds," Warfield said to the men.

They all jerked around at the noise of someone approaching. Casper and his men burst into the clearing firing at another guerilla who'd almost run into them trying to escape Warfield's team.

"Man!" Casper said, lowering his rifle.

"How is he?" Turner asked.

"Don't seem too bad. Looks as if they wanted to play with him first," Warfield answered.

"Then he's lucky. I saw one of ours staked to the ground with his skin peeled off and left for the animals to eat. That's what they were going to do to him. We need to get out of here," Fletcher said, peering into the trees.

Holland cleaned and bandaged the wounds where the guerilla had made three parallel marks from the breast to the lower stomach.

"What happened?" Robinson asked Glover.

"My fault," Glover whispered. "I saw three of them along the trail, and all I thought of was our guys they'd killed. I tried to change position to take them out, but they heard me and my weapon jammed."

"I told you about your temper," Warfield said.

Glover grunted.

"Can you walk?" Holland asked.

"Help me up," Glover said weakly. "Where's my weapon?" He tried to maintain his balance while looking around.

Bankston picked up three Viet Cong weapons and inspected them before giving Glover one. "You don't want it if it jammed. Take this one."

Glover took a step. "Let's move out," he said. Casper and Warfield caught him as he stumbled.

"We got you, brother. We got you."

***

"Whoa," Robinson exclaimed as he peered at the mound near the edge of the clearing.

"What?" Casper asked as he approached Robinson.

Robinson pulled at the wood slats beneath the dirt. "I thought this was an anthill until I saw something shining through."

"Whoa is right!" Warfield said. The others gathered around the two as Robinson uncovered four large camouflaged earthen pots filled with weapons.

"Look at this," Casper marveled. "RPGs, Bangalore torpedoes, grenades, pistols, mortar tubes, rifles, knives, hundreds of cases of ammo, and a surgical kit."

"If this is a rallying point, they'll be back," Fletcher said. "And we shouldn't—"

"Shhh!" Warfield pointed into the jungle. "Listen."

Casper motioned the men into position at the edge of the jungle facing the clearing and the noise, disregarding Fletcher, who faded into the bush. The sound of foliage breaking, which sounded about two hundred meters away, grew closer.

The men scrambled to hide in the tree line, waiting.

Glover slumped over a piece of dead wood, wounded, exhausted, and resigned, but with his weapon ready. Turner took deep breaths, one after another. Warfield's hands trembled so badly, he was afraid he wouldn't be able to aim. Holland shivered as a cold chill sliced through his body, but he was ready, he told himself. It was them or us—couldn't be both.

Minutes later, they came. They surprised Casper moving so quickly through the foliage, possibly lured by the sound of shots fired and the tracks the American soldiers had left on the trail.

There were about twenty of them. Twelve fell in the first barrage of bullets and grenades. The remaining VC fired back before retreating. Bankston killed two more as they ran through the jungle. Afterward, the only noise breaking the dark silence was the breathing of the men and the moaning of wounded enemy.

***

Warfield's eyes widened as he stared in disbelief. He'd seen it but couldn't believe it. Turner had shot Fletcher—one bullet to the chest. Warfield looked around, checking to see if anyone else had witnessed it. Turner looked at Warfield, the only one of the seven within eyesight. Their eyes locked before Warfield nodded. Turner nodded back.

Warfield understood. Just before Turner shot Fletcher, he'd seen Fletcher raise his rifle and point it at Casper's back. Warfield had yelled, but Casper couldn't hear above the din of gunfire. He was relieved someone had intervened. But Turner?

***

Casper waited another three minutes before standing and walking into the clearing, weapon up, eyes darting from the wounded men to the area where the VC had retreated.

One by one, like black ghosts, the other men moved to the clearing. Robinson, his eyes cold and face frozen except for the constant twitch on the right side of his mouth, shot the wounded VC. "Sarge, Frankford, Ward, Sampson…" Robinson said softly after each shot. A frowning Casper stared at Robinson before shaking his head and taking another head count.

"Fletcher?" Casper asked, looking around.

"He's dead," Turner replied glancing at Warfield.

No one asked how.

Warfield, Robinson, and Holland lay waiting at the edge of the trees in case any of the Viet Cong returned.

After stripping Fletcher of his tags, they dug a hole next to his body and rolled him into it.

Casper motioned at the stockpile. "Grab what you need, including the surgical kit for Holland. Strip the others of their stuff. Throw what you don't want on the weapons cache, then let's get two of the Bangalores and blow this shit."

The men ducked even though they were behind trees. The explosion followed by an even larger one, then one greater than the last, darkened the sky with dust, dirt, and debris.

"There must have been more hidden nearby," Casper said to Warfield as they listened to the continued explosions. "Maybe underground."

"Cool," Warfield responded hoping that blowing up the weapons symbolized an end to all the death he had witnessed. He was hopeful, but not too.

CHAPTER 47

I'm okay with what happened," Warfield whispered to Turner as they walked together along a narrow trail.

"What happened?" Casper asked.

Warfield, surprised Casper walking behind them had overheard, just shook his head.

Casper joined Warfield and Turner. "Hey. Whatever happened, I'm okay with it."

Warfield looked at Turner, who walked a little farther before nodding in consent.

Warfield took a deep breath. "May his soul rest in peace."

Casper waited, looking back and forth between Turner and Warfield.

"That lowlife tried to kill you," Warfield said.

Casper stopped to hear Warfield better. "What?"

"Fletcher tried to kill you," Turner repeated.

"How?"

"He circled behind you during the ambush," Turner said.

"How'd you..." Casper tilted his head.

"I saw him raise his weapon," Turner said, looking straight ahead.

Warfield looked at the ground.

"Then who got Fletcher?"

Warfield and Turner looked down.

"I did," they said in unison.

Turner glanced at Warfield.

Warfield glanced back. "We both did."

Casper looked at both of the men. "Ain't no need in covering it up. I'm grateful for whoever did it."

"It was me," Turner said. "That dude had the devil in him, man. If he had gotten to you, it would have been over, Da helping us or not. I knew that. I felt it. I wasn't going to let it happen."

The three walked in silence for a few minutes. "Do you think I should tell the others?" Turner asked.

Casper looked at the ground before answering. "Negative, man. We already got enough to deal with. Keep it to yourself."

***

"What the...?" Warfield gasped, ducking and backing out of the cave.

"What's wrong?" Casper asked as he climbed the last twenty feet to the cave entrance.

Warfield stared into the darkened entrance, his rifle raised. "Something's in there."

Da laughed. "No problem."

Casper raised his rifle, too, as he slowly moved forward. "No problem? Then what's in there?"

Da made a flying motion with his hands.

"Birds?"

Da went deep inside the cave and brought out a dead bat.

Casper stopped. "Bats?"

The word filtered to the other men. "Bats!"

Casper walked with Da into the cavern, slightly unnerved by the fluttering, squeaking, and chirping overhead as they went deeper. He stood for a minute, waiting for his eyes to become accustomed to the dark, then turned to walk back to the men clustered around the entrance.

"It's okay if we stay near the front of the cave," Casper told the men.

"Don't they bite?" Bankston asked.

"If you mess with them," Turner said.

"How do you know?" Bankston asked.

Casper smiled at Bankston. "You questioning the professor?"

"I just know. Plus Da wouldn't have brought us here if it wasn't safe," Turner replied.

"Well at least it ain't a tiger," Holland said.

Turner's response seemed to satisfy the men, but they sat around near the front of the cave with ponchos over their heads.

***

It was June 28, ten days since they'd been dropped off, and the fourth day in the cave. Casper looked around. The heat, hunger, and the jungle had taken their toll. The men were emaciated, having eaten only palm shoots, berries, and the little rice cakes they'd taken off the dead Vietnamese. They'd spent the last few days in the cave trying to recuperate, but the lack of food worsened the problem.

They would be lucky to make it a half-mile, much less the miles necessary to find a safe haven with American troops.

"Where's Da?" Warfield asked.

Robinson went to the rear of the cave. "Da?"

Robinson returned and raised his hands. "Maybe he went looking for more food."

"I hope so," Glover said weakly.

Hours passed as the sun began to set and the heat became bearable. The men waited.

The next morning, Bankston and Casper looked at each other blankly. Da hadn't returned.

"He ain't coming back," Holland said. "I saw him looking east and saying, 'Beaucoup VC. Number 10.' We're on our own."

"Can't blame him," Robinson said resignedly. "As much shit as we've been in."

Casper stood and looked at the six men. "Well. This is our fifth day here. We can't stay in this cave forever. We need to get out of here. We can't depend on anybody leading us out. We've got to find the way ourselves. And we can't depend on anybody finding us. We have to find them."

He could tell by the men's faces they agreed, but no one moved, and no one looked directly at him.

Robinson gazed out over the trees. "Glover can barely walk, Casper. Warfield's got foot sores. Holland's wounded."

"What if we lay something on the ground so a plane or helicopter could see it," Holland asked.

Casper pointed to the sky. "You hear any planes or helicopters flying around here?"

"What if one of us went out to get help?" Robinson asked.

Warfield looked at his friend. "And the VC take him out? We'd be in here another three or four days waiting. We need to stay together and keep on pushin'."

"Warfield is right," Casper said. "We've all got to move out or remain in the cave and die of infection and starvation."

No one spoke.

Casper looked in the direction the men had come, then turned. "You know what we did back there? We defied all odds. You guys defeated a superior force. At the end, they were the runners. We were like…"

"Wolverines," Turner offered.

"Wolverines?" Warfield asked.

"An animal that can defeat other animals twice its size," Turner replied.

Casper put his hand on Turner's shoulder. "You know, it's been my privilege to serve with you guys. It's been my privilege to know each one of you, to know your heart. At first I had my doubts. I mean, look where you came from." Casper hesitated and looked around the cave. "And look who you are now. You are warriors, man, true warriors. We've been through hell, but we are here today because we overcame. We became one," Casper said opening his hand and closing it into a fist. "We looked after each other. We fought for each other and I love you guys for that."

After another moment of silence, Warfield clenched his fist, "Wolverines."

"Wolverines fight to the finish. They don't give up," Turner said.

Robinson and Holland dapped each other.

"Yeah," Bankston added, "Warfield's right. We need to keep on pushin'."

"Wolverines," Glover said in a gravelly voice.

"So then, we're Wolverines?" Casper asked.

After a few more minutes, Holland rose slowly, wincing, looking at Warfield. Robinson gradually rose and helped Warfield to his feet. Bankston and Turner picked up Glover.

Each step was excruciating for the men, either from experiencing pain or watching the painful movement of their comrades. They barely covered three miles that day, resting every hour, and, in spite of the danger, taking any trail they could find. Resting at another creek bed, Casper walked among the men, giving encouragement. "We can't be far."

"How would we know?" a stone-faced Robinson asked.

A faint boom of a howitzer interrupted their conversation, causing the men to look up. Warfield looked at Holland. "That's ours."

Holland frowned. "It sounded miles away."

"Don't matter," Casper said. "At least we're nearer than we were."

Turner walked with Casper. "I saw a few hills from the cave. If we could get closer and get more elevation, maybe we'd see where they're firing from."

Casper squinted in the direction of the sound. "We might also see where they're firing at so we can avoid the area."

"Let's go," Glover said, weakly pumping his fist.

***

By the next day, the soldiers could see the rise. There were a series of hills running two to three hundred yards high at their peak. Bankston and Robinson scouted the closest of them.

The howitzers let go another salvo. The echoes faded in the distance.

"We can make it to the top," Bankston puffed, returning forty minutes later. "And if we follow the creek bed I saw from up there, we should be headed where the big guns are."

"Holland and Warfield, can you make it?" Casper asked, pointing at the hill.

The two looked at each other. "If it will get us closer, yeah," Warfield answered.

Holland nodded.

Casper lifted Glover. "I'll help with this brother. Let's see what we can see."

It took two hours for the men to reach the top, grasping at any trees and vines that would help them move upward. Every part of Casper's body ached, but he didn't show it because each of the men was worse off than he was.

Some energy returned when he looked out from the top of the hill. The view allowed them to see at least three miles east. There was a valley below with a small stream running alongside the foot and a narrow path beside it. Their side facing the stream was a steep drop— and impassable.

Casper explored the hill, looking for an alternative route to descend, finally finding one to the south, the way they were headed. His stomach dropped, though, when he saw the fresh boot prints. Somebody had been there. He ducked behind a tree, looking, and listening, before joining his men.

"Be alert. We don't know who else might be up here."

"Why would anybody be up here?" Robinson asked.

"Just be alert."

Robinson scratched his initials in the dirt as he thought of his situation, his father, and the promise he'd made. After calling around to find out how his son could avoid the draft, Drew Robinson eventually accepted the futility of trying. He sat his son down at the dining room table. "I wish I knew the right people so you wouldn't have to go, but since you do, son, you do what they tell you. Do it to the best of your ability, and don't worry about things you can't control. Let God be your guide."

Robinson listened as he did whenever his father spoke. And as always, he would do what his father asked. But it was the request his father, a custodian at Shaw High School, made as he dropped his son off at the hotel where he would board a bus to Fort Benning, Georgia, that weighed the heaviest on his mind.

"Come back in one piece, son."

"I will, Dad."

He'd kissed his mother, who'd been sobbing from the time he'd awoken until he stepped out of the car. "It will be okay, Mom. Really."

Really? He rubbed his chin and leaned against a tree. Here he was, with no control over the outcome. Maybe he could buy some control with the $25,000 they had talked about, but there was one thing for sure: He couldn't—no, he wouldn't—let his father down. His father had invested too much time in Robinson's future.

Robinson scratched his father's initials next to his as he thought back to his sophomore year in high school. He had been agonizing over a trigonometry course at the kitchen table when his father sat across from him.

"Anything I can help you with, son?"

Robinson had laughed. "No, dad. Did they even have trigonometry when you went to school?"

His father had chuckled. "Not that I remember."

Robinson smiled as he recalled his father waking him at six in the morning. "Come downstairs. I want to show you something."

On the kitchen table was Robinson's trig book and some typewriter paper next to it with his dad's handwriting.

"Let's go through these problems," his father had said, opening the book and referring to his notes.

His dad had stayed up all night reading the first five chapters and solving the questions at the end of each chapter. Robinson looked in wonder at his father, a man with a sixth-grade education, as he explained each of the questions to his son and how to solve them.

"Your father might not be educated," his mother, a schoolteacher, had told Robinson years ago, "but he's not stupid. And to take time to learn and then teach you shows how much he really loves you."

The weight of the promise was heaviest when he had time to think, time to wonder why he wasn't dead or wounded. Bullets had flown past him on four different occasions. Why he hadn't been shot must have been divine intervention. Robinson rolled his eyes at the thought. But, with all that had happened, he was beginning to doubt it existed. Sampson would have.

"You are mighty quiet over there, Robinson. Thinking about your girlfriend?" Warfield asked.

"No. My dad."

It was during moments like the trigonometry episode when Robinson felt the deepest of gratitude for having been born into a family with a mother and father who were like heroes to him—each strong in their own respect and each loving in their own way. So when his father made that simple request, to come home in one piece, how could he not?

Yes, the situation was dangerous—people were out to kill them if the jungle didn't first, but over the past four days, Robinson felt better about the prospects of fulfilling that request. He felt better about the men he was with, and he felt better about himself being in the jungle because they'd all changed. They had to if they were to survive.

Reverend Poole had always preached that life should be revered, cherished. But *revered* and *cherished* weren't words used where he was now. *Kill* or *be killed. Adapt* or *die.* Those were the most important words, and those were the words foremost in his mind. They were survival words.

The howitzers boomed again.

Casper pointed in the direction of the sounds. "They are firing from over there. Let's rest here, get our strength back, and move down to the stream in the morning."

Casper didn't share his earlier discovery of the footprints, hesitant to spook the men any further. When everyone settled, he explored the rest of the hill, only satisfied they were alone after a half hour of surveillance.

"Where were you, Casper?" Warfield asked.

"Just looking around."

The men shared the last of the rice cakes and slept. Casper kept watch. He looked at the six remaining men and shook his head. Despite what they'd gone through— the heat, the rain, the diseases, the battles— they'd accomplished little except to survive.

Some might say they'd won the battles they'd waged because they'd killed more VC than they'd lost of their own. Casper grunted. But did body counts distinguish who was right—or just who was left? And with all the firepower in America's possession, we can't defeat a small, backward country like Vietnam? Was it some Supreme Being's way of telling us we shouldn't be here? He'd ask Robinson when they were back at base.

Early morning, Casper was trying to map the most direct and safest route to the howitzers when an ominous sound of men moving snapped Casper back to attention. He peered over the hill, looking in all directions but saw nothing. Just then, the dry bushes crackled as soldiers in khaki-and-green uniforms appeared. Their outfits identified them as NVA, the regular army of the North Vietnamese.

A searing sensation knifed through Casper's stomach as he ducked, then peeked again. They kept coming, moving along the creek bed, stopping, then dispersing, most moving quickly through the jungle, their presence cutting off any hopes of his men following the stream.

Were the boot prints theirs? Probably. Nobody would set up under a hill unless they knew it was vacated.

Casper tiptoed to each man, waking and shushing them at the same time. He pointed his rifle toward the NVA. Each of the men quietly grabbed his weapon and watched Casper for orders.

The soldiers waited as Casper squatted, thinking. If they tried to move in almost any direction, they would be captured as soon as they left the hill. Their only option was to stay on the hill until the NVA moved on. But how long would that be? Days? Weeks? He stared straight ahead as he ran his hand across his face. As close as they were to home base, there was still a long way to go.

Casper looked through his field glasses. As far as he could see, there were NVA. He chewed his lip in frustration. There were two choices: die of starvation if the NVA were setting up a permanent camp or be captured. Casper started to lower his field glasses when he noticed movement through the trees about two and a half kilometers away. He raised his field glasses again, squinted, put them down, then raised them once more. "Damn!" he whispered.

"What?" Warfield asked.

Casper handed Warfield the field glasses and pointed over the trees to a distant opening in the jungle canopy.

"Those are ours!"

"Yep."

Bankston joined them. Casper pointed downward then outward. Each had a similar look of surprise, despair, and finally, resignation.

Bankston frowned as he slid backward. The other men watched carefully as Casper, Bankston, and Warfield approached them.

Bankston rubbed his rifle barrel, repeatedly. "This ain't good."

Casper signaled the men to gather. "The enemy is directly below us—a lot of them. They are waiting to ambush our soldiers coming this way." Casper glanced at Turner, but Turner, eyes narrowed, said nothing.

Glover rose on his elbow. "We got to warn them."

The men turned to Glover, surprised, thinking he was out of it.

Glover looked at Casper. "Attack."

"Too many," Warfield said.

Bankston leaned his rifle against a rock. "If we attack right before our guys come in contact, it will be a warning."

Robinson shook his head. "Yeah, but then they'll attack us."

Warfield paused and rubbed his forehead before speaking. "We got the hill. They can't get up here from there."

"They might from there, though," Casper said, pointing to the thick vines and bushes south of the hill where he first saw the boot prints. "Plus, they got the numbers, they got mortars, and they got the big guns."

The men sat in a circle as Casper went back to the edge to scan the area once more. "Our soldiers will be within range in less than ten minutes. What do you think?" he asked when he returned.

***

With all the turmoil, fear, and deaths, the past days had been a series of miracles: Having Sarge as a leader, winning those battles with the VC, seven surviving when there probably should have been none, Turner thought as he stared at the ledge of the hill. Most people never experienced one miracle. They'd exhausted their quota long ago. Had the miracles run out, or was there one more in the hopper? But at this point, who cared? He was tired, bone tired—tired of running, tired of fighting. He sighed. Right was right.

***

"A lot of our guys will die if we do nothing," Turner said.

Holland sniffed. "Who gives a damn about them? They didn't care about us."

"It wasn't them who sent us out here," Casper responded. "Plus, if we stay here and do nothing, we will either starve or be captured. We can't go anywhere if they remain."

"Maybe we should wait," Robinson said.

Bankston glared at Robinson. "For what? And starve to death after all we been through? Lay down like wimpy-assed sissies?"

"You are starting to sound like Fletcher," Robinson retorted.

"No. Actually you are," Bankston said. "He's the one always talking scared."

"I…"

"Gentlemen," Casper said, quietly but forcefully. "Let's talk this out rationally. We've come too far together to fall apart now."

"Attack," Glover whispered again.

Casper looked at the men, their faces grim as they pondered. "We don't have much time, gentlemen. What will it be?"

The men sat silent. Robinson scuffed the dirt with his feet. Bankston sighed. Warfield tapped his leg repeatedly.

"If we fire a few rounds each and pull back before they can retaliate, we might be okay," Turner said.

Warfield looked at Turner. "At least we get to choose our poison."

"If we do save those guys," Turner continued, "it will probably be the most decent thing we do in this war."

The men sat in silence before Holland put out his hand and stared straight ahead. "Wolverines."

After a few seconds, Casper covered Holland's hand with his. "Wolverines," followed by Warfield, Glover, Turner, Bankston, and finally Robinson.

"Wolverines," they whispered together.

***

In some ways it made sense to Casper. In other ways it would be suicide if the NVA directed all their firepower toward them, whether they pulled back or not. If they fired for ten seconds then withdrew from the edge, as Turner suggested, then all they'd have to worry about would be mortars and the VC charging up the path to the south. He sighed. *Hope you'll be proud of us, Sarge.*

CHAPTER 48

The men spread about ten yards apart and crawled into place. Each soldier who still carried a grenade pulled it out. Casper spread his hands wide, then closed them into a fist. The men responded with the same motion. In another second, Casper raised his fist to shoulder level and thrust it forward three times. The men threw the grenades and commenced firing.

Bankston targeted the two mortar men. The rest fired into a cluster of men who appeared to be giving commands.

The Vietnamese soldiers scrambled for cover, and within seconds returned fire. A wall of bullets concentrated toward the hill made the seven American soldiers hug the earth as they scooted back from the hill's edge. The noise was deafening. It seemed every NVA who'd dispersed to the jungle had reappeared to shoot at them.

Casper motioned his fighters to continue edging backward as the bullets tore trees and foliage to shreds. He pointed south of the hill. The men crawled in the direction of the area where the enemy would attack if they tried taking the hill.

Seconds after the initial barrage, Casper heard the American M-16s, 50- and 60-caliber machine guns, and grenades exploding. The firing toward the hill stopped as the staccato speech of one of their leaders gave instruction.

Casper wished he'd paid more attention in language class. Minutes later, mortar shells dropped amid the NVAs' position. The seven dug in even more as a shell hit the side of the hill. The howitzers boomed as those shells fell perilously close to the soldiers on the hill. Shortly after, the drone of helicopters could be heard as their guns opened fire on the enemy.

Casper sweated, waiting for an assault on their hill, but it never happened. Maybe they thought they had taken us out when there was no return fire, Casper thought. Or maybe they had to concentrate on the superior firepower of the soldiers they'd tried to ambush. Either was good for him.

The fighting lasted three hours as the seven soldiers lay waiting and watching. In the distance, Casper watched helicopters filled with troops sink below the tree line to deposit the replacements, then rise with men who were probably wounded or dead.

During a lull, Casper peeked downward to a creek and a trail littered with dead khaki-and-green–clad bodies his men had killed. In time, the sound of shooting became sporadic.

"What now?" Warfield asked no one in particular.

The men continued to watch the path for any enemy.

A Huey, flying higher than typical, hovered over the battleground, then flew over the creek bed. Casper, Bankston, and Warfield waved excitedly as the helicopter flew past them, then turned and flew over them again.

In another forty minutes, an assault squad of American soldiers entered the area below the hill, looking up. The men on the hill waved again as the men below cautiously waved back.

***

"Who the hell are you guys?" Lieutenant Dillard Maynard asked.

"We're from the 25th, sir," Casper answered.

"25th what? What battalion? What company?"

"Division headquarters, sir."

The lieutenant's head tilted as he looked at each of the men. "Headquarters? How the hell did you get out here? Where'd you come from?"

"Cambodia, sir," Turner answered.

"What the hell?"

"Yes, sir," Robinson affirmed.

The answers seemed beyond the lieutenant's comprehension, so he changed the subject. "You responsible for them?" he asked, pointing to the dead NVA along the creek.

"Yes, sir."

"Then you're the ones who saved our asses."

"Yes, sir."

The lieutenant called to his RTO. "Reese. Call in a chopper to take these men back to base, then call Captain Valentine to tell him what we found."

"We going back, too, sir?" a rifleman asked.

"Yeah, but they get their own chopper."

PART III

CHAPTER 49

October 23, 1969

The call from Terrence Means in New York was unexpected.

"I got some good news."

"Shoot! I mean what?" Anthony Andrews chuckled.

Means laughed, too. "I got a call from Marcus Glover. I didn't even know he was in the city. He got busted for attempted homicide in Cleveland, but got released after they found it was self-defense."

"How'd he find you?"

"He's got some relatives here. He found I was active with the Panthers because he'd met a couple of our guys in the joint. One of 'em put him in touch with my dude, Foster, and Foster called me."

"Where is he?"

"Here. He needed to get away and a place to flop after getting out. I accommodated him."

Anthony walked with the phone, almost tripping over the cord. "Can I talk to him?"

"Marcus! The phone!"

"Hello."

"Hi, Marcus. This is Anthony Andrews, a reporter. I—"

"Means told me about you."

"Well, first—congratulations on beating your case."

"Yeah. Sure. Thanks."

"And congratulations for getting out of 'Nam alive."

"Thanks again."

"So you understand I'm trying to find out what happened?"

"Yeah."

"So what are you doing now, Marcus?" Anthony asked.

"I'm lookin', man. The best I've found is a porter job I guess I'll take. I can't find work in my field."

"Which is?"

"I studied mechanical engineering."

"Wow. I'm sorry. But don't give up. Never give up."

"Yeah."

"Look, I want to talk to you about the mission."

The phone was silent.

"Marcus?"

"Yes."

"Can we do that?"

All Anthony heard was a sniff.

"Marcus?"

"Not yet."

Anthony's stomach sank. "I understand."

"Do you?"

Anthony was at a loss for words. How could he explain how well he understood? "Wouldn't anybody know better than you, Marcus. Would you contact me when you want to talk?"

"Okay."

"Can I talk to Means?"

"Yeah. Anthony?" Means asked.

"Is there any way you could persuade Marcus to talk? It'd be in his best interest if I'm able to get enough information to prove these soldiers were railroaded."

"Yeah, but he's got to do it at his own pace, Anthony."

Anthony understood only too well. Moving at one's own pace was important. It was the way a man stayed in control.

CHAPTER 50

Piece by piece, Anthony thought as he tapped his desk with a pencil. A little information here, a little information there, and hopefully the puzzle would start to come together. He looked at his notes and stopped at Furman Soledad's name. What else might *he* know?

Anthony wished he had something new to share with Soledad, but quite possibly, Soledad might have something for him, he thought as he picked up the phone.

"Mr. Soledad?"

"Yes. You find out anything, Mr. Andrews?"

"Not yet. Sorry."

"Oh."

"But I do have some questions."

"Yeah?"

"So when we last talked, you mentioned Jeremiah being herded somewhere with other soldiers. You remember him saying anything about the other men?"

"He mentioned a soldier named Sampson he went to basic with."

"Do you remember Sampson's full name?"

"Mitchell, I think."

"Anybody else?"

"No. He didn't have many friends besides me."

"Okay. That's helpful. I'll be in touch."

Anthony sat on the couch staring out the window as the dusky gray light darkened into nightfall. At first he refused to acknowledge that his singular focus was on finding The Seven to the exclusion of anything else. It had become, he admitted to himself after making fifteen calls to find Myron Turner with no luck, a progressive addiction—one that was becoming as strong as his need had been for alcohol.

Because besides uncovering the plight of the soldiers, his quest might provide answers to a question that to date had eluded him— how to get the war out of his head and get his wife and daughter back.

***

Myron Turner and Leroy Casper never returned Anthony's calls. Robinson was polite enough but hung up after five minutes of conversation. And even though he had their numbers, no one answering could tell him how to get in touch with Xavier Warfield, Clarence Bankston, or Raphael Holland.

Warfield's mother was somewhat helpful. "Xavier stayed with us for about a month, then he told us he had to get a place of his own. We haven't talked to him since then. If you talk to him, tell him we're worried about him, okay?"

"Yes, ma'am. I will."

"Clarence is moving to Cleveland," Bankston's mother said. "He wants to be around his army friends. He told us they're the only ones who understand him. I expect he'll call once he gets settled."

"Raphael? Don't nobody know. He out in the street somewhere," the voice on the other end said.

"Okay," Anthony had responded to each of the three. "Please tell him a reporter called who wants to help with his situation."

Anthony waited for the phone to ring. He hoped to talk to and convince at least one of The Seven he had their best interest in mind. When he went out, Anthony checked his answering machine as soon as he returned home. No messages. Not even someone trying to sell him something.

Anthony became so discouraged he considered having a drink before mentally slapping himself in the head. Was this where it ended? The story never told? Each of the men going his own way—scared, scarred?

But then, maybe they weren't. Maybe he was the only one. Maybe he was the only weak one. But that couldn't be. If they weren't affected, why didn't they talk? Was it the other-than-honorable discharge, or did the mission play a part? Did they talk to each other? It appeared they did if Bankston was moving from Mississippi to be with them, but why wouldn't they talk to him?

He sat back grimacing. The thick folder with his notes and articles lay on the kitchen table where it had remained unopened for the past three weeks.

What else could he do? Without their cooperation, nothing would happen. Anthony sighed. The least he could do was to get away for a while, go to Cleveland, and visit the Williams family as Chucky had suggested. But he was torn between leaving home—risking not being there if Carla returned—and getting some comfort and answers from the Williamses who were like another family to him.

Anthony hung his head. Fat chance of the former happening. Carla's father had been clear: Even if she returned, he still was not where he needed to be. He had more work to do.

***

"Raymond?" Anthony asked over the phone.

"Yes. Who's this?"

"Anthony."

"Anthony! Your ears must be burning."

"Why. What happened?"

"Cread just asked about you. Wondering how you are and why you haven't stayed in contact."

"Man, if you only knew. But that's why I called. I'm coming to visit."

"Great!"

"How's everybody?"

"Everybody's good. They'll be happy to see you. When are you coming?"

"About two weeks. I'll be staying at the Majestic Hotel on 55th

Street."

"No you won't."

"Huh?"

"You'll stay with me. I've got an extra bedroom."

"I don't want to interfere with you and Myra."

"We, um, we're not together anymore."

"Aw, man. I'm sorry."

"Things happen."

Anthony toyed with the phone for a few seconds. "I'll call you a few days in advance?"

"That'd be good. It will be good seeing you."

"Same, Raymond."

Anthony placed the phone down, wondering what had happened between Raymond and Myra, who were as close as he and Carla had been. Was their break up a harbinger of things to come?

Nah, he thought running his hand over his jaw and looking at the ceiling. Nah.

***

So many issues pulled at Anthony as he drove the highway. Could a person be both elated and depressed? He looked forward to seeing the Williamses, a family with whom he'd bonded with as a reporter for the *Arkansas Sun* seven years ago. Had it been that long?

The inability to connect with any of the missing soldiers wore on him, but the sadness foremost in his mind was the disconnection between him and his family. He had to make things right.

Chucky's suggestion to visit Cread, a hardened World War II veteran, was a good one. Cread had admitted the war had changed him, but he'd seemed okay with it. But how? Anthony glanced at the list of the soldier's names he had placed on the passenger seat. Cleveland had helped him grow when he'd visited before. Could Cleveland also help him heal?

***

Driving down 105th Street brought back vivid memories. There had been a riot a year earlier, and some of the buildings Anthony remembered had been demolished. He smiled as he approached Massie Avenue. Riley's pool room and the Café Tia Juana bar still stood.

Raymond had told Anthony to meet with him, Cread, and Uncle Thompson at Thompson's house that evening. Before Anthony reached the screen door, his adopted aunt, Ludie, ran out to smother him with kisses.

Thompson smiled broadly as Anthony entered the house.

Anthony hugged his adopted uncle. "Uncle T."

Cread and Raymond hugged Anthony.

"Anthony," Thompson held Anthony at arm's length and looked into his eyes. They stood like that for a while before Thompson spoke. "You've changed, son."

Thompson turned to his brother and nephew. "What do you think, Cread? Raymond?"

They both nodded.

Ludie laughed. "He's just tired."

"Naw. Something's different," Raymond said. "I noticed over the telephone."

"It's been a while," Anthony offered.

Cread smiled knowingly. "It's not just time."

***

After the men had eaten and cleared away the dishes, they remained at the dining room table. Thompson put his hand on Anthony's shoulder. "So, Anthony, enough with the small talk. We've brought you up to date about us. What have you been up to these past years?"

Anthony clasped his hands. "Where do I start?"

He told them about his job and how much he enjoyed working with the people at the *Post*.

"What about Carla?" Ludie asked from the living room.

Anthony's face reddened. "She's okay, Aunt Ludie."

"You still have just the one child?"

"Yes. Mali. She's six now."

"Yes. I remember now. I always liked her name. Next time you must bring them, too," Ludie responded.

"I will."

Thompson smiled as he studied Anthony's face. "I remember Carla being sharp as a tack."

"She still is, Uncle T."

"So you report on local news or what?" Cread asked.

Anthony smiled briefly. "Mostly local, Cread."

Cread raised his eyebrows waiting.

Although Anthony was eager to share his battle experience and tell them of his broken marriage that had caused him so much grief, he deferred. Compared to what the Williams family had experienced having to leave Arkansas so quickly rather than be jailed or possibly killed by Klansmen, his problems were insignificant. And he was afraid his inability to cope would make him look weak. "Nothing important."

"Really?" Cread asked as if reading Anthony's mind.

"Yeah."

"Okay. If you say so."

Feeling as if he should offer something, Anthony said, "I'm working on one story, though."

"What about?" Thompson asked.

"I was attached to the 25th Infantry Division in Cu Chi, Vietnam and found that fifteen mostly non-combat soldiers were sent on a secret mission. Just seven survived. The Army covered up the real story, so I'm trying to interview them since six of the men live in Cleveland, but I'm not having any luck."

"That would be international news," Cread said with a half-smile. "Did you know Raymond was in Vietnam?"

"What?" Anthony jerked around to look at Raymond.

Raymond nodded.

"When?"

"Got out about a year ago."

Anthony hung his head. "Wow. I have been out of touch. What unit?"

"I was in the 27th Infantry, Wolfhounds."

"You see any action?"

"Yeah," Raymond answered as he got up to go to the kitchen.

Cread watched Raymond leave and then leaned back. "He's still working out some things, Anthony."

"I understand." Anthony took a sip of water and let out a deep breath. He took another sip before setting the glass down. Embarrassed his hand had begun to tremble again, he moved it to his lap. "I was in a battle, too."

Cread cocked his head. "But you were a reporter."

"Not that day."

Raymond returned from the kitchen, having overheard. "So what happened?"

Anthony told all that had happened to him but left out the part about Carla leaving him because of his temper. He told the full story of The Seven as the men listened without interruption. He lowered his head. "I want to tell their story—set things right for them—but I've hit a dead end. So I thought seeing family again might at least give me some comfort."

"Let's talk after dessert," Raymond said. "I might have some ideas."

CHAPTER 51

Y ou said you had a list of names?" Raymond asked.

"Yeah," Anthony responded.

"Let's see it."

Anthony pulled it out of his hip pocket. "It doesn't matter. None of them will talk anyway."

Raymond squinted as he read the seven names. "None of these sound familiar."

"They probably arrived after you left."

Raymond handed the list back to Anthony. "What are you doing tomorrow?"

"Nothing."

"I want to visit my Aunt Cordelia who arrived here from Mississippi. You want to come? After Aunt Ludie's breakfast, you'll need the walk."

"Sure."

"After that, we can see if we can get with some of the guys on your list."

"I've just about given up."

"How long you been at it?"

"About four months."

"Four months doesn't seem that long to make things right for those soldiers."

Anthony remained silent for a few seconds before responding. "You're right."

***

"So how are you doing, Raymond?" Anthony asked as they walked down Massie Avenue.

Raymond looked down. "I'm better. I'm at Cleveland State working on my bachelor's degree. Everything's working out." Raymond hesitated. "I'm best when I'm alone, though, you know? Solitude works for me. I'm betting on time taking care of the rest. At least it's what Cread tells me."

"You're lucky to have Cread and the rest of your family around you."

"I am. What about your family, Anthony?"

"Carla and Mali?"

"No. How are your mother and father?"

"They're good. I talk to them at least once a month."

"Too bad they aren't nearer."

"True. But they would never leave Arkansas." Anthony thought briefly about his parents. His father would have been jealous he chose to visit the Williams family instead of his own. His mother would be, too. But dad seemed to have some special dislike for the Williams. Probably because Anthony bragged about them so much. That in ad-

244

dition to the Williams being a working-class family as opposed to the upper-class with whom his father identified. So, he chose his second family over his first? Oh, well.

"At least you have your wife and child."

Anthony bowed his head. "They left me."

Raymond stopped to look at Anthony. "Why?"

"I developed a temper. It got out of control. I did and said stupid things, so Carla took Mali and left."

"I'm sorry, Anthony." Raymond paused. "I'm not sure why Myra left me. When I got back from 'Nam, she was gone. Nobody knew where. I guess I was gone too long."

"I'm sad to hear it, man. She was such a beautiful young lady. I hope she's okay."

"Me, too." Raymond patted Anthony on the back. "At least you know where your wife and daughter are. And your temper, it's probably a temporary situation. You'll heal. It doesn't happen overnight, though."

Anthony looked down. "I'm a little embarrassed telling you this."

"Why?"

"From what you told me, you were knee deep in battle several times. I was in one firefight."

"True," Raymond said, "but I was mentally prepared for it." He laughed. "As much as you can prepare." He stopped and turned to Anthony. "You weren't, and from what you've told me about the seven soldiers, they weren't either. It can make a difference." Raymond continued to walk. "I can tell you, I'm better than I was. Every day is a better day. It's what I tell myself each morning, and then you make it happen."

"You know, Raymond, every time I'm with you, you give me something to think about."

"I'm just the messenger, Anthony. My uncles and cousins gave me their knowledge. I'm just passing it on."

Anthony looked down. "I probably need to work on making it happen for me before I try helping anybody else."

"You know what I remember about you, Anthony?"

"What's that?"

"You are smart, and you are dedicated. Don't get hung up on whatever shortcomings you think you have. Don't let your situation stop you from making a difference in those boys' lives. I believe you can do both."

Anthony pressed his lips together and nodded. "I guess I'll have to. I've gone too far to turn back now."

***

"You still shoot?" Anthony asked as he pointed toward Riley's pool room as they turned onto 105th Street.

"So much going on, I don't have the time to practice."

Anthony looked up and down the street. "The Five hasn't changed too much."

"Not in this area. One Hundred and Fifth Street is about the same way you left it. The Glenville riot took out a few buildings, though."

"Nothing like the riots overseas," Anthony said.

Raymond laughed. "I heard those were up close and personal."

"And for a good reason."

"I figured it wouldn't be long before something jumped off," Raymond responded.

The two men turned off 105th Street onto Morrison Avenue. They hadn't taken but a few steps when someone yelled from across the street.

"Lieutenant Williams?"

Raymond and Anthony turned.

"Arthur Warfield, sir," he said, saluting.

Raymond grinned. "Warfield." He ignored the salute and hugged the man. "I'm out of the army, so no saluting necessary."

"You will always be my lieutenant, sir."

Raymond tilted his head toward Anthony. "This is Anthony Andrews, a reporter."

"Nice to meet you, Mr. Andrews. You are walking with the best officer I ever served under—a straight-up guy."

"Glad to meet you, Mr. Warfield." Anthony cocked his head as he looked at Warfield. "So you served?"

"Two and done."

"You have any relatives in the army?"

"My first cousin."

Anthony grabbed Warfield's arm. "Named Xavier?"

Warfield's eyes narrowed as he withdrew his arm from Anthony's grasp. "How'd you know?"

"I've been trying to meet him," Anthony responded.

"For what?" Arthur Warfield asked.

Raymond patted Warfield's shoulder. "Anthony is cool. He's trying to run down a story about fifteen support soldiers sent on a mission where just seven returned."

Warfield looked at Raymond. "Xav mentioned it, but he didn't go into detail. I do know he didn't come out of it too well."

"I can imagine," Anthony said.

"Can you?"

"He's been in some shit himself," Raymond said.

"I thought you said he was a reporter, sir."

"A reporter who got caught up in an ambush, killed some VC, and saved a company from being attacked from the rear," Raymond answered.

Arthur Warfield stared into Anthony's eyes for a while then nodded. "Yeah. Yeah. Okay. Where?" Warfield asked, a little more conciliatory.

"Outside Tay Ninh."

"You tell Xav that?"

"No. Our conversation was about thirty seconds long."

Arthur Warfield shook Anthony's hand. "All right. Well, it's nice meeting you."

"You, too, Mr. Warfield, and if Xavier ever wants to talk, would you take my number?" Anthony asked giving Warfield his card.

Warfield nodded, took it, and then turned to Raymond. "Lieutenant, you live around here?"

"Yeah. On Parkwood."

"We got to get together."

"Any time, Warfield. Let me get your number and I'll give you mine."

Anthony slammed his fist into his palm as he watched Arthur Warfield walk away. "I'm feeling hopeful, man."

Raymond smiled. "It's one small step, but I'm feeling like you, Anthony. This might be the break you've been looking for."

CHAPTER 52

Raymond rang the bell and knocked on the door a few times. "Aunt Cordelia must have stepped out." Raymond knocked once more. "I wanted to find out about my great-uncle Willie Crenshaw, who's still in Mississippi. He'll be ninety-four this year and still lives on his own."

"Wow. Good for him," Anthony said as the two left to return to Thompson's house. "One of the soldiers who didn't return was named Willie."

"It's a common name."

"Willie Stinson. He was their sergeant."

Raymond stopped. "Willie Stinson? Was he from Cleveland, too?"

"Yeah."

"You sure?"

"It's what the roster said."

"Damn! How come his name wasn't on the list?"

"He never came back. Do you know him?" Anthony asked.

"If it's my Willie Stinson, we lived on the same street for a while."

"What? You've got to tell me about him."

"I lost track of him some time ago, but let me get this straight. Willie was in Vietnam?"

"That's what I understand."

Raymond pulled out the piece of paper with Arthur Warfield's telephone number. "We need to talk to this Xavier cat and find out what he knows about Willie."

"When's the last time you saw him?"

"We were just kids, but he was a great friend. Actually, he was more than that. I'm writing an essay about him as an assignment for my English Composition class."

"I'd like to read it."

"As soon as I'm finished. And if it's the Willie I know, you'll have an even better story than mine."

***

Anthony and Raymond sat in the kitchen of Raymond's apartment as Raymond dialed Arthur Warfield's number. "Warfield, this is Raymond. I realize we just talked this morning, but I've got something important to ask you. I found out a good friend of mine might have been with Xavier on that mission. His name is Sergeant Willie Stinson. Run it by your cousin and give him my telephone number."

The phone at Raymond's apartment rang fifteen minutes later. "Hello?" Raymond answered. He motioned Anthony to go to his bedroom and pick up the other line.

"Uh. This is Xavier Warfield. You Lieutenant Williams?"

"Yes. How are you doing?"

"All right, sir. Making it."

"I appreciate you returning my call. So you knew Willie Stinson?"

Anthony almost felt the urgency in Raymond's voice.

"Sarge? Yes, I did."

"What did he look like?"

"Like a body builder. Dark skinned. About five feet, eleven inches."

"Did he say where he went to high school?"

"Yeah. East High and Tech."

"It's him. Any idea what happened to him?"

Warfield paused. "No. I'm sorry. Nothing. We've been trying to find out, but…"

Raymond sighed. "Okay. Let me know if you hear anything."

"Will do."

"Look. I've got Anthony Andrews, the reporter with me. Do you mind talking to him?"

There was a long pause. "My cousin told me he met him. He knew Sarge, too?"

"No. But he's trying to find out what happened to you guys and what happened to your sergeant. Can you help him?"

Warfield paused again.

"Warfield," Raymond said, "we've all been to war, including Mr. Andrews. We understand, man. He's trying to get to the bottom of the shit they put you through, and you need to help us, so he can help you, your boys, and Sergeant Stinson. Understand?"

"Yeah, LT, I understand."

"Good. Can we meet?"

"Yeah. I guess."

CHAPTER 53

Anthony watched as Xavier Warfield entered, wearing perfectly creased black wool slacks, an open-collar blue cotton shirt, and black leather shoes that almost gleamed in the dimly lit kitchen of Raymond's apartment. The men shook hands and sat.

Xavier Warfield stared at Raymond for a while. "Aren't you the pool shark?"

Raymond laughed. "Used to be."

"Whoa. I remember you. When I was coming up, I wanted to be like you. You beat me out of fifteen dollars one time when I thought I had game."

"You still shoot?" Raymond asked.

"Yes. You?"

"No. It requires time I don't have right now."

The three sat at the kitchen table talking about 105th Street while Warfield tapped out a rhythm with his fingers.

"Thanks for coming," Raymond said.

"My cousin mentioned you were an outstanding officer. I respect that," Warfield replied. "There weren't a lot of those."

"I appreciate that." Raymond dipped his head toward Anthony. "Mr. Andrews here is a good friend of mine. When I found out what he was trying to do—set things right for you guys who got screwed over—I thought I'd try to help him."

Warfield placed his folded hands on the table. "Okay."

"There's no way you should have been sent on a field mission like that, much less receive an OTH for your service. If Mr. Andrews here can help you guys, would you work with him?"

Warfield shrugged, his fingers started drumming on the table again. He pursed his lips before looking at Raymond. "The whole thing was crazy."

"I understand," Raymond answered, "but it doesn't mean you have to live with it and get punished, too."

"Yeah," Warfield said.

Raymond leaned toward Warfield. "And I know no better person than someone who's been subjected to something similarly crazy to make it right."

Warfield glanced at Anthony and nodded.

"So can you help?" Raymond asked.

Warfield paused a few seconds before answering. "Yes."

Raymond put his hands on Warfield's and Anthony's shoulders. "Let's make this right."

"Tell me about yourself first, Warfield. Some history— how you got drafted and how you became one of the fifteen men sent on this mission," Anthony said.

Warfield gazed out the window. "I grew up not too far from here on Lakeview Avenue. Went to Patrick Henry Junior High and the 'Ville."

"The 'Ville?" Anthony asked.

"Glenville High."

"Right."

"I got a job at Ford Motor Company and was doing okay before this dude tried to rob me. I ended up shooting him, and they gave me a choice: the army or jail."

"So how'd you get sent out on patrol?"

"There was a fight. Some of the Cleveland guys got involved. I joined in, became one of the fifteen."

"You want to talk about what happened to you and the other fourteen?"

Warfield glanced at Raymond. "Not now, if you don't mind. Maybe later?"

"Sure." Anthony was happy to have gotten as far as he did. "Did you know any of the other seven before you were drafted?"

"Glover. He was the reason I got caught up in that mess."

"What happened?"

"I was in HQ when Glover called me out. He said we were going to fight. Glover was a hothead, and any little thing would tick him off, so I thought this was one of those times.

"All through junior and senior high, Glover would get into fights and call me for backup. I was always there for him because he was my friend, but when I saw what was happening on base, I backed off. He ran and grabbed me and almost threw me into the fight, so I had no choice but to scrap."

"Anybody else you knew before the fight?" Anthony asked.

"Robinson and Casper. The others? Not well."

Anthony looked at the list. "Okay. What about Robinson?"

"The preacher? He was okay. Pissed people off with his constant praying, but he changed. Came around to becoming a good soldier."

"Are you in touch with Robinson?" Anthony continued.

"No. He kind of faded out when he got back. I guess we all did to some extent."

"Casper?"

"A good dude. I've seen him at a few parties since we got back. He ain't as quiet as he used to be."

"Bankston?"

"Sniper. Did what he was told and killed a lot of VC."

"Holland?"

"Holland. I remember him doing a lot of drugs on base. That's about it."

"Turner?"

"The professor. A righteous dude. He saw things."

"What do you mean?" Anthony asked.

"He predicted some things before they happened. He helped a lot in us returning from Cambodia."

"Cambodia?" Raymond and Anthony asked together.

"You didn't know?"

"Cambodia was off limits," Raymond said.

"It could have been. They never told us, but that's where they dropped us."

Raymond looked down and then at Warfield. "It's lucky any of you got back."

"True."

"How long were you in the field?" Raymond asked.

"Eleven days. It was supposed to be three."

Anthony's eyes narrowed. "Wow. Somebody's got some explaining to do. Tell me more."

Warfield glanced at his watch. "I apologize, but I've got a date tonight. I have to clean my apartment and prepare the food."

Anthony stood and shook Warfield's hand. "Okay. I appreciate you sharing this with us. Can we talk again?"

Warfield shrugged as he walked toward the door.

"Would you do me one big favor, Warfield?" Anthony asked.

"What's that?"

"If you see any of the others, would you tell them we talked, and I would like to speak to them, too?"

Warfield stopped at the door and spoke without turning. "Eight of us didn't make it. The rest of us are lucky to be alive. Most of us are just trying to settle into life in the United States and forget this whole thing. I can't promise you anything."

"Remember one thing, though, Warfield. You were wronged. I want to make it right."

Warfield tapped his fingers on the doorframe a couple of times, then closed the door behind him.

"What do you think?" Raymond asked.

"Cambodia? No wonder everyone was closemouthed." Anthony looked at Raymond. "You think they were supposed to come back?"

"Good question."

Anthony shook his head and then he looked at his notes. "Well, I'm as close as I've been, thanks to you. I don't see it getting any easier, but we are advancing."

Raymond smiled. "Advancing. That's an appropriate term."

CHAPTER 54

The phone rang five times before Xavier Warfield picked it up.

"Warfield?"

"Yeah."

"Glover, man."

"Hey, brother. You still in the big city?"

"Nope. I'm back in Cleveland looking for a place to lay for a minute."

"No problem. I got a couch," Xavier offered.

"That's cool."

"Why'd you leave?"

"Not my kind of place, man. New York is noisy; everybody seems to be stressed out, and it's expensive. I don't need none of that," Glover replied.

"I hear you. Where are you?"

"At the Greyhound bus station."

"You need a ride?"

"I'm good. What's your address?"

"It's 1838 East 90th."

"Off Chester Avenue, right?"

"You got it."

"Cool. See you in a few."

***

Warfield smiled at the knock, as if Glover was tapping some secret code for admittance. He swung open the door and hugged his friend. "How long a ride you have?"

"About sixteen hours, man. The bus stopped in every little-ass city on the way."

"You get any sleep?"

"Some."

"You want to crash now?"

"Naw, man. Too wired. You got beer?"

"Yeah."

"So what's up with you?" Glover asked.

"Cool as can be under the circumstances. Glad to get out of the house, though, with Mom's trailing me everywhere except the bathroom asking if I'm okay."

"I heard that."

Warfield popped open a Budweiser for himself. "I had an interesting day yesterday, though."

"Yeah?"

Warfield took a sip. "Yeah. This reporter…"

"Andrews?"

Warfield stopped sipping and held the beer can two inches from his lips. "You know him?"

"Yeah. I talked with him when I was hanging with Means."

"What did you talk about?"

"I didn't," Glover responded.

"Well, my cousin, Arthur, ran into his former lieutenant named Williams, who lives not too far from him. This reporter guy was with Williams. My cousin loved his LT. Said he was the coolest officer under fire he'd ever met. But get this, the lieutenant knows Sarge."

Glover bounced up, almost knocking his table lamp over. "What? How?"

"They lived on the same street growing up."

"Are you kidding?"

"Nope. After I described him, he said it was his man."

Glover sat back down. "Wow."

"And the reporter was in a firefight. Can you believe it? He killed some VC and saved the company from being surrounded."

"Really?"

"Yep. You could tell he had been in it. All you had to do was look in his eyes."

"What'd you guys talk about?" Glover asked.

"Ahh, just about some of the guys. He wanted a profile on us."

"What'd you say about me?"

"The truth: hotheaded; always getting me in trouble."

Glover chuckled. "If I had that day to do over, though, I wouldn't have fought."

"Quit lying. Yes you would have."

"Not if I could have seen the future."

"You'd be speaking for all of us on that," Warfield said.

The two remained silent for a few minutes, sipping their beers.

"You okay?" Warfield asked.

"Chest itches a lot."

"You know what I mean."

"I'm good."

"If you aren't, they say you're supposed to talk about it to somebody who understands."

"Who are 'they'?" Glover asked.

"Some older vets I talked to at a rally against the war."

"You went to a rally?"

Warfield stood. "Hell yeah. The war was bullshit, man."

"At least it was to us."

"They say they have a group who get together. They invited me to join."

Glover chuckled. "It probably just took one look to tell *you* needed help."

Warfield shrugged. "We got our own group, though."

"The Wolverines," Glover said.

"The Wolverines," Warfield repeated.

The two sat quietly for another few minutes before Glover looked at Warfield, "That might not be a bad idea."

"The get-together?"

"What do you think?" Glover asked.

Warfield tapped his knee a few of times. "It couldn't hurt. We've been in touch here and there, and it would be nice for all of us to see each other again. Why not?"

***

The next morning Glover stretched and ran his hand through his hair. "I can get used to this couch. I fell dead asleep last night. Best sleep I had in a long time. What time is it?"

"Eleven-forty-five," Warfield responded.

"Wow. That couch *is* good."

Warfield laughed. "Cool. It's there as long as you need it, brother. By the way, Turner said no to the meeting."

"I figured that. He was always a little different."

"Shy," Warfield said.

"Is that it? He had a gift, though."

"Saved our asses."

"What about the others?" Glover asked.

"I got Holland calling Casper. Holland's in. Robinson's a maybe."

Glover stretched, then yawned. "Think he got his own church by now?"

"I don't know, man. I wonder if he even goes to church after Cambodia."

"Anyway, I'll keep calling rest of them."

"You think this will help?" Warfield asked.

"Can't hurt."

CHAPTER 55

I'm sorry I couldn't stay longer, Raymond, but I've got to get back on the job," Anthony said.

"I understand. It was good seeing you, though, even for this short a time."

"Thanks for all your help."

"You're doing a good thing, Anthony. I imagine most people would have given up by now."

"I was close to doing that a few times."

Raymond looked at Anthony. "I'm sure, but there's something else I've noticed about you since we first met."

"What's that?"

"As mild-mannered as you seem, you got some pit bull in you. It's why you could pick up a rifle in Tay Ninh, and it's why you'll get to the bottom of the Cambodia thing."

Anthony smiled. "You think?"

"I know a fighter when I see one."

Anthony looked down. He'd never thought of himself as a pit bull, but looking back on his life, maybe he was. And he hadn't even told Raymond about knocking out a light-heavyweight boxer.

***

Anthony's mindset as he drove from Cleveland was different from the one he had driving to Cleveland. He'd made inroads with one of the soldiers, and he felt more peaceful after talking with Raymond. Now, if only he could reconnect with his wife and daughter.

As he pulled into the driveway of his home, he looked first at his front window and smiled. The window was intact. That was a good sign.

That night he slept peacefully in his bed for the first time in months. The next morning he took a long, hot shower, fixed a light breakfast, sat in the living room and tried to read the issues of the *Post* he'd missed while traveling.

Even though Anthony had expected it, the doorbell startled him. He tried his best to restrain from dashing to the door and wrenching it open. He rubbed his hands on his thighs, then fumbled with the lock before opening the door.

"Hi, honey."

"Anthony."

Anthony grimaced. She usually greeted him with "baby."

"Why didn't you use the key?"

"I haven't been here in a while, Anthony. I thought it best I ring."

"Where's Mali?" he asked, looking over her shoulder.

"I thought we should talk first."

"Okay." Anthony closed the door and slumped into the high-back chair. "But I want you to understand... nothing like that will ever happen again. I swear. I—I know my temper scared you."

"It didn't scare me, Anthony," Carla said, leaning back on the sofa across from the chair and crossing her legs, "but it scared our child."

"I know. I…"

"What happened to you, Anthony?"

He frowned and shook his head.

"I realize you've had some painful experiences in your life, but you seemed to have been handling it. Was it Vietnam?"

Anthony remained silent.

"You never talked about it. What went on over there?"

Anthony rubbed the back of his neck. "I—"

"Tell me, Anthony," Carla said, leaning forward and staring pleadingly at her husband.

Anthony thought about The Seven and how hard it was for them to talk. It was something he understood well, but he had to try. He hesitated before speaking, clasping and unclasping his hands. "I saw death. I saw pain like nothing I'd ever seen before." He stood and paced for a minute. "I killed people, Carla. I went to report on the war, but I ended up…"

Carla sat for a moment waiting for Anthony to finish but spoke when she realized he wouldn't, or couldn't. "I figured something happened, but you never talked about it."

"I–I didn't because it would remind me all over again. I tried to forget. Get away from it."

Carla leaned back, quiet for another minute. "I can't pretend to understand, but I've heard about the problems some men have in combat. Uncle Clayton was in combat in World War II. Aunt Dee mentioned he was never the same."

Carla laid her purse next to her on the chair after realizing she had been grasping it so hard her fingers hurt. "Have you talked to anyone about it, Anthony?"

"Yeah. Chucky. And I just came back from visiting the Williamses in Cleveland."

"Oh?"

"Both Raymond and Cread were in the war."

"Raymond, too? What did they say?"

"They said I needed to be around people who understand." Anthony sat next to Carla. "I'm better, Carla. The nightmares don't come so often anymore, and I've quit drinking."

Carla looked up. "When did you start?"

"In Vietnam for a short while and then again after you left."

Carla stood and walked into the kitchen and the dining room. "You've kept the house in good shape, for an alcoholic. It doesn't appear you need any help taking care of the place."

"Oh, but I do," Anthony responded.

Carla came back into the living room, a half-smile on her face.

"Okay, baby. Just kidding about the alcoholic comment. Here's the deal: I come back first. We try this out for a month, just the two of us. Mali will stay with my parents until then."

Anthony smiled. "That would be great."

"Give me a few weeks to get our daughter squared away and I'll come home. If the month works for us, then we can try to be a family again."

CHAPTER 56

It had been an uneasy two days for Anthony since Carla had returned. Anthony mentally tiptoed around the house, trying his best to avoid any emotional landmines. He considered making a small toast to himself on the evening of the second day but decided against it.

Their first night out, Anthony and Carla ate at their favorite restaurant, Harvey's, on Connecticut Avenue. Anthony ordered an appetizer of steamed oysters with the canvas-back duck entrée. Carla ordered the oysters, too, but had fried chicken, a specialty of the restaurant. Neither drank any alcohol as they made small talk, glancing at each other like sixteen-year-olds on their first date.

Carla and the waiter both laughed at a joke Anthony told, providing Anthony with some relief as he nervously played with the food on his plate. He recognized a few of the patrons but refrained from hailing them for fear of breaking the tenuous but relaxed mood he had developed with his wife.

"How's your food, honey?" Anthony asked.

"Good. They must have a sister in the kitchen," Carla giggled.

After dinner, the two engaged in more small talk. Carla looked up after laughing at another of her husband's jokes. "Honey, we're the only people left!"

Anthony looked around at the empty restaurant and laughed.

"Have we been here that long?"

The air was breezy but warm as Carla slipped her hand into Anthony's as they walked to the car. The relief that washed over Anthony from that single gesture erased any remnants of apprehension prowling around inside his mind. He pecked Carla on her cheek as he held the door for her. She smiled and returned the kiss.

That night in bed felt like the first time they'd ever lain together. Anthony, leaning on his elbow, ran his hand tentatively across Carla's stomach as she lay quietly in her nightgown, accepting but not reciprocating.

Anthony's senses were so heightened, his need so intense, it took all his resolve not to ravish her. But he sensed an unfamiliar guardedness.

It didn't stop him from savoring her skin, her hair, her smell, her curves, and her crevices, though, gently holding, caressing, kissing before the first tremble and the slightest sound of acceptance escaped her pouted lips.

It seemed an eternity before she turned, running her hand over his chest, pecking his forehead, then his cheek. One, then two more sighs slipped from her as his strokes became more intense, more intimate.

One tear slid down her cheek as she finally reached for him, holding him like a child, placing her lips to his ear. "I love you, Anthony."

His emotions, scattered to the wind, didn't allow for speech. He could only nod as she lay back, her arms above her head.

"I love you, too, Carla," he cried as their exhausted, quivering bodies erupted for the fourth time that night.

Later, as they lay spoonlike, breathing quietly, a smile crossed his face at the realization she had missed him, too.

***

"Whose are these, Anthony?" Carla came into the kitchen holding a pair of stockings the next morning.

"They're not yours?"

She stared at him, head cocked. Confusion turned into dread as he recalled that night with Constance. "Nothing happened, Carla."

Carla glared at him, shook her head, and threw the stockings at him.

"Carla, nothing happened," he tried to explain as she stormed up the stairs with him behind her.

At the top of the stairs, she held up one hand, stopping him. "Anthony."

"Are you going to let me explain?"

Anthony's impassive expression and his ominous tone made her put her hand down. She stood there, her hands on her hips.

Anthony took a deep breath, counted, then walked past her into the bedroom, and sat on the bed. He motioned her to sit, but Carla remained standing.

"A lady was in the house. She followed me home from a bar. I'd had a fight. I got drunk—very drunk. When I woke up the next morning, she was here. We didn't do anything because I was too drunk. She confirmed it. I asked her to leave when I came to my senses."

Carla stood staring at Anthony. "You got drunk? Got into a fight?"

"Yeah."

"Then you bring a woman into our house?"

"She followed me."

"We're not talking about a stray dog, Anthony. You brought a woman into our house." Carla looked at Anthony, at the ceiling, then back at Anthony. "Drunk, fighting. Is this what you've become?"

"Nothing happened, Carla."

"Who was she?"

"Constance Hanson."

"Constance…the boxer's wife?" Carla asked.

"Ex-wife."

"Wife, ex-wife. It makes a difference? And who did you fight, Anthony?"

"Marvin Hanson."

Carla put a hand to her forehead. "Jesus, Anthony." She looked at her husband as if he were an alien. "You fought a boxer? What happened?"

"I knocked him out."

"You knocked Hanson out. Right. Now I know you're lying."

Anthony raised his hands. "You think I would be here as opposed to George Washington Hospital if I hadn't?"

"Okay. Okay. So you knock him out. Evidently she was with you then."

"Look, all I remember was going to the Shanty for a few drinks. This woman sits next to me and starts talking. She's laughing and puts her hand on mine, and I get snatched out of the chair. I remember throwing some blows and walking out. That's it. I'm not clear about the rest until I wake up and see this woman in our house. I asked her to leave, and she did."

Carla put her hands back on her hips and stood in front of him for a few seconds, glaring into his eyes, thinking before asking. "Would you have done anything if you weren't drunk?"

"If I hadn't been drunk, she would never have been here."

"How do I know that? Huh? If you are doing everything else—going to bars, drinking, fighting—why not that?"

Anthony raised his hands. "Because you know me."

Lips pursed, Carla sniffed. "I don't know if I do."

Anthony took a deep breath. "Look, Carla, there's nothing else I can tell you. If you don't believe me, I'm sorry. I can't fight but so many battles right now. I can't," he said as he got up and went downstairs.

"We're not finished, Anthony."

"I am," he said as he walked out the door.

***

"Where have you been? It's three o'clock in the morning."

The voice in the dark startled Anthony. He turned on the living room light to see Carla sitting up, a blanket over her legs.

"Out. You stayed up all night?"

Carla nodded. "Did you drink?"

Her subdued tone surprised him. "No. Just driving. Clearing my head."

Carla took a deep breath and pushed the blanket aside.

Anthony braced for the salvo.

"You know, I was so happy to come back home. I wanted to call you so many times after I left. Maybe I should have. Maybe I shouldn't have left. If I hadn't, maybe we wouldn't be having this conversation."

Anthony exhaled and sat on the couch with her. "I don't know how else to tell you this, Carla. We've been through a lot, but I've never cheated on you. I screwed up. I admit it. In my right mind, it would have never happened. I wasn't in my right mind. That's all I can tell you. Nothing happened.

"Too much has been going on in my life to jeopardize what's been most important, what I hold on to when I'm searching—trying to find a quiet place in my head. I understand if you don't believe me, but what I told you is the truth."

Carla stood and folded her hands in front of her. Her look softened. "The only reason I want to believe you is because you've never lied to me. But you've got to understand how absurd it sounds. You bring a woman—an ex-model—into this house. She obviously disrobed, slept in the same bed with you, but you did nothing. How many people do you think would believe your story?"

Anthony looked Carla in the eyes. "Anybody who knew me."

Carla sat, repeatedly smoothing her hand over her robe. "Okay, Anthony, I've got to give you the benefit of the doubt. You've changed, but I can't believe you changed so much you would screw up our marriage, even if you were drunk. It would be so out of character for you it would be scary."

She sighed, clenched her fists by her sides and looked to the ceiling. "When does life become normal again?"

"It will soon, Carla. I promise."

"I'm going to follow my instincts. You've been under a lot of stress. I don't want to be the one that adds to it." Carla took a deep breath and exhaled. "I can barely picture you drunk and fighting, but hard as I try, I can't imagine you with another woman. You aren't the type. I know that. I feel that." Carla got up and poked her stiffened fingers into his chest. "But if I ever find you lied, dude, I will cut your throat."

"That's the main reason I wouldn't," Anthony said out of Carla's hearing range.

CHAPTER 57

Bill Walden laid an article from the *Richmond Times Dispatch* on Anthony's desk. "Here's something I found while researching another story. It's six months old, but I thought it might interest you."

Rampage in Charlottesville

Police report a former army lieutenant colonel, Leonard Rainey Bertram, fatally shot his wife and severely wounded two males, Arnold Fern Fricker and Rhyne Leonard Foster, in the lobby of the Buckingham Hotel late Friday evening.

Bertram and his wife, Heidi, had recently reunited after his return from Vietnam. Bertram's last assignment was executive officer of the 25th Infantry Battalion in Vietnam.

"You're still collecting articles on the 25th in Vietnam, Anthony, right?"

"Yes."

"Did you know this Colonel Bertram?"

"I did. He was my liaison at the 25th," Anthony replied.

"And Rhyne was a former reporter for the *Washington Post*. Always in trouble," Walden said. "I wonder what he's gotten into now."

Anthony read the article again, wondering how he'd missed it. "This is old news, but I'd like to talk to the colonel. I've got a few

278

questions pertaining to my research on the fifteen men."

Walden shrugged. "Why not? Also, check to see if there's more to Bertram's story. And find out how the hell Rhyne was involved."

***

The Virginia State Penitentiary with its dull, gray concrete walls and buzzing fluorescent lights was crowded that Friday. The visitors, mostly women, carrying or walking their children across the worn tile floor, sat at the two-way windows. Anthony planned to spend a short time interviewing the colonel that afternoon and return for a longer session on Saturday.

Colonel Bertram looked so different from the man Anthony had known in Cu Chi, that Anthony thought they had sent out the wrong prisoner. The tall, square–jawed, sharply dressed executive officer Anthony remembered slumped as he walked. His hair was unkempt, and he was unshaven. But what most unnerved Anthony were Bertram's eyes: They shifted back and forth like those of a newly caged tiger. Anthony watched through the glass wall as Bertram shuffled to his chair, flopped down, and picked up the phone.

"Colonel. Remember me? Anthony Andrews from the *Washington Post?*"

Bertram squinted at Anthony before his eyes widened with recognition. "Yeah. Yeah. I remember. You shot some VC, saved some lives."

Anthony grimaced. "Yeah"

"What are you doing here?"

"My editor thought since I knew you, I could interview you about what happened."

"Not much to it."

Anthony waited for Bertram to continue.

Bertram scratched his unshaven jaw. "People were still talking about you killing those gooks long after you left."

"Just trying to stay alive."

"Ain't we all?"

"How are they treating you? You need anything?"

"How about a Huey and an extraction team?"

Anthony watched as a forced smile flashed across Bertram's face.

"So tell me what happened for you to be here."

Bertram looked down for a while before looking up at Anthony.

"Two tours."

"Two tours?"

"Yeah. A lot of marriages have problems after one, but two tours, and a lot of them seriously start to unravel, you know?"

"So your wife was resentful of you being away for so long?"

"You could say that."

"How'd you find out?"

"Trailed her, as I would any enemy. I didn't believe it at first. Heidi came from a good, church-going family," Bertram said, snorting, "but I guess that don't count for much these days." He stared at the wall behind Anthony.

Bertram looked back at Anthony. "How's your marriage, Anthony?"

"Huh?" The question caught Anthony off guard.

"You're married if I remember."

"Yeah. Some problems, but I think they're worked out now."

"Well, watch her. They can't be trusted."

"So, Colonel, why shoot her? Why fire on the other guys?" Anthony asked, ignoring Bertram's comment.

Bertram scratched his jaw again. "I don't know. I guess I snapped."

"When did you get suspicious?"

"I went to surprise her when she was supposed to be at Bible study. We'd had this argument, so I bought these roses, just, you know, something to show how much I loved her. She wasn't at the church, so I got worried, started looking. When she came home, I asked where she'd been, and she told me Bible study.

"After that I followed her. I caught them two days before I shipped out to Fort Benning. She was supposed to come with me but said she would come later."

Bertram's facial features hardened. Just his lips moved as he continued. "They were at this party at a restaurant outside of town," he said in a monotonous voice. "I waited until they came out, laughing, holding hands, not a care in the world—her, him, and this other guy—

as if they had been doing this for years. I can't remember much after except I pulled out my forty-five and began shooting."

"Did you know the guy Rhyne who was with them?"

"Seen him around. Never liked him much. Now I know why."

The more Bertram talked, the more Anthony wondered. The colonel was already shell-shocked. Was that all it took to kill—coming home to more mental chaos than you could handle when you thought it was behind you?

Anthony decided to change the subject. "I see you got promoted since we last saw each other."

"Yep. And Colonel Bolt, who sent the fifteen men out, remember him?"

"Sure."

"He's a general now."

Anthony's mouth fell open. "What? How?"

"It's a crazy world."

"What do you mean?"

Bertram scratched his knee. "Your soldiers destroyed a major weapons cache." Bertram chuckled. "It was one of the caches the 1st Cav soldiers were looking for. Bolt and others took credit."

Anthony put his hand to his forehead. "Unbelievable."

"You tellin' me."

"So, he gets rewarded for being involved in an illegal mission."

"Wouldn't be the first time." Bertram sat up in his seat. "But you really came down to ask me about those soldiers, right?"

"I can't lie that it didn't cross my mind. I've been in contact with a few of them."

"I figured you would be, eventually. You were bulldog persistent in getting that story."

Pit bull, Anthony thought. He liked pit bull better. "You want to tell me what happened, Colonel?"

"Time's up," the guard said as he stood behind Bertram.

"Okay," Anthony stood slowly. "You sure you don't need anything?"

Bertram gave Anthony a half-smile. "No. Thanks, Anthony. I got everything I need," as he waved his hands around.

"I'll see you tomorrow."

"I'll be here."

CHAPTER 58

The colonel looked a little better the next day. He had shaved, and his eyes were brighter. Even his speech was sharper.

"They'll probably give me the chair for what I did," Bertram said quietly. "I've become okay with that." He paused. "It's funny how just a few minutes in your life can dictate your whole future."

Anthony nodded. "How well I know, Colonel."

"Just like those young men. They shouldn't have had to go through what they did."

"So why did they?"

Bertram took a deep breath. "Well, first, the black soldiers didn't initiate the riot. Then to put fifteen of them in the stockade was wrong."

"Was Bolt a racist?"

"I wouldn't say that. He promoted a black officer and had good rapport with his black troops until the riot. I think he felt betrayed."

"That the black troops would fight back instead of lying down and taking it?" Anthony asked. "Sounds like a plantation-owner mentality."

"Bolt was also up for promotion. A riot under his watch was detrimental to his advancement."

"So, he acted out of anger."

"Probably. I wouldn't have punished those young men like that, though," Bertram responded.

"If you felt that way, why didn't you say anything?"

Bertram sighed. "The army. Everything is based on 'go along to get along.' Officers who challenge their superiors jeopardize their advancement."

"So you became a lieutenant colonel because you didn't?"

"That, among other factors."

"What happened with the fifteen?"

Bertram bent his head a long while, staring at the floor before looking at Anthony. "The North Vietnamese Army had established some twenty bases along the borders of Laos, Cambodia, and Vietnam. Sihanouk's regime had weakened by 1969, and the NVA were able to move all types of supplies through Cambodia from the north to the south along the Ho Chi Minh Trail.

"In some areas, they cleared out entire villages so their movements would be undetected. The villagers who resisted leaving, they killed.

"Even though it was illegal, the top brass decided incursive strikes were necessary to stop the flow of supplies, so we sent small raiding parties into Cambodia to ambush, attack, and disrupt."

"What did that have to do with the fifteen soldiers?" Anthony asked.

"Our raids hadn't gone well. In a previous foray, the VC wiped out the whole team, and the higher-ups were desperate for a successful mission. The 1st Cavs's next strike would go in deeper than usual to take out two major storage facilities—one deep into Cambodia and one near Vietnam's border. We knew there was considerable enemy activity in the area, so Bolt comes up with the idea to send these fifteen soldiers into the area as decoys."

"More like sheep let loose in the wolf's den," Anthony said.

"True. As you've found out by now, most of these guys were clerks, cooks, and general support. They'd never been in combat. Bolt figured while Charlie was preoccupied with the fifteen soldiers, our men could complete their mission.

"When Bolt and Major Tilden from the 1st Cav sent them out June 18th, I guess they had planned to extract them when the operation ended, but a few days later, when someone leaked the 25th had conducted an illegal raid, Bolt, Tilden and their immediate superiors tried to cover it up before it went public.

"The same day of the leak, the 1st Cav soldiers radioed they were in trouble. You could hear the gunfire and the screams, then silence. Shortly after that, all we heard were Vietnamese voices, so Bolt and Tilden, assuming they'd been wiped out, froze any rescue attempt thinking nobody had make it out alive."

"But some of the fifteen did."

"Yes, they did."

"That's why all the secrecy when they got back."

"Exactly. The careers of Bolt, Tilden, General Wyatt, and a few others were on the line if anyone out of the chain of command found out."

"I'm sure. Who found them?" Anthony asked.

"They found us, ironically enough. Valentine's company happened to be on a sweep that day."

"Why ironic?"

One of the fifteen had served with Valentine. He had taken choppers out several times before, looking for any survivors, according to logs we found later."

"How'd he know about them?"

"The warrant officer who dropped them into Cambodia was a friend of his."

"Nobody stopped Valentine from going out on his own?" Anthony asked.

"Nobody had a clue. He and Warrant Officer Mitchell were close friends. Somehow they got away with it."

"That's why he was missing during the operation I was on."

Bertram leaned back in the chair and nodded. "They went a number of times to the drop location, but finding those men would be comparable to looking for a mouse in a cornfield, yet he continued to look." Bertram chuckled. "But it was the seven soldiers who ambushed the NVA and saved Valentine's company's asses—a hell of a turn of events."

Bertram laughed outright. It was the first time Anthony had heard Bertram laugh. "You should have seen Bolt's face when the word got out seven of the soldiers had returned."

"That's why they were sequestered so quickly."

"Yep," Bertram answered. "I'm sorry for the runaround, Anthony, but we were under strict orders."

"I understand."

"They presented a monumental problem for him since it was reported they were MIA/KIA. When these guys got back, a lot of paperwork had to be reshuffled."

"I can imagine."

"So then he declared them AWOL for not reporting back on time even though it was Bolt's fault they didn't." Bertram raised his hands. "You know what else is interesting, though?"

Anthony waited.

Bertram grinned. "They were talked about like heroes even among the guys they'd fought in the riot, for saving Valentine's company and blowing the weapons cache." The smiled faded as he continued. "So Bolt had to make sure these guys are not only isolated but gotten rid of as quickly as possible. They were discharged immediately with other-than-honorable discharges."

"Because they were AWOL?"

"Yep."

"The Inspector General's office looked into it, but the cover-up was so complete from so many angles, they got frustrated and gave up. Plus, there was a lot of pressure on them from some higher-ups who made them let it go."

"What about Valentine?"

"I'm not sure, but they probably withdrew charges against him for not accompanying his troops on your mission in exchange for his silence."

Anthony leaned back. "But what if they received information detailing the incident—the time, place, individuals, and contact information?" Anthony asked.

"I'd imagine they would reopen the investigation, and I would also imagine the general would be screwed along with a lot of other brass."

Anthony gazed at the prison bars. "Good." He looked down at his notes, "Three last questions."

"Shoot."

"Someone threw a Coke bottle filled with gasoline through my window with a message that said 'Forget about it.' Any ideas?"

Bertram's half-smile reappeared. "You know Bolt is a D.C. resident?"

"No."

"He's got long arms, Anthony. More than likely it was one of his men."

Anthony shrugged. If that was true, at least he wouldn't have to deal with Hanson anymore. "All the men involved got less-than-honorable discharges. One—Ernie Daniels—got a dishonorable discharge. Why?"

Bertram put a finger to his forehead. "Daniels, Daniels. He worked in headquarters?"

"Yes."

"Ah. The bright one. Bolt never liked Daniels. He thought Daniels was too smart for his own sake, and he might have been the one to leak the Cambodian operation. He also suspected Daniels was the reason the 25th's rosters were missing."

"Did he send them?"

"No." Bertram scratched his knee. "I did. Evidently you got them."

"You?"

Bertram nodded.

"Why?"

"Not the reason you think. Bolt and Tilden needed to be chopped down a notch. They not only screwed over those fifteen and the 1st Cav troops, but they were getting ready to do it again with other soldiers."

"Are you kidding?"

"I kid you not. Some within the hierarchy egged them on after the investigation waned. They'd gotten an all-clear signal to try again, and they were about to. It was probably the same people who squelched the Inspector General's investigation. I didn't want that to happen, so I sent you the rosters hoping you would blow the cover off things."

"Did they do it again?"

"Not that I know of."

Anthony decided not to tell Bertram that Daniels had committed suicide. He was at a loss determining what he would tell Daniels's sister.

Anthony checked his notes. "There's one guy still missing."

"I heard."

"You still got contacts on the outside?"

"Yep."

"Any info on him?" Anthony asked.

Bertram scratched his jaw. "Maybe. I'm going to give you the name of an assistant adjutant over there who used to serve under me in the States."

CHAPTER 59

October 30, 1969

Anthony had called Xavier Warfield after talking to Bertram. "A Colonel Bertram shed a lot of light on what happened to you guys, and I have some information on Sergeant Stinson."

"Really?"

"Yes. I'd like to lay out the story to you as I know it, whenever you want to hear it."

Warfield called back the next day. "Mr. Andrews? I told the guys you had some information about Sarge. We want to meet."

***

A light drizzle fell. The temperature in Cleveland was about fifty-five degrees. The sun shone through the clouds as if it were fall instead of winter. Even if there had been twelve feet of snow, it would have still been a beautiful day for Anthony.

Anthony was elated but also nervous to finally be able to meet the seven soldiers. He sat back and watched as the men gathered in the Cory Methodist Church basement early Friday evening, hugging one another while talking in hushed tones as if still in combat mode.

Anthony watched Casper grab a recoiling Turner and kiss him on his forehead. Bankston arrived last, but as soon as he entered, the men gathered, spread their fingers, closed them, brought their fists together, and whispered "Wolverines!"

"What was that you did with your hands?" Anthony asked.

"Something Sarge taught us," Robinson answered. "The fingers of a hand are the most dangerous when they are closed together. We were the fingers that became a fist."

***

Casper looked down as he remembered the last time he saw Sarge give the fist. It was when Sarge had told Casper to leave him behind. More than four months later, Casper still struggled with obeying Sarge's last order. If he had disobeyed, would Sarge be with them today or would all of them have been killed instead? He took a deep breath. How could he second-guess a man who had been responsible for their survival? Yet the question still lingered: How do you leave a man like him behind?

***

"Where'd you come up with the name?" Anthony asked.

"When we were at our lowest," Casper answered, "we named ourselves. Pound for pound, the wolverine is one of the fiercest animals in the forest."

"Wolverines!" Casper shouted. "Wolverines!" the men responded.

Anthony had waited for the men to greet one another before he announced, "I'm sorry to be the one with the bad news, but as I told Mr. Warfield, I asked Colonel Bertram about Sergeant Stinson."

The slight wind blowing against the window screen was the only sound in the room.

"I called the source Colonel Bertram gave me and learned they've found Sergeant Stinson's body."

Casper slammed the table with his fist "Damn."

"What? And you're just telling us?" Holland blurted.

Silence swept the room.

"I apologize, but I wanted to wait until you guys got settled," Anthony said.

"Where'd they find him?" Warfield asked.

"Outside Firebase Henry."

Casper looked at Warfield. "Firebase Henry. That means he'd made it back? He was almost home."

Glover scratched his jaw. "How? He was wounded and barely able to walk."

"From what I've been able to gather, the VC captured Sergeant Stinson in the area near the border of Cambodia and Vietnam. A guerilla prisoner told his interrogators Sarge escaped after killing a guard with a trowel."

Glover grunted. "That's Sarge."

"He killed five more with his guard's weapon after they found he had escaped, but he couldn't outrun the other captors and apparently was shot down." Anthony waited as some bowed their heads.

"The captured guerilla took them to the area where they last saw him. The search team found the body of a black soldier, but it was decomposed beyond recognition. They confirmed his identification by the name on his jacket and his dog tags. The remains were shipped three days ago. His funeral is Saturday."

A few of the men looked at one another and murmured, "Sarge."

***

Sarge is dead. Turner took a deep breath. His mind had been buzzing since they'd returned to Cu Chi because he couldn't sense what had happened to their leader. He had hoped he would receive some kind of sign Sergeant Stinson was alive, but he hadn't. Even with Anthony's announcement there was still some uneasiness, something that wouldn't quite let him close the door on Sarge.

CHAPTER 60

Turner surveyed the room, looking at his friends. He was glad he'd decided to come when Warfield called for the seven of them to meet. It was the second time they had all been together since leaving the service four months ago. Turner had never been emotional, but he loved these guys.

At their first meeting, he remembered the men sharing their coming home experiences with each other and how they'd dealt with their transition back into civilization.

The first thing Xavier Warfield said he did when he returned home was to buy a pair of Stacy Adams shoes, a brown Bill Blass pinstripe suit, a white silk shirt, and a .38 caliber handgun. "The first three were optional, the last a necessity," he had said. When the Army took away his weapon in Vietnam, he felt naked. Warfield couldn't explain why except he felt much safer with a gun than without one.

His first night home, his mother, whom he loved dearly, hovered over him, watching Warfield so intently it irritated him. His father was the opposite. "You okay?"

"Yeah, Dad. I'm okay."

"Welcome home, son," he'd said, hugging Warfield before going to bed.

After a sleepless three hours where Warfield jumped at almost every sound, he took his mattress, pillow, sheets, and gun to the basement and fell asleep within the hour.

"Why are you sleeping on the floor down here, Xav?" his father, with his mother standing behind him, had asked the next morning.

"You're going to have to bear with me for a little while, Mom, Dad." He didn't expect them to understand, so he didn't feel obligated to explain.

***

The first thing Leroy Casper told the men he did when he came back was to go straight to his house. He needed the comfort of a home, his mother's cooking, and to catch up with his girlfriend, Ida, and his friends as soon as he could. He figured the busier he was, the better.

Casper became hyper in creating diversions for himself, like going out to cookouts, picnics, movies, the zoo, and even to a play. The night was for nonstop parties and anything else that would keep his mind busy. Ida, smart as could be, but a party girl herself, loved it. His friends just laughed, but Casper had a plan. He figured at some point when he slowed down, maybe the images would be gone. That was his hope.

***

The first thing Raphael Holland said he did when he returned was to seek out his Uncle Farley, who was an ex-con and a drug dealer. Holland stayed with marijuana and Wild Irish Rose wine for a while before graduating to heroin while working the streets for Farley.

The drugs served Holland well, obliterating at least for a short period the memories of sheer terror he had experienced, especially the tiger's roar that awoke him almost every night. But there were consequences, and Holland realized early on he had merely replaced one bad dream with another.

With the help of his Aunt Mildred, Holland went cold turkey in her basement and pledged to himself he would find another way to erase the memories before he did something the Viet Cong hadn't been able to do—kill him.

***

The first thing Marcus Glover told the group he did when he arrived in Cleveland was purchase a mosquito net because just one in a room made his skin crawl. He had visited four stores before he found one, but, even with the net, there was no peace until the insect was dead. The second thing he did was call Oscar Adams. The pool room fight had weighed on his mind even in Vietnam.

"Oscar? This is Marcus."

There was silence on the other end of the line.

"I called to apologize about the fight, man. I hope you accept it."

There was more silence before Oscar responded. "Okay."

"Cool. So how are you doing?"

"I'm good, Glover. Sandra and I got married."

"Great. Well, I wish you both the best."

"You, uh, and she never…?"

"Naw, man. Never."

"Good. Thanks. I-I understand you were in the war."

"Yeah, but I've got to go. Take care."

"Yeah, Glover. You, too."

***

The first thing Clarence Bankston said he did when he came home was to inform his parents he was moving to Cleveland. As soon as the plane landed at Jackson-Evers International Airport, he'd decided. He already missed his buddies and couldn't fathom living in Mississippi after having fought for the country.

Bankston was afraid he might hurt somebody real bad if provoked. It would be better to leave Mississippi and be around his friends who understood what he had been through. Plus, the way they talked about Cleveland, it had to be five times better than living in Mississippi.

***

Erving Robinson confided only to Turner. He was too embarrassed to tell the others. The first thing Robinson did when he got off the bus was head to Ebenezer Baptist Church where he'd been raised. It was Saturday. There would be people there.

As the brick two-story church came into view, he hesitated, hung his head, and turned to go home to surprise his parents instead.

"Maybe later," he'd said to Turner. "Maybe later."

***

The first thing Turner did when he got to Cleveland was rent a room at the Holiday Inn on East 55th. He had saved $1,830 of his army pay. Two weeks would barely dent his savings. Turner hadn't called his mother because he needed to rest. Too many issues were agitating him; too many unanswered questions were bouncing around in his head.

He understood Sarge when he said he would buy peace of mind if he could. Well, this was the next best move: Rent a room, only go out to eat, and sleep the day and night away, which he did.

Being a loner, it didn't bother Turner that he passed on calling his family or friends. Two weeks of cooling out wouldn't hurt anything, but it certainly might help.

CHAPTER 61

D o you want to talk about Cambodia?" Anthony asked.

Glover scratched his chest. "Why don't you tell us about Tay Ninh, first?"

Anthony gathered himself and haltingly told the men about the firefight. The men were quiet, looking at Anthony, then one another with bowed heads, sidelong glances, and an occasional nod.

"How did you come out of that?" Warfield eventually asked.

"Not too good. But compared to your experience, mine was minor."

Casper snorted. "Any situation where you can be killed is major."

The men murmured agreement.

Anthony then opened up, describing his bouts with alcohol, his nightmares, his temper, and the flare-up that made his wife leave him. Speaking of his family situation caused a hitch in his voice.

"So there were two reasons for my initial trip here: The first was to spend time with my other family; the second was to get with you guys. I wanted to find out how you are coping and tell your story, so I can make things right by you. I'm glad you invited me back."

After a few moments of silence, Casper shifted in his chair. "Cambodia." He paused. "They sent us out to sea in a boat with no paddles. If it weren't for Sarge, we'd all be dead."

There was another long silence before Holland spoke. "First, you don't send men out who haven't had any jungle training."

"It would be the same as sending David to fight Goliath without a sling," Robinson added. "Then you give some lame instructions and some false hope that if we do everything we're supposed to, we get to come back to base."

Warfield, dressed in a brown jumpsuit, tapped the table as he had in Raymond's kitchen. "Maybe we were supposed to meet soldiers from the 1st Cav and get extracted, but it never happened."

Glover sniffed. "And if the soldiers we were supposed to meet were the ones who were killed, we knew we were through."

Finally loosening up, they told Anthony about the ridge that was their rendezvous point and how they had climbed to an area where they watched the Viet Cong ambush other American soldiers more than a mile away.

***

Even at that distance, Holland remembered the awe and fear of watching American soldiers being killed and the remainder chased. Even though they had been out of harm's way, the dreadfulness of watching others being killed was almost as terrifying as being there.

Nothing, though, compared with the horror of the attacking tiger. Holland mentally erased the thought, as he did each time it surfaced, and returned to the conversation.

***

The men talked about taking the hill occupied by the enemy. What Glover remembered was the churning anger he felt when Sarge got shot as he and the others charged the hill, killing five VC in less than a minute.

Robinson described running from the enemy and leaving a wounded Sarge behind. "So when we turned and saw Casper didn't have Sarge, we started to take him out, thinking Casper had ditched him because he was too heavy. We heard grenades and weapons firing, then nothing. You had nine black soldiers, tears streaming down our faces, running for our lives."

Bankston rubbed his jaw and frowned. "It's funny, though."

"What's that?" Anthony asked.

"None of the VC followed us."

"Not right away," Robinson corrected Bankston.

"What happened next?"

"We tried to find our way to base when we discovered we weren't even in Vietnam."

"Man, we almost died right then," Robinson said. "It was as if all the energy was sucked out of us—everybody trying to figure out why we had been put there and how we would get out of a place we knew nothing about."

"I think we would have given up if it weren't for Sarge's wisdom."

"Like what?" Anthony asked.

"He taught us it's not the smartest or the strongest who survive, it's those who adapt," Warfield responded. "That kept us going, kept us thinking."

"He also taught us that will was more important than skill," Glover said. Glover tapped Casper on the shoulder. "Plus we had Casper's leadership."

"Near the end, I could barely walk," Warfield said. "Holland was wounded. We had sores, cuts from the saw grass and wait-a-minute vines, and we had jungle rot. We were exhausted—mentally, physically, and spiritually. And Glover was so sick, he could hardly stand."

Anthony watched as carefully as he listened. The war hadn't been kind to them, as evidenced by Robinson's facial tick, which Anthony assumed came from combat and Warfield's constant drumming on his leg with his fingers. When any of the seven talked, their eyes were still, mostly vacant and staring, even though they might not have meant them to be. Where a typical person might move his hands to make a point, the men's narrations were accompanied at most by the slightest of head movements.

Anthony ran his hand over his face. He saw himself in each of them and their need to be normal again.

Robinson gazed out the window. "If we had run into any more VC, we would have been dead out of luck. I mean, we sat looking at each other, trying to figure how we could go any farther."

"That bad?"

Holland looked around. "Man, you should have seen us. You should have smelled us. You'd have to go to the Bowery to see somebody as bad off as we were. We had no food, no ammo and were losing hope."

Bankston glanced at Robinson. "All Robinson here said during the last few days was, 'Could care less.' And that's about how we felt. As if nothing mattered anymore."

"Couldn't," Turner responded.

"What?" Bankston asked.

"Couldn't care less."

"Whatever, Professor."

Robinson punched Casper in the shoulder. "Yeah, but Casper made us continue. I'm so glad I didn't shoot you for leaving Sarge, Casper."

Casper grunted. "Me, too."

"So how did you survive without food?" Anthony asked.

"We ate what the monkeys ate—fruits, leaves, roots…," Bankston replied. "It was nowhere near enough, though."

"And grubs," Robinson added.

Anthony frowned.

Robinson looked apologetic when he saw Anthony's reaction.

"It's why I didn't mention it," Bankston scolded Robinson.

Warfield's lips turned down. "I don't want anybody to know I ate grubs."

Holland laughed. "That was the least of our worries."

"Whose idea was that?" Anthony asked.

The men looked at one another.

"Da, this Cambodian boy who helped us find the way back. Anyway, we figured if the monkeys were our cousins, then maybe their digestive system was similar. At least it's what Turner said." Bankston laughed.

"We would have eaten a monkey, too, but we didn't want to give our position away with rifle shots and then a fire."

Bankston looked at Glover. "We gave the food to him first. When he didn't die, we ate it."

"What?" Glover said, glaring at Bankston.

"Just kidding, man. Just kidding."

Glover's face softened. "I couldn't have made it without you guys, though. I was messed up."

"We all got messed up one way or another," Casper said.

They became quiet again.

Anthony bowed his head. "I know," he murmured to himself. "I know."

He also knew that although their passage from Cambodia was over, the end of the war was assured only for the eight who had died.

CHAPTER 62

Casper's eyes softened as he spoke. "Sarge helped us survive in so many ways."

"Because he held the enemy back?" Anthony asked.

"No. Because he prepared us well—and he did prepare us well," Casper answered. *"Will more than skill"* echoed in Casper's head every time he mentioned Sarge's name.

"Like?"

"He trained us to fight as a team and taught us the one other thing that probably saved our lives."

"What?"

"He told us if we were to get out alive, we had to be united—be one, think like one, move like one. So every night we would go through 'what ifs,' and we would figure out how we could have dealt with the situation as a team. He taught us we had to want to win." Casper hesitated. "It's difficult to explain, but Sarge trained us that the mental was as important as the physical."

Anthony nodded. "I understand that."

"We kept wondering why Sarge kept putting us through those drills if we were just reconning, but he had us thinking ahead," Bankston said. "It was as if he knew he wouldn't be with us at the end."

"When Charlie ambushed us, they were so close, we should have

307

all died, but we counterattacked as Sarge taught," Casper said.

"Counterattacked?"

It would have been easier to run from an ambush, but besides Sarge drilling them on the maneuver, Casper had already been there in another ambush. Men were falling like bowling pins from the on-slaught until Sergeant Henderson had yelled. "Charge!" It was their only chance, and Casper had learned the lesson well. Instead of them being wiped out, twenty-four died, but twenty lived because they'd followed Henderson's order."

"Yeah. Because if the enemy is within fifty yards and you retreat, a one hundred percent casualty rate is almost guaranteed," Casper answered, providing the same reasoning Sarge and Henderson had given the survivors.

"We were lucky, too, though," Warfield added.

"Yeah, we were," Holland agreed.

Warfield scratched his neck. "I'm not sure why they ran. They had us."

"Not to change the subject, but did anyone get a good look at the one they carried away so fast?" Warfield asked.

"No. Why?" Casper asked.

"I swear it was a woman," Warfield said.

Robinson huffed. "Get the hell out of here. A woman? No way."

The men looked at Robinson. It was the first they had heard him curse. "I'm just saying," Robinson said, his face reddening.

"If it was a woman, I got her at least twice," Bankston said.

"Theirs is a different culture," Anthony offered.

***

Turner looked at Robinson and felt a deep sadness for his friend, more so than he did for the rest of the men. It appeared he had lost more than the others. Robinson had certainly changed more. Holland had changed a lot, too. Where Holland had hardened, though, Robinson had turned from caring to cold. Turner felt it. Robinson had been the one with the morals, the "love your brother" attitude. When he shot those men in the head without blinking, without regret, without praying, Turner had cried inwardly for him. Sampson was right. They had been in hell, and the devil had claimed the most righteous of their souls.

***

"How did the eight die?"

There was a long silence. Anthony could hear some of the men take a deep breath.

"One died from a sniper. The others died in firefights," Warfield said glancing at Turner.

***

Bankston's heart had dropped when his cousin Darius Ward was killed in the attack. He would have cried, but something closed up in him. The anguish that came from his cousin's departure was released through the barrel of his weapon. The more VC he killed, the more his anger was assuaged. But relief was fleeting. It was as if he had transformed into a vampire. But instead of seeking a victim's blood to continue to live, he needed their deaths to relieve his grieving.

***

Anthony made a mental note to call Furman Soledad about his friend Jeremiah Kendrick Franklin, one of the deceased.

Anthony turned to Turner. "You haven't said much of anything."

Holland looked at Turner, too. "He hardly ever says much."

Glover smiled. "Yeah, but when the professor does..."

"How'd you get involved in the brawl?" Anthony asked.

Turner removed his glasses and cleaned them on his shirt. His tone darkened as he spoke. "Somebody hit me. I don't like being hit."

"We were lucky to have Turner," Casper said, draping his arm over Turner's shoulders. "He saw things."

"Like what?" Anthony asked.

"He made suggestions, like taking the high ground on the ridge when we would have been wiped out if we had stayed where we were. He was also the one who suggested we ambush the VC chasing us instead of running like Fletcher wanted us to do."

Anthony looked at Turner. "You had combat experience?"

"No. Just lucky I guess."

Casper laughed. "It was more than luck."

"Intuition?" Anthony said.

"Mostly my Basic Training," Turner answered.

Anthony looked at his notes. "So, this Fletcher—the one called Rabid—how was he involved?"

Warfield cleared his throat. "He was second in command, but he got killed."

"That probably saved our lives," Glover said.

"How so?"

"He wouldn't listen to anybody. Thought he was still running his gang," Glover answered.

"When he died, Casper took over," Robinson said, "and he led us the rest of the way."

"Right into two North Vietnamese Army companies," Casper chuckled.

Bankston smiled. "Wasn't your fault, man. We were lucky to be moving at all."

"We were so close to home, but we came up on what we found out later was these NVA, who were getting ready to ambush our soldiers. But we got them first," Holland said.

"How?" Anthony asked.

Glover leaned forward in his chair. "We ambushed them."

"I heard that from the colonel, but it seemed so bizarre to me. So you are saying that seven men took on two NVA companies."

"We had a height advantage, the ability to take cover, and we had the element of surprise," Casper said.

Warfield drummed his leg. "We had to if the troops walking into the ambush were going to survive."

"That took a lot of guts," Anthony said.

***

"Twice," Warfield said. Warfield noticed his fingers had not stopped tapping his leg since he had sat down. He clenched both fists to stop before shuddering at the memory of hearing Charlie coming through the jungle and his hands trembling so badly he was afraid he would not be able to aim, much less shoot. Will more than skill, he told himself as sweat had poured into his eyes blurring his vision. He was afraid to take his hand off the trigger to wipe them, fearing the tremors would not allow him to grasp the weapon again.

It wasn't until the enemy began to fall that he felt confident he and his brothers would prevail. Only after the firefight did he dab at his eyes to see all of them still standing. It was the most beautiful sight of his life.

The weirdest thought, though, crossed his mind as they walked away from the slain enemy. Trumpets blasted in his mind, and a game show emcee yelled, "Mr. Warfield, you have just won a new lease onnnnnnnnn life."

The second time, on the hill, it was easier. Warfield remembered watching three enemy soldiers fall from his bullets. His hands hadn't shaken that time. And as he watched the men fall, he felt nothing—no fear, no remorse, no relief.

***

312

Bankston spoke up. "It sounds like suicide for somebody like us, but we had to. And it worked. That's when they picked us up and brought us home."

"Seems like you guys should get medals," Anthony said.

"Right," Casper said, chuckling.

"So what happened when you got back to base?"

Robinson smiled. "When we set down, it seemed like everybody on base stood outside, waiting."

"I know," Anthony said. "I stood with them."

The men looked at Anthony.

"I watched you get off the chopper—seven black men looking like you were one step from the grave. But as tired as you looked, you began marching back to base. I wondered why."

"We were soldiers," Casper responded.

"The whole scene seemed strange, so I began investigating."

"I'm glad somebody cared enough to," Robinson said. "Anyway, the MPs put us in their jeep when we got to base and took us to the empty barracks that had been mortared. We stayed there for two days with two MPs standing guard."

"How'd they treat you?"

"They fed us, gave us clothes, sent a doctor look at us. We could wash and everything, but weren't able to leave the barracks," Warfield replied.

313

"Then this adjutant comes in and starts processing paperwork. Right after, Colonel Bolt comes in. He's looking at us like we're the enemy."

Warfield took a deep breath. "He tells us that because of the riot and because we were AWOL, we would get less than honorable discharges, but if we stayed clean for a few years and never mentioned Cambodia, it would be changed to honorable."

"Like we would believe anything he had to say," Glover said. "In two years who knows where he would be?"

"He asked us everything about Cambodia," Robinson offered, "but you could tell he didn't give a shit about us. If I had still had my weapon, I would have wasted his ass."

The men looked at Robinson again, smiling.

"So a few days later, we were all discharged," Bankston said, spreading his arms wide. "And here we are!"

Anthony stood and distributed a piece of paper to each of the men. "I want to share something with you before I forget. It's something my wife gave me and asked to share it with you."

Casper read it out loud: "It is better to conquer yourself than to win a thousand battles. A Buddhist saying."

Glover slipped the paper into his wallet. "You got that right. Sampson would have agreed, too."

CHAPTER 63

Warfield looked around the room. "You know what? We need a drink."

Casper smiled. "Yeah, we do. But we can't do it here."

Holland pointed at Robinson. "The church must have been his idea."

Before Robinson could speak, Anthony interrupted. "No. It was mine. I know someone who's a member."

Casper stood. "No problem, Anthony. But when we find that bar, you got to buy the first round."

"I'll buy, but I'm not drinking," Anthony replied.

"Understood," Casper said.

***

Inside the Café Tia Juana, the men sat quietly for a while before Casper raised his glass. "Here's to Sarge, the baddest ass on this planet."

"Hear, hear," the men responded.

Warfield raised his glass. "Here's to Sarge, the main reason we're still alive."

Holland raised his glass. "Amen to that."

Robinson glared at Holland and then laughed. "That's my phrase."

"To Sarge," Glover said.

Bankston sighed. "What hurts most is that we weren't able to say goodbye to him, to thank him.

The men fell into another silence before Casper spoke, "There's another major regret, too."

"What's that?" Anthony asked.

"We weren't able to retrieve our buddies' bodies."

The men sat quietly again before Robinson spoke in the softest of voices. "Here's to Frankford, Somner, James, Matthews, Sampson, and Ward."

The men all raised their glasses.

"What about Fletcher?" Anthony asked.

"Yeah," Glover said. "He taught us something, too." He snorted. "He's gone. Might as well." He raised his glass a quarter inch from the table.

"He never understood us," Bankston added. "He never understood Sarge."

"His world was too small," Turner responded.

The men all turned to Turner, and one by one nodded slowly as they absorbed his words.

"And Da," Bankston said after a long pause. "We can't forget about Da!"

Warfield raised his glass again. "And we almost killed him."

Casper chuckled. "Yeah. That's the luck part."

"Remember what Sarge said? 'Use what's available,'" Holland said.

"And take what's necessary," Robinson added.

"Is that why we ended up with all those AK-47s?" Glover asked.

"They didn't need them anymore," Casper said.

"Sarge never liked the M-16s anyway."

Their hushed voices in the loud bar indicated to Anthony they were still contending with the circumstances that brought them together. But in spite of the unanswered questions each of the men probably had, Anthony reveled in their company, glad to know they were fighting their way back again, except this time it was to sanity.

"This isn't over, you know," Anthony said to the men during one of their silent moments. "I'm writing your story, and I'm sending it to the president, politicians, and top brass in the army."

"Want to take bets on how far that'll go?" Warfield asked.

A few of the men snorted.

Glover folded his arms. "Who cares about seven black soldiers being punished for fighting back? Who gives a damn?"

Turner looked down before speaking. "It's not over."

The men looked at Turner, waiting for more, but as usual, Turner was through.

"I'm also sending the story to the press," Anthony said. "Look, I'm not giving up on you guys. I want your story told. I want the people who sent you to Cambodia to be punished, and I want you to receive honorable discharges."

Warfield looked at Anthony. "That's asking a lot."

"No more than you deserve," Anthony responded resolutely.

Casper draped his arm over Anthony's shoulder. "I think everyone here would agree that any time you're in Cleveland and you want to get together with us, let us know, Anthony. You just acquired a third family."

"Can we make him an associate member of the Wolverines?" Warfield asked.

"Good idea. Show of hands?" Casper asked.

All seven raised theirs.

Anthony felt a rush of warmth flow through him. "Thanks, guys."

CHAPTER 64

The eight men filed into Boyd's Funeral Home and sat in the rear. There weren't many people in attendance, maybe thirty-five. It surprised Anthony. The casket, draped with an American flag, was closed, but a picture of Sergeant Willie Stinson sat on top. It appeared to be a recent photo of him in a short-sleeved shirt standing next to a jeep.

Anthony noticed Raymond Williams near the front row and waved.

The funeral program's obituary was as short as the eulogy. Excited after reading it, though, Warfield pointed out one sentence to the others: Sergeant Stinson served honorably, receiving the Silver Star for gallantry in action.

A few of the men whispered shouts of "yes" as they dapped and hugged, causing others in the room to turn around at the commotion. Anthony held up his hand in apology.

Casper hugged Warfield, who had his hand draped over Glover's shoulder.

Raymond approached the men.

Warfield extended his hand. "Lieutenant?"

"Warfield."

Anthony introduced Raymond to the rest of the men.

"Anthony told me your story. I'm so glad he was there. If you guys need to know anything about Anthony, it's that he's got your back."

"We believe it, Lieutenant," Casper said.

"I've got to pick up my uncle from the airport. It's a pleasure meeting all of you. I'm sure I'll see you again."

"Can you believe it?" Bankston said, playfully punching Holland in the chest after leaving the building. "A silver star and an honorable discharge."

Even Turner smiled. "Great."

Casper draped his arm over Turner's shoulder. "If it is to you, you know it is to us."

Robinson couldn't stop giggling as he looked to the sky.

Anthony, feeling uplifted himself, grinned as the men celebrated. It seemed each of them had shed a little of the anguish they had carried for so long. Whether the relief was permanent or not, and Anthony thought it would be, Sergeant Stinson was still showing his men the way back.

"I'll miss you guys," Anthony said as they walked to their cars, "but I'll press on to get you guys cleared."

"If nothing else happens, at least *you* know our story," Warfield said.

"And if nothing else happens, I hope you do write it," Turner added.

"Consider that part done, Turner," Anthony responded. "It's a story everyone needs to hear."

CHAPTER 65

It was 9:00 P.M. when Anthony arrived home. Carla met him at the door.

"How'd it go?" she asked.

"Great," Anthony responded. "Each of those guys deserves a medal."

"I'm guessing you're tired from the drive."

Anthony looked up with a half-leer, half-grin on his face. "Why? What did you have in mind?"

"Oh, Anthony. You have a one-track mind. I was checking to see if you were hungry and if you wanted to wait until tomorrow to tell me about the trip."

"Yeah. I'm a little bushed," he said, going through the mail addressed to him. One of the envelopes was nine-by-twelve inches and immediately piqued his curiosity. He opened it first.

There was a letter inside, along with additional pages.

Anthony,

Here's the essay I wrote for my class about Willie Stinson. I'd appreciate your feedback.

Raymond

The next morning, Anthony made coffee and pulled out Raymond's essay.

Wow. Anthony thought after reading it. *I'm sorry I never got to meet Sergeant Stinson.* He smiled as he picked up the phone to dial. "Raymond?"

"Anthony. Did you get it?"

"Yes, I did. This is an excellent essay. He must have meant a lot to you."

"Yeah. I'm not sure he realized how much. When he left, I tried to find him but was unsuccessful. He never attempted to find me, though, which was disappointing. My family stayed on that same street for the next fifteen years. He could have visited at least once."

"It's a shame, because you two seemed to make each other better."

"That's true on my part," Raymond responded. "He definitely made me a better person. And now I'll never see him to thank him."

"Well, if you ever want a job as a reporter, look me up," Anthony said.

"Any writing suggestions?"

"Just one. Keep doing what you're doing."

PART IV

CHAPTER 66

June 21, 1969

If the tug on his pant leg had been any harder, Stinson would have turned and shot. Instead, he rolled on his stomach, aiming his .45 at the tugger. The slight, dark-skinned man bowed quickly and put a finger to his lips, motioning Stinson toward him. The man had no visible weapon, which allayed some of Stinson's fear, but he was still wary. Who was this guy and where'd he come from?

Stinson had managed to roll sideways for about ten yards along the bank before sliding down a slope another ten yards to avoid the bombardment directed toward his former position. He'd thrown his last grenade and left a rifle pointing toward the enemy to gain a few more seconds.

When the man beckoned him, Stinson tried crawling backward, but was unable to move in that direction too well after having taken another round in his buttocks. Luckily it was just a flesh wound. For some reason, he trusted the little man, though, and continued inching toward him. Suddenly, two other unarmed men with a litter came and laid it next to Stinson. A cautious Stinson rolled onto his new transportation, watching their every move as the men scurried farther into the jungle with their load.

After about twenty minutes, they stopped. Stinson grunted in pain as the one carrier dumped Stinson unceremoniously into the arms of another, who had crawled into a hole in the ground. The man laid

Stinson on the dirt floor, placed Stinson's weapons and gear next to him, jumped out, and slammed the opening shut. Stinson could hear the faint scuffle of feet as they moved off.

They must be South Vietnamese trying to help a soldier, he thought as he assured himself that if they were enemies, they would have taken him out by now. And if he was a prisoner, they wouldn't have left him with his weapons.

There was no telling who or what awaited him if he tried to escape, but in his condition, it was a moot point.

As Stinson crawled through the dark, attempting to familiarize himself with his surroundings, he was able to measure his new home. The hole was about ten-by-ten feet, but only five feet high. The height was okay because he couldn't stand for any length of time anyway. He pushed at the makeshift door to check if it was locked. It moved upward. Feeling relieved he would be able to leave at any time, Stinson lay down.

Hours passed. The patter of rain drops was the only sound as Stinson rested against the wall. What seemed like days went by before someone opened the top and dropped in rice cakes filled with fish, a spicy green vegetable, water, a clay pot, a poncho, and a blanket. More time passed before someone dropped leaves and bandages. He assumed the leaves were medicinal, so he placed them over his wounds, wondering how much damage the bullet shards had caused.

Stinson busied himself playing mind games, trying to ignore the throbbing pain as he mapped out how he would get back to base once he healed and what his first real meal would be.

He alternately cursed the weakness his wounds had caused and praised the fact he was still alive. More time passed before someone removed the cover and a person was lowered into the hole. He reached for his .45, but from the brief glimpse of light, his visitor appeared to be a woman holding a bag.

"*Chào*," he said.

She didn't respond.

"Who are you?" he asked.

She remained quiet as she lit a lamp and pushed him into a reclining position to remove his bandages. Whatever she used to probe his wounds hurt like hell, but he never felt like she wanted to harm him.

He muffled his groans with the blanket as the instrument dug into his wounds, then the woman poured a hot, oily liquid over the injuries. She applied fresh bandages, and when finished, she tapped on the ceiling. She held up her bag and the pot they had given Stinson for elimination. Hands reached in to remove her. More food and water plus the emptied clay pot were dropped as he lay back on the dirt floor, bandaged, but weak. The deliveries became a daily routine.

As he ate one day, Stinson tried to determine how long he'd been in the hole, but couldn't. He did know that even with the attention he got, he would go crazy if he didn't get out soon.

He wondered whether Turner was making it, if Glover had ever smiled, if Fletcher had ever looked out for anybody but himself, and if Casper was serving as a stabilizing force. Had he taught them enough to survive?

What was all this fighting about that young men like his were continually offered as sacrifices? After all the killing, torture, and maiming, would the world actually become a better place?

And Stinson wondered how much each of the men would change, because they would change. Some would succumb to the horrors and fight the battles over and over, seeking the solace of drugs and alcohol to dim the memories. Some would carry on, hoping the nightmares would fade in time. But each would change, and each would move on, carrying his own personal snake.

Time passed, and Stinson sank deeper into the hole in his mind, becoming giddy for no reason, then crying. He had to muffle the high-pitched laugh that came when he least expected it, followed by a sense of abandonment, then indifference, then anxiety.

Although he looked forward to their visits, no one ever spoke when they came, which added to his isolation. A slow panic would set in as soon as they left, leaving him alone with his thoughts. With no one to affirm or deny the validity of what he was thinking, Stinson began questioning his own understanding of reality.

Thoughts of his wife, Darlene, and their son, Jerome, played across his brain. He struggled to recall the best memories of when they were together to maintain some semblance of sanity.

***

"You remind me of a friend I used to have," Stinson had said when they first met.

"Why?" Darlene Jackson asked.

"You don't believe in backing down."

"And you do?" she said, throwing a hook that hit the basketball rim before falling out of bounds.

"This is our fourth game, and you haven't won yet."

"It doesn't mean I can't."

Stinson had smiled. He had come to the Forest Hills basketball court to practice when he thought no one else would be there, but she was, shooting jumpers, foul shots, and driving to the basket.

They had nodded to each other as she continued to practice. Curious, because he had never seen a girl with her talent, Stinson stood and watched. Her game was so smooth, with spins and turns befitting a ballerina, that her striking looks were secondary. She had the sharp, angular features of a model without the daintiness.

"You going to play or just spectate?"

Her questions snapped him out of his trance. "One-on-one?" Stinson asked, surprised she would ask.

"Anybody else here?"

"All right. What's your name?"

"Darlene. Yours?"

"Willie."

"She tossed him the ball. "Alright, Willie. Take it out."

Stinson was good at sports, not girls, so although he was very comfortable playing one-on-one, he felt awkward playing Darlene.

Stinson caught the ball and launched a jump shot that circled the rim before rolling out; she dribbled past the foul line, faked him with a cross-over dribble and sunk a twenty-footer. Stinson smiled. It was on.

"Where'd you learn to play?" Stinson asked after the fifth game.

"My dad, and I played for Shaw High. Where'd you play?"

"I didn't. Just playground."

"Really?"

"What's that mean?" Stinson asked.

"With your game, the only reason I can think of why you didn't play organized ball is because you don't like authority. I know a few people like that. Are you one of them?"

Stinson's face flushed. "So you think you got me pegged?"

"What do you think?"

"I think you need to work on your game and quit trying to be a psychiatrist."

Without saying a word, Darlene jumped up, picked up her ball, and left the court.

***

Two months after he'd met her, Darlene remained on his mind. He'd almost given up on ever seeing her again when one afternoon he casually glanced at a bus across the street that had stopped at the 79th Street and Euclid Avenue intersection. Stinson's eyes brightened in recognition of the passenger with close-cropped hair and chocolate skin. He couldn't see her face, but he knew.

He ran to catch the bus, even though it was going opposite the direction he was headed, and almost got hit by a car. The bus pulled off, leaving a puffing Stinson behind. Disheartened, thinking it might have been his final chance of ever seeing her again, he began the ten-block walk toward the warehouse where he worked.

A tap on his shoulder while he waited at a stoplight four blocks later caused Stinson to jump.

"You lookin' for me?"

"Where'd…?" he asked as he unclenched his fist.

"Someone lied. They told me you were fast," Darlene said, her hands on her hips.

"I…"

"Well?"

Stinson scratched the side of his head. She'd asked about him? "I–It's great to see you, r–really great."

She giggled at his awkwardness.

Stinson stuffed his hands in his front pockets. "I didn't think I'd ever see you again."

"You probably shouldn't have. You dogged me out on the basketball court, and then you dogged me out verbally. There's only so much doggin' a woman will take," she said, her hand, head, and shoulders moving with each word.

"Yeah. I'm sorry. It was rude. But you do know you injured me, right?" he said as he showed her a scar on his hand.

"That little scratch?" she said, laughing. "A real man wouldn't even mention it."

"Oh, wow."

Darlene sniggered. "I'm just playing." Then she punched him in the chest. "I want a rematch, though, man. I ain't playin' about that."

A year and a half later they married. She made him wait that long before they had sex, but he didn't mind. He made up for it every night after as the two coupled with twice the intensity of any of their basketball games, exclaiming in wonderment at the searing sensations they'd caused within each other.

She gave birth to Jerome nine months later. And two years afterward, he joined the Army. Stinson bit his lip when it came to him that the Army had probably sent Darlene an MIA notice. He hoped she was handling the news well. She should have. She was tough. *I'll be home soon, honey. Hold on.*

***

Stinson tried counting the days by the visits he received. Since they came once a day, it would be close to a month and a half he'd been cooped up. As soon as he was able to stand, he pushed at the ceiling and peered out, only to be greeted by more darkness.

The next day he did the same. Even though it was daytime, he could see little because of the brush surrounding the hole. He continued to peek to determine whether it was day or night, but after a few quick glances, he decided not to push his luck. The next time he opened the hole would be when he left.

Days passed, and Stinson could stand for longer periods. Eventually, his strength grew where he was able to test his leg more strenuously by doing abbreviated squats. He stretched as best he could until he could do limited exercises with only moderate pain.

When he felt he was finally able to move out, he waited until dark, then gathered his weapons and wrapped the food and the full canteen he had saved for his journey. Stinson wrote the Vietnamese word for thank you, *"cảm on,"* on the dirt floor, pushed the cover up, pulled himself out, and knelt on the ground to get his bearings.

His sense of smell and sight were enhanced from weeks of deprivation. Everything seemed so lush and loud. The bird and animal sounds pulsated through the jungle. It was as if he had stepped into another world—a world he hadn't expected to still be a part of.

He tested his leg to make sure it was able to hold his weight when he walked. He took a few tentative steps. The soft dirt under his boots gave him some comfort as he moved forward. Stinson cut a branch from a tree to carve a cane, looked at the big dipper to get his bearings, and began his journey southeast.

CHAPTER 67

August 21, 1969

The serenity Stinson first experienced under fire remained as he limped along a stream flowing southeast, hoping it would lead to a larger body of water and eventually to an army base.

It was necessary he travel at night and sleep during the day because his wounds would not allow him to move fast enough to escape anyone who might chase him. He carried an AK-47, a .45 pistol, a bandolier, three magazines of ammo, a poncho, a knife, food for four days, and a walking stick.

How far was base camp? Stinson thought back to the chopper ride. They had been in the air about ten minutes, which meant they would have traveled about twenty to twenty-five miles plus the approximately twenty miles they'd traveled on foot. And according to Ramsey's map he had since lost, northwest.

At night, Stinson listened carefully to the sounds of the jungle—the chirping of the birds, the hooting of the monkeys, and the thousand other noises that reverberated through the denseness. There was a rhythm to them that signified a certain order. What Stinson listened for even more carefully, though, was a break in the rhythm—some indication there might be others beside the jungle's normal habitants. Since his presence caused a disruption in their sounds, anyone or anything else would, too.

Occasionally, Stinson would massage his leg, encouraging it to stay strong. If his calculations were right, and at his pace, it was possible he would need to travel for at least five days. And although the leg was an impediment, he ignored it, placing the pain from it in a compartment in the back of his mind.

It worried him that he'd heard no sounds of battle, no big guns, no aircraft, nothing. Maybe there was a lull. Or maybe he was too far away for the sounds of war to reach him.

What worried him most was whether his men had made it back. To see his boys again was more than enough incentive to make it. Their survival would be his greatest accomplishment.

***

During the day, Stinson found high ground, used the poncho as a shelter, and attempted to sleep against a tree. But he was only able to obtain a quick doze before he would hear something that would wake him.

During the early evening of the second day, after abandoning the stream for higher ground, he spotted a ridge like the one he and his men had been on. His stomach sank at first, thinking he had somehow traveled in circles, but when he looked back, he was relieved to see distant landmarks, like the clump of tall Banyan trees and a valley he had crossed two hours earlier. The ridge would be his new landmark.

By the fourth day, he had run out of food. He tried to remember what he'd been taught about what he could eat—or more importantly, what he shouldn't eat. Palms, figs, bamboo shoots and some insects were okay, Stinson remembered hearing that in one of the classes. *So that's what it will be,* he thought. No use taking a chance on something that would make his journey any worse than it already was.

Those thoughts were on his mind when a small clink caused Stinson's heart to sink. It was a sound only a human with a weapon would make. He turned slowly, trying to pinpoint the location when he felt the nudge of something metal in his back.

"Dau hang!"

He knew the words. He'd spoken them himself to a guerilla he'd found hiding in a burned-out pagoda on a sweep outside Ho Bo Woods. There were three VC. They took everything, including his boots. The three talked among themselves and laughed at something one of them said while pushing him to walk ahead, giggling as he limped.

It was twenty minutes later when he heard the faint boom of howitzers. They sounded distant, but his emotions were jangled by the faint reports. Here he was on or near friendly territory, but unable to make it home.

A sharp pain in his leg caused Stinson to stumble as they approached a muddy clearing carved out of the jungle where sunlight barely penetrated the branches and vines draped around and above the open space.

There was no barbed wire, guard towers, or searchlights. The only building Stinson saw was a thatched hut. And the only object in the clearing was a large vase filled with water.

The smell, though, was the smell of death, an undeniable stench only a human in the last days of his life would emit. Stinson grimaced as he entered the compound looking for another American.

It was when his captors nudged Stinson to a bamboo cage hidden by the trees that he realized he would have to get out of there as quickly as possible. Seven soldiers lay on filthy blankets on a dirt floor wearing tattered clothes. Not one of them looked like they weighed more than a hundred pounds. Four lay with their eyes closed.

One hardly breathed. Pus oozed from one eye, and blood smeared his pants at the crotch. Another of the sleeping captives moaned continuously, one arm wrapped in a dirty bandage, his pants soiled by his own excrement. The three sitting up stared blankly at him as he found a space in a corner.

None of his captors spoke English, but their short staccato demands were apparent: Stay there until they said otherwise.

Four of the captives were Marines. One was a pilot, and two were Army, he was told by Ferris Grant, one of the Marines, and the only one who seemed lucid enough to communicate. But with his swollen throat, he was hard to understand.

"How long have you been here?" Stinson asked.

Grant held up two fingers. "Scott and Callahan, about a year, and Christian, two. Those three," Grant rasped, glancing at the captives who appeared to be one step from dying. "I can't tell you. There used to be fifteen more of us, but they moved some north, I think, three months ago. We'll probably be moved, too."

Stinson surveyed his surroundings as he listened to Grant give him the lowdown.

"Don't talk to Christian," Grant whispered, motioning to the pilot sitting in the opposite corner. "Whatever you tell him, he'll tell them."

"Which of the Vietnamese speak English?" Stinson asked, glancing at Christian staring at the sky.

"That person's not here. He comes once a month to give instructions. He's the one who makes us talk."

"Makes us talk?" Stinson asked.

"Torture. And you will talk," Grant said, nodding. "We all do eventually, but it's what you say," he said conspiratorially, "that counts."

Stinson looked at Grant for more information.

"Tell them anything but the truth."

Stinson ran his hands through his hair. "Okay." It was even clearer what he needed to do.

***

It took Stinson a few days to understand his captor's routine. Each day in the morning, the Americans were given water with some kind of gruel. They were allowed to move around the compound for a few hours while being watched by at least two guards. Then they were herded back to their bamboo enclosure.

At mid-morning, one guard would take whoever was able to walk out to pick edible roots. There were one or two at most who made it. Although still feigning excruciating pain as he walked, Stinson volunteered.

"We need to start planning our escape," Stinson whispered to Grant.

Grant said nothing for a while. He finally looked at Stinson, inhaled, then exhaled, his eyes drooping and his voice was so low Stinson could hardly hear him. "I'd barely make it twenty yards. And you don't look like you'd make it much farther."

Stinson looked at Grant. "But I will, in time."

The second week, Robert Garson, one of the three, and the worst off, died. The VC hauled his body to the middle of the camp, rolled him onto Stinson's poncho and dragged him into the jungle.

Stinson felt his leg getting stronger, but not as sturdy as he needed it to be. He exercised and massaged it impatiently each day whenever the guards weren't around.

At the end of the third week, one of the VC caught Grant stealing food. Other than yelling at Grant, no one punished him, which Stinson thought was strange.

The fourth week, the English-speaking Viet Cong appeared. His khakis were pressed, and his boots shone. He stood tall and spoke in crisp, commanding words that had the guards scurrying to fulfill his commands. A yellow chevron with a red background on his sleeve indicated he was a lower-level officer.

Stinson braced himself mentally when the officer and two of his underlings approached. The officer looked at Stinson and then Grant, his eyes gleaming like a hyena eyeing a wounded prey. Grant whined softly. Suddenly, another of the officer's men ran up to him speaking rapidly. The officer hurried to a jeep and sped away from the compound.

The same day they pulled Grant from the hut. He screamed, "No, no, please, I'm sorry," as the guards beat him into silence with a bamboo pole. The silence lasted less than five minutes followed by an eerie wail that seemed to go on forever. Stinson shivered as the howling turned into horrifying screams that intensified, interspersed with "Oh, God!" before there was silence again. Grant did not return.

***

The first time Stinson felt well enough to attempt an escape was five weeks after his capture. But, Ortega Rivera, another of the soldiers in poor health, died. All the captors went on alert as if they anticipated some kind of an uprising.

A week later, Stinson's fear became a reality. He got sick. He couldn't keep any food down. He perspired constantly but felt no real pain, just a nagging cramp in his stomach. As thin as he had become, he figured he'd lost another ten pounds because of his illness, which caused him to defecate continuously. He looked at the emaciated bodies of the other prisoners and couldn't help but wonder if that would be his fate.

After close to a month of drinking as much water as his captors would allow and avoiding the chunks of rancid meat in the soup, Stinson's health improved and his strength slowly returned.

Six weeks later, the VC carried Private Armand's body away, the third of the soldiers in the worst of health, after two days of throwing up blood. After Armand's death, the guards argued among themselves. Stinson guessed their squabble concerned who was to blame. Dead captives didn't make as strong a statement as live ones.

One benefit came from the deaths. Stinson's leg had almost healed. He'd become healthier because of the upgrade in food. Instead of the usual foul-smelling soup, their captors had begun to feed them the same soup they ate.

The officer in charge had not returned, to Stinson's relief, and he had not been mistreated, probably because of the deaths.

The prisoners who could work were still sent out with a guard to obtain edible roots. Since they had dug up most of the roots near the compound, they had to go farther to find any. And when Stinson was placed back on detail, he made sure not to show his captors he had improved as much as he felt.

It was two months into his capture when Stinson was taken out during a light rain to dig for roots on his own. None of the other prisoners were in any shape to travel that far. As usual, Stinson dragged his leg and pretended to fall twice as they proceeded to an area about a half-mile from the compound.

The rain had subsided, leaving a light mist hovering over the trees. Except for the occasional chirp of a bird, the sounds in the surrounding jungle were muted. Stinson stretched his leg as he did every time after a long walk and began to dig.

The tool the prisoners were given was a trowel with a wooden handle and a scoop-shaped metal blade. Stinson balanced the trowel in his hand then gripped it tightly, testing his strength.

As he dug, he positioned his body so he could watch his guard who rested against a tree five yards away. The sun rays piercing through the mist caused Stinson to sweat profusely. His escort had leaned his weapon against a tree and barely looked his way.

After Stinson filled his basket, he picked it up and walked toward the guard who was sitting and picking his teeth. He looked up, motioning Stinson to head back toward camp. As the guard stood and turned to pick up his rifle, Stinson jumped him, shoving the trowel into his throat. The Viet Cong's eyes widened as he feebly reached for his weapon. Stinson kicked it away.

The trowel had pierced the guard's vocal cords allowing him to make only gurgling sounds as he tried to crawl toward the rifle. Stinson grabbed it, flipped out the bayonet, and stabbed him in the back. Looking to see if anyone had heard the struggle, Stinson dragged the body into a small ravine, covered it with leaves, and took off.

He had debated going back and killing the other guards, which would have given him more time to escape, but it would have been chancy. If they weren't all in one place, it would turn into a firefight he would probably lose. Plus, in his condition, he would need all the time and strength at his disposal. Even then the outcome would be a toss-up.

CHAPTER 68

October 2, 1969

"Do you know where you are?" the doctor asked.

"No," the man whispered.

"Then you probably don't remember how you got here."

The man's eyes narrowed as he tried to focus, looking around before turning back to the doctor. "No."

"You are at the 6th Convalescent Center in Cam Ranh Bay."

The man's forehead wrinkled as he looked around again, slowly. An orderly dropped a metal tray at the end of the hall, and the mam jumped at the noise.

The doctor frowned at the dropper, who hastily retrieved the tray and exited the large room.

"You are very lucky. You lost a lot of blood from three bullet holes in your back and shoulder. You also had some head trauma from a blunt object. Yet, here you are healing well. I expect if you continue to improve, you might be able to go home in a month or two."

The man lowered, and then raised his head slightly as the doctor checked his vitals again.

"That soldier has a strong constitution. He must have been an athlete in the past," the doctor said to the head nurse as they walked the hallway.

"I never got the full story on him," the nurse responded.

"According to a Sergeant Farrell, there was gunfire just outside their perimeter. He led a squad out to check and found our Sergeant Stinson lying in a pool of blood, gaunt, with no boots, wearing torn and dirty clothes as if he'd been living in the jungle most of his life.

"He looked more like a Montagnard peasant than a soldier. His appearance probably helped him make it back.

"He told Farrell he had escaped a POW camp. The sergeant drew a map of the camp on the ground and said 'You have to get them' before he passed out.

"It's good Farrell found him so quickly; otherwise, he'd be dead."

The nurse sighed. "He's one of the lucky ones, and I'm so glad. I'm tired of losing so many of these young soldiers."

The doctor turned to visit another patient, then stopped. "Oh. Something else. There were two dead VC twenty yards away. When Farrell checked the sergeant's weapon, it was empty. The sergeant had killed them with his last two bullets. If he had missed, he probably wouldn't be here."

The nurse shook her head. "I'd sure like to hear the rest of his story."

"You will if his memory returns, and I expect it will."

CHAPTER 69

November 15, 1969

Stinson's elbow bumped against the restroom stall door at the Seattle airport as he tried to change into his civilian clothes. Neither the faint stench of urine nor the tile floor speckled with spots where previous visitors had missed the toilet bothered him after the sights and smells he'd been subjected to. Even the grunts from two stalls over—probably due to constipation—were a welcome sound. They were the sounds of life in the United States.

With a Houdini-like effort, he made the switch. It was the first step in his self-imposed journey to remove the stench of war from his body then his mind. He felt a lot different about Vietnam when he departed than he did when he first arrived in that beautiful, dank land, and he wanted to remove any vestiges of that nightmare of an experience.

So many dead, and for what? He glanced in the mirror before he sat back in the wheelchair and flinched. He barely recognized the thin, wearied face staring back.

Even after changing clothes, the angst of war still seemed to hover over him like his personal rain cloud. There was no satisfaction in knowing he wasn't the only one affected. He remembered looking at the war-weary soldiers as he was wheeled to his seat on the first leg of the plane trip from Tan Son Nhut to Seattle, Washington. Even in their sleep they displayed a bone-tired fatigue. Some sat staring straight ahead, a few talked, but only another sergeant, his seat mate, babbled as if he would be shipped back if he ever stopped. So Stinson slept, or at least tried to, through the entire flight.

***

Stinson sat at the half-filled airport restaurant in a corner, his back to the wall, slowly sipping a Coke, envying the people who walked past the restaurant entrance. Some bounced along, a few engaged in animated conversation, and others walked quietly but confidently to their destinations, all of them looked…comfortable.

Stinson rapped a beat on the table with his fingers as he hummed a song whose title escaped him. It had been the only melody he remembered during his ordeal. He continued to hum to alleviate the anxiety of returning home. It wasn't that he didn't look forward to seeing Darlene and his son, Jerome; it was just that he wasn't ready.

What he really wanted to do was to go somewhere and continue his sleep—hopefully, a dreamless one. The Army had informed Darlene he was coming. He hoped she didn't want to celebrate, but he couldn't deprive her if she did. Yet he wondered how she would feel about him when she finally saw him. They were going to take him to the VA hospital first. Stinson looked at the clock. He'd call her once he got settled.

"You're ready to board, sir. I'll wheel you over to the boarding area, and they'll take it from there," an older, dignified attendant said.

Time already? A slender thread of apprehension weaved its way into the weariness that had become his constant companion. He paid his bill and grabbed the carry-on he had bought to replace the Army-issued duffle bag, now the resident of an airport waste receptacle.

There were people everywhere, more people than he was ready to handle. Stinson lowered his head as the attendant wheeled Stinson toward them, joining the milling throng, lost in a swirl of thoughts. Somewhere during his tour, he had come to hate crowds. Unlike the jungle, the jumble of people lurching toward their destination felt confining.

Right before he reached his gate, he watched as three men bumped an army sergeant E-6 wearing his Class A uniform, simultaneously. The sergeant cursed before his arm shot out to grab the man on his left.

The lean, long-haired man wearing sunglasses tried to jerk back, but the sergeant's grip on the front of his loose-fitting yellow-and-green silk shirt immobilized him. His two friends turned to rush the soldier, but hesitated.

Stinson understood. He'd seen the look on the sergeant's face and sensed his need to lash out. The men paused, seeing something in the soldier's lean, muscular body that signaled almost an eagerness to take them on. The crowd shifted, and the noise swelled as those closest looked on.

The long-haired man tried to jerk away once more before his eyes met the segeant's. There was a flicker of resignation as a wallet magically appeared in the thief's hands. The sergeant took it without releasing the man, flipped it open with his right hand to inventory the contents, slid it back into his pocket, and pushed the man away.

The sergeant didn't even turn at the noise of shoe leather slipping on the tile and the dull thump of a body hitting the ground. "Civilians. They'll never understand," the soldier muttered.

"Roger that," Stinson said to himself, smiling.

The noise level lowered, and the people in the crowd continued moving toward their respective destinations.

It seemed like everyone who was in the concourse was lining up to board Stinson's plane. Disappointed the airplane would be crowded, Stinson hoped whomever he sat next to wouldn't be a talker. If he could grab a few hours' sleep, maybe he would feel better by the time he arrived in Cleveland.

"War is hell, ain't it, troop?" the lean, dark-faced passenger with a scar along the right side of his face said as he sank into the seat next to Stinson.

"How'd you know I served?"

"No one gets their hair cut like yours on purpose. Colonel Roger McPherson. Welcome home."

For some reason, Stinson felt relieved. "Sergeant Willie Stinson. Thank you, sir."

The colonel glanced at Stinson and smiled. "Sergeants, the backbone of the Army."

Stinson remained silent.

"Stationed?" the colonel asked.

"Cu Chi, 25th Infantry Division, was with the Wolfhounds for a while, sir."

"General Ellis W. Williamson." The colonel paused. "I lost a lot of men saving one of his battalion's asses at Parrot's Beak."

Stinson stared out of the window. "You think it was worth it, Colonel?"

"What, saving their asses?"

"No," Stinson responded, "the war. Was the war worth it?"

Colonel McPherson sighed wearily. "Only time will tell, son."

Both, lost in their own thoughts, eventually dozed off without saying another word until the plane landed. The colonel turned to Stinson as he stood to depart. "You gonna be okay, Sergeant?"

"Yes, sir."

McPherson looked at Stinson as a father would a child. "Son, each of us carries a heavy weight from combat."

Stinson looked down and nodded.

"Remember one thing."

"Yes, sir?"

"You are not alone."

"Yes, sir."

As Stinson looked up to watch the colonel, erect and proud, stride toward the plane's exit, he wondered why he hadn't noticed it before. Maybe because the colonel's bearing belied the obvious, but it was evident now. Colonel McPherson's left arm was missing. Stinson sat and watched as all the anguish he'd felt temporarily lifted like a fog being blown away by a gentle wind.

CHAPTER 70

S tinson gazed out the plane's window and watched as a black lady ran across the tarmac. His first thought was a question. How did she get there? His second thought was that he hoped she caught whatever she was chasing. But as she got closer, Stinson's eyes widened. It was his wife.

The hydraulic lift lowered Stinson as Darlene stood waiting, tears pouring. As soon as his wheelchair hit the ground, she rushed him, smothering him with kisses and hugs.

"How'd you know when I was arriving?" he asked.

"The Army called me, but nobody could tell me a time, so I called all the airlines until I found your flight. "I was a mess. They had you listed as missing in action, then killed in action, and then when they told me they'd found you, I lost it. I guess I scared our child to death."

"Yeah, I can imagine."

"They told me not to worry when I saw you in a wheelchair because it was temporary," Darlene said, making a statement and asking a question at the same time.

"I can walk now."

"No! I know you, Willie. They said to make sure you stay confined to this chair until the doctors have evaluated you."

"Where's Jerome?"

"Aunt Francine is bringing him to the hospital. Why didn't you call?"

"I was after I got to the hospital. I was hoping I'd be standing when you came."

"You don't stand until they say you can, Willie, and that's an order," she said sternly.

Stinson grinned as he looked at Darlene. Seeing her had fulfilled all his wishes. While recovering in Cam Ranh Bay, he had received an unofficial visit from a Cornell Latimore, an adjutant general clerk in Cu Chi.

"I'm two weeks short," Latimore confided, "and I see this name come across my desk. There were rumors about you and the others, but until I saw your name, I didn't put much stock in them. So now I see it's true. Y'all survived that mission. I wanted to come meet you before I got out of here, Sarge."

"Do you mind?" Latimore asked, pointing to a chair near the bed.

"No. Have a seat."

"Where were you exactly, Sarge?"

"Somewhere in Cambodia, I understand."

"So that's true, too."

"What did you mean by y'all?"

Latimore handed Stinson a piece of paper. "I figured you'd ask. As far as I can tell from an MP friend, here's who I know made it."

Stinson read the handwritten note: Casper, Glover, Robinson, Warfield, Turner, Bankston, and Holland. He frowned as he leaned back in his bed. "Just seven?"

Latimore raised his hands.

But considering the circumstances, Stinson was grateful any had made it. "Seven." He took a deep breath before exhaling.

***

Darlene didn't know how to tell her husband tactfully, so she blurted it out, "They had your funeral last week."

"They must have found the body."

"What body?"

"When I was in the jungle, I saw a black soldier's body. It was pretty messed up. He was air force, according to his uniform. I buried his clothes, dressed him in my shirt, and put my dog tags on him. I hoped that if the VC found him, they would think they'd found me."

"Wow."

"It seemed to work until I ran into two VC scouts a few hundred yards from a firebase." Stinson placed his hands on hers. "I'm sorry to have put you through that."

"It's okay now; you're here." Darlene rubbed his shoulder. "Reverend Jemison gave the eulogy."

"Little Eddie Jemison?"

"Yes."

"How'd he ever become a preacher?"

"Like most, I guess. He was called."

Stinson sniffed.

"He was all I could afford, honey."

Stinson patted her hand. "It's fine, Darlene. It didn't count anyway." Stinson was silent for a moment, then chuckled. "I wish I could have been there."

"Oh, Willie. No you don't. You would have scared those people to death."

"Who was there?"

"Johnny Mack, the Carsons, Phillip Johnson and his lady, Maurice. Gladys is bringing the guest book over later. Then, there were eight men s in the back. They made a commotion about something before settling down."

Stinson raised his head. "What did they look like?"

"I remember one real big guy. One of the short guys looked like Sammy Davis, Jr., one...

"Do me a favor, baby," Stinson said, fingering the paper Latimore had given him. "I need a phone book."

CHAPTER 71

"Any story on the Colonel Bertram case?" Bill Walden asked Anthony as they both sat in Walden's office reviewing a story Anthony was working on.

"Yeah, Bill, but it goes beyond Bertram. The story I want to write begins and ends with Bertram, but it's actually about fifteen black soldiers sent on a mission they weren't expected to survive."

"Okay. So, the information you've been seeking is coming together?"

"Yeah. Finally. It's a story about an unbelievable journey by primarily support personnel who only learned to soldier while in the field. It's a story about a sergeant who showed them what it took to be men first and a team second. It's a story of survival."

Walden put down a sheaf of papers. "Tell me more."

Anthony took Walden through the whole story.

"Jesus. And all this is documented, sourced?"

"Yes. Bertram and the men were very helpful, very open."

"When will I have it?"

"You'll get it by Friday of next week, Bill. I've already written it in my head."

"If it's anything like you've described, you'll probably want to write more than a story for the press."

"I plan on it."

***

A Long Way Back—A Story of The Seven

By Anthony J. Andrews

This is the story of seven survivors of an ill-conceived mission created to punish soldiers involved in a brawl at Cu Chi in June 1969.

Vietnam was America's first fully integrated campaign. This created chaos in some parts of this Asian country since the war coincided with the rise of the black power and the Civil Rights movements. Further complications arose when the draft, which some labeled discriminatory, accounted for an increasing number of African Americans called to service.

Alleged discrimination and animosity between some of the black and white troops in Vietnam, combined with the established white power element rubbing against the growing black power movement, heightened racial tension. This hardened the solidarity among each of the groups while eroding the amity the army attempted to preach: "We're not white or black, we're green."

Cross burnings, the flying of the Confederate flag, and other highly inflammatory displays were countered with black power fists and peace signs painted on helmets, constant flouting of hair regulations, black-only barracks and dapping (the power handshake) among the black soldiers.

The combination of clashing symbols, conflicting ideologies, and real and perceived biases caused fights, shootings, fraggings (injuring or killing a fellow soldier, often officers and NCOs, generally with grenades), and even riots.

Although there doesn't appear to be any definitive record of the frequency of riots in Vietnam, there were a number, including the Long Binh stockade riot in 1968; Qui Nhon in 1968; Cam Ranh Bay in 1968, where some Navy personnel donned Ku Klux Klan attire after the assassination of Dr. King; Cam Ranh Bay in 1969; and the USS Kitty Hawke in 1972.

The grievances were dealt with by officers in a myriad of ways. Some conceded discrimination existed and launched reforms to improve the conditions of black servicemen who complained of being assigned to more combat, given menial jobs, unequal promotions, and disproportionate punishment. Others ignored the complaints and punished those who protested. A few found more unique ways of dealing with those they accused of causing the unrest. This is one of those stories…

CHAPTER 72

Bertram stood as the men entered the Virginia State Penitentiary visiting area. Anthony shook Bertram's hand. "I told them I had someone I wanted them to meet."

Casper extended his hand. "Sir, so glad to meet you."

"I'm no longer a sir, son, just Prisoner 1458409."

Warfield extended his hand, too. "We know what you did, and we wanted to show our appreciation."

Bertram smiled broadly as he looked at the seven former soldiers. "Anthony told me I had a surprise visit, but…" He looked at Anthony. "How were you able to get all of them in here, Anthony?"

"Believe it or not, Colonel, you have admirers here. The warden is a Korean War vet, so he understands," Anthony responded.

"It must have cost a bunch to get these men down here."

Anthony laughed. "Not really. I received a raise. It covered the car rentals. I figured you are worth that and more."

"Look, if you ever need anything, Anthony is not the only person you can call on, okay, sir?" Robinson handed Bertram a paper with their names and telephone numbers. "We don't live around here, but we have friends who do."

Bertram stood as if to hug Robinson, but glanced at the guards and said, "Thanks, guys. You don't know how much I appreciate the gesture."

"If it weren't for you, sir," Turner said, "our lives going forward would have been a monumental struggle."

Bertram smiled. "I'm glad I helped."

"Time's up," the guard said.

The men stood and saluted as they led Bertram away. Bertram beamed and saluted back.

CHAPTER 73

Ly Trung Trac's primary goal was peace of mind. She knew she was the only one who could achieve it, nurturing and coddling it until it grew large enough to protect her, bathe her in its beatific light, and buffer her from the horrific sounds of men and their weapons, the ghastly smell of death and defecation, and the grisly sight of mangled and twisted bodies. Only she could grow this peace.

But she was impatient because it hadn't grown quickly enough. It was like a water buffalo calf, stumbling, gaining its footing, then wobbling a step or two instead of the graceful, powerful giant she hoped it would become, protecting her mind and spirit from the dark, butting away the horrid blackness that crept through her defenses at night.

Her hair had grown long again, her beauty unmarred as she gazed in the Boeing 707 washroom mirror. It was a wonder the darkness inside hadn't surfaced, disfiguring her skin like some disease. Trung sighed. She should have felt proud of her accomplishments. The Americans had named her "The Black Tigress" because of her prowess in battle and her clothing. Her tactics had been simple: When the enemy advanced, they retreat; when the enemy camps, they harass; when the enemy tires, they attack; when the enemy retreats, they pursue.

Her superiors relayed messages to Trung on how she was revered by her countrymen and feared by the invaders. They shared that even rumors of a Black Tigress sighting caused enemy battalions to go on alert.

Before the misfortune with the black soldiers, Trung had been victorious in almost every other encounter with the Americans, losing just five men in sixteen skirmishes. Her strength was hit-and-run, and she did it best with a small group, attacking troops on the move.

When she had been given forty men—the most she'd ever led—Trung had not only lost twenty-nine in Cambodia, but she had been shot.

"Excuse me," she said in the softest of voices to her elderly male seatmate as she slid into her window seat. She looked at the vastness of space, the clouds and the shafts of light that pierced their denseness. She had been like that light in battle—except for the one time in Cambodia.

When she first encountered the black soldiers, they were undisciplined, unruly, and unready. But within a week, like the cub that becomes the tiger, they had grown. The men had become so adept she had lost face because of her inability to crush them.

What happened, though, that the bumblers had become a force? What changed?

Although it was a question she had asked before, Trung had since guessed the answer—the one who stayed behind, the warrior. From his fierceness under fire, he had to be their leader. It was obvious he'd been wounded from the blood on the foliage and soil, but he'd held them off for more than ten minutes, killing five more of her men before disappearing. To where?

It was like the magic show she had seen once as a child where the conjurer waved his hand, saying "poof," making a whole pig disappear. Trung was incensed they hadn't found the leader when the firefight ended. And in their search for him, they had lost track of the remaining men. And when her men did find them…

A grimace flashed across her face. It didn't matter now, though. Soon she would enter the belly of the beast, as Uncle Hong had described her destination. Her only concern would be traveling to a new place, hoping her forged identity would not be uncovered. She was apprehensive yet optimistic as she looked forward to life in a new world.

The trip was necessary because of the large reward the Americans and South Vietnamese government had placed on her. With so much money at stake, even the most loyal of comrades might have been tempted. Then there were the wounds she had sustained in her last battle. She was no longer of any worth to the war effort because of her shattered leg and arm.

Her mother, father, and Uncle Hong, a businessman who had prospered selling weapons to the North Vietnamese, provided her with the names of relatives living in the States.

"You served well," her uncle had told her while she lay recovering in a cousin's village hut after being treated in an underground hospital. "I convinced the North it is best you depart this country and leave your legacy intact. It would do the cause no good to see you in this condition—or, worse, caught. And the United States is the last place anyone would look. Like your famous namesake, your compatriots will sing of your triumphs for years to come," Uncle Hong had said as he provided Trung her passport and funds.

Once she was able, Trung traveled through Laos to China to be treated further. After healing and much deliberation, she agreed the United States should be her final destination since she had family there.

As the plane descended, she watched a migrating flock of swallows fly in formation. Unlike the birds, she would probably never return to her home. Her mother had cried when Trung gave her goodbyes, hugging her so hard it had hurt. Mother knew.

Trung leaned back into the seat. Although serenity was her goal, could she ever achieve it without avenging the deaths of her kin, of her beloved soldiers? Would she ever gain peace until the American soldiers had paid for the death and destruction they had wrought?

She clenched her hands as she tried to contain the bitterness sweeping through her. Her homeland was destroyed by invaders, and the men she had fought represented all that was bad with America. What was there to gain for them?

They would go home and live satisfying lives while her countrymen suffered—but not if she could help it. She had seen the faces of some of those men, and she would remember. And if they ever reappeared in her new life, they would remember her.

CHAPTER 74

Stop playin', man."

"I'm not, Casper. I swear. Sarge just called me," Holland said.

"What you been smokin'?"

"Nothing!"

Casper paused. "Who's there with you?"

"Nobody, man. I swear. This ain't no joke, Casper. Sarge is alive."

"Holland, we just attended his funeral."

"I know, man, but would I lie to you about something like that?"

"Then somebody's playing a joke on *you*. What'd they say?"

"They said, 'Holland, are you sitting down?' Nobody's got a voice like Sarge. I said, 'Sarge?' And he says, 'It's me.' Man, I almost fainted."

Casper was silent on the other end.

"Casper? Casper?"

"Where is he?"

"He's at the VA hospital."

***

The tears were contagious as Glover, Casper, and Robinson stood in the waiting area. "Holland and Turner are on their way." Casper sniffed. "Warfield had to work."

"On Sunday?" Robinson asked.

"Yeah. A new job."

"Well, I hope they handle this better than you guys," Stinson muttered as Darlene wheeled him down the hallway toward the waiting room. "Warriors don't cry. Damn!"

"Sarge," they cried out in unison before bawling outright as they tripped over one another running to hug him.

Stinson shook his head. "All that talk I gave you about manhood, and this is how you turn out, some snuffy-nosed momma's babies?"

"Sorry, Sarge. You just don't know, man," Casper said, walking beside him. "I ain't ashamed. You just don't know, Sarge."

"All we talk about is what you were to us, what you did for us, what you taught us, how you saved our lives," Glover said, wiping his eyes. "I ain't ashamed either."

The men sat and looked at Stinson for a while, smiling and pulling tissue from the dispenser one after another.

Holland, Turner, and Warfield rushed in together. "Sarge," they yelled as they smothered him.

"Hey, hey," Stinson said playfully fending them off. "I almost got hugged to death by them three clowns, now you going to finish the job?"

"How'd you find Warfield?" Casper asked.

"He walked off the job. Told his boss he had some serious family business to attend to," Holland answered.

"I hope you have a job when you go back," Sarge said.

Warfield raised his hands. "Don't matter, Sarge. This was way more important."

"Men, meet my wife, Darlene."

She hugged each of the men. "Willie has told me about each of you."

"How, Sarge?" Casper asked.

"Yeah, Sarge. How'd you make it out?" Robinson asked. "Last we heard there were all kinds of weapons going off, then silence."

Stinson leaned back in his wheelchair. "I was hoping you wouldn't blame Casper for leaving me behind as I demanded."

"Negative, Sarge. We figured it out. And we knew how pigheaded you could be," Warfield said.

"But what happened after?" Holland asked.

Stinson rubbed his furrowed brow, shook his head slowly, and stared at the wall. "I don't remember everything. I do remember being saved—by these Cambodians, I guess. I can't remember how long I stayed in this hole in the ground. They gave me food and treated my wounds. Once I got better, I tried to make it back but got captured.

"They took me to this POW camp, but I escaped, moving as best I could, and hiding in the jungle. I remember VC chasing me. I remember getting shot. I remember shooting, before falling into this gully

367

and headfirst into a rock, tree, or something. When I woke up, I was in Cam Ranh Bay. I swore it was heaven."

Casper beamed. "If anybody was going to make it, it would be you."

Stinson looked at the men. "I always felt like I would. This one song kept playing in my head."

"What song, Sarge?" Holland asked.

Stinson hummed the song.

Glover laughed. "It's 'Keep On Pushing by the Impressions. It's what Casper told us when we didn't think we could go any farther."

Stinson laughed, too. "Yeah? It's the subconscious working. Right, Turner?"

"Right, Sarge."

***

It was like a slab of concrete was removed from Turner's brain. No more wondering about Sarge. No more questioning himself. It felt so good to be so wrong.

***

Stinson laughed. "Plus, I didn't want Fletcher to make me out a liar."

"About what, Sarge?" Holland asked.

"I remember," Casper said. "You told him one of us will die out here, and it won't be me."

Stinson grimaced. "Something like that."

"Well, you were right," Warfield said.

"I'm aware. And I hate that because I felt responsible for all of you, including Fletcher."

Stinson looked at each of them. "So there were seven of you?"

The men nodded.

"Bankston made it, too?"

"Yeah, Sarge. He had to go back to Mississippi to pick up some items he'd forgotten, but when he called Casper and Casper told him about you, he turned around and started driving back. He should be here some time tomorrow," Glover said.

"So tell me your story. How'd you make it back?" Stinson asked.

"Our story is as wild as yours. I don't think they could write a novel about you or us and make it believable," Turner said.

***

Darlene handed Stinson the phone after the two had returned to his room. "It's for you, honey."

"Sergeant Stinson?"

"Yes."

"This is Anthony Andrews, a reporter at the *Washington Post*. I've been following the story of you and your soldiers since they returned to base camp. I just heard. This is incredible. We thought we had buried you. I'm so grateful to hear your voice."

369

"Thank you, Anthony. My men briefed me on how you helped them, and I want to tell you, I'm eternally thankful."

"My part was easy. You're the one who kept them alive."

"That's what they tell me, but in the end, they kept themselves alive."

"I'll be in Cleveland next weekend. My first priority will be to meet you. I definitely want to meet the guy who saved soldiers' lives without even being there." Anthony paused. "There's another person eager to see you, too. He'll be visiting you today if he's not already there."

"Who's that?"

"He should be there shortly. Be well," Anthony said as he hung up the phone.

Stinson looked up at the knock. A familiar face peeked in.

"Permission to enter?"

"Raymond!" Stinson tried to stand, but Darlene held him down.

After chewing out his men for crying, Stinson had to hold back his own tears. "Raymond, you don't know how glad I am to see you."

"I'm surprised, since you'd been dodging me since you left Thornewood Avenue," Raymond said, laughing. "This must be Darlene." He turned to embrace her.

"Pardon my French, ma'am," Raymond said to Darlene before addressing his boyhood friend, "but you look like shit."

Stinson chuckled. "Same old Raymond. But it's not as bad as it looks. I can still beat your ass."

Raymond laughed and embraced Stinson. "Same old Willie. It's been a long time."

Darlene held Raymond's hand. "I've heard so much about you, Raymond. He talks about you nonstop. It's as if you were a part of the family."

"I know I've got some explaining to do," Stinson said.

Raymond pulled a seat next to Stinson's wheelchair. "So, explain."

Stinson looked out the window, gathering his thoughts. "You were the best friend I had, Raymond. I cried when I had to leave Thornewood. It felt good living there, but I was embarrassed, too. You had your life together, and I didn't."

Stinson paused. "And it kept getting worse. I kept traveling in the wrong direction—fighting, gangbanging, robbing."

Raymond laughed. "I heard about some of your exploits."

"The best thing that happened to me was Darlene, so I joined the service before I hit bottom. I thought it would help me get my life back together so I could come home and take care of my family."

"I thought about you a lot over the years, wondering where you were, how you were doing," Raymond said.

"The same with me."

"I was looking for you because I needed to tell you what that year and a half we spent together meant to me, and I wanted to tell you how much of an influence you were on me."

"Really?" Stinson asked.

"Seems like that's your calling, brother."

Stinson chuckled. "Seems like it."

"Did you know I was in the service, too?"

Stinson looked up. "When?"

"Got out over a year ago."

"That's a shame."

"Why's that?"

"We would have made a helluva team over there."

Raymond laughed. "You better believe it, brother."

CHAPTER 75

December 13, 1969

Walden patted Anthony on his back as they sat at a table with some of the *Post's* staff, Anthony's wife, Carla, and his daughter, Mali, during the *Post's* annual Christmas party. "Your article about those seven soldiers is finally getting some legs, Anthony."

"It's about time. I sent it to the Pentagon, the State Department, the Joint Chiefs of Staff, and some members of Congress. I even sent it to President Nixon."

Walden grimaced. "I already know how that went."

"I did get a response."

"I hoped you would," Leonard Shanklar said. "It's a shame how they treated those soldiers."

"Not the kind of response I wanted, though," Anthony responded. "Members of the House Armed Services Subcommittee denied anything like that incident could ever happen, that the story was designed to create more racial tension and stoke more protests against the war."

"Typical," Walden said. "Our boss, Bradlee, had a problem with the article, too, but the senior staff rose to your defense, including Shanklar."

Anderson nodded at Shanklar. "I'm grateful, because I wondered about Bradlee."

Walden chuckled. "Not to worry."

"Congressman Stokes from Cleveland was the only person to respond positively," Anthony continued. "After he obtained more information and met with the survivors, he requested an inquiry. They stonewalled him at every turn, but the congressman was persistent."

"Like you." Walden laughed.

"When he called me a month ago to say The Seven were being interviewed by the Inspector General along with Major Tilden, General Wyatt, Colonel Bertram, General Bolt, and several of General Bolt's former staff members, I knew we had broken through," Anthony said.

"Anthony picked us up and danced us around the room for fifteen minutes," Carla laughed.

"I've always been a little leery of the army meting out punishment to its own, especially top brass," Walden said.

Anthony slid his hand around Carla's waist. "Except this embarrassed the President after The Seven were the cover story in both *Time* and *Newsweek*. CBS ran a Mike Wallace interview with Colonel Bertram, and it's been run in at least ten major newspapers throughout the country."

"Since Nixon said no troops were ever in Cambodia in 1969, he had some explaining to do. Guess who's going to have to fall on their swords?" Walden asked.

"Let's hope so. By the way, I was able to obtain this from General Westmoreland," Walden said with a sly smile.

DEPARTMENT OF THE ARMY

WASHINGTON, D.C. 20310

1 December 1969

MEMORANDUM FOR LIEUTENANT GENERAL WILLIAM F. FARRIS

SUBJECT: Directive for Investigation

Confirming oral instructions given you on 24 November 1969, you are directed to explore the nature and the scope of the original U.S. Army investigations of the alleged Cambodian incursion incident that occurred between 18 June 1969 and 30 June 1969. Your investigation will include a determination of the adequacy of the investigation(s) or inquiries on this subject, their subsequent reviews and reports within the chain of command, and possible suppression or withholding of information by persons involved in the incident.

Your investigation will be concerned with the time period beginning January 1969 until Mr. Anthony Andrews sent his letter, dated 27 October 1969, to the Secretary of Defense and others. The scope of your investigation does not include, nor will it interfere with, ongoing criminal investigations in progress.

The procedures contained in AR 15-6 are authorized for such use as may be required.

You are authorized to select and use on a full-time basis officer and civilian members of the Army whom you deem necessary for the conduct of the investigation. Your deputy is designated as Mr. Charles Carson, Assistant General Counsel, Department of the Army. Should you require other assistance, please let us know.

You will inform us at an early date of the expected completion date of your report.

W.C. WESTMORELAND	STANLEY R. RESOR
General, U. S. Army	Secretary of the Army
Chief of Staff	

"Whoa!" Anthony said, punching Walden playfully on the arm.

"I thought this would be an appropriate gift since the Worth Bing-ham Award Ceremony is not until next year."

Anthony laughed as he held the paper, reading it again before handing it to Carla. "If this bears fruit, these two," he said, hugging his wife and daughter, "the redemption of The Seven, and the proper punishment to whoever was involved will be the only award I'll ever need."

CHAPTER 76

Anthony received good news twice in one day. His book, *A Long Way Back*, was picked up by the first publisher his agent contacted. Then he received an unexpected call.

"Mr. Andrews?"

"Yes."

"Myron Turner."

It had been months since Anthony had talked to any of the men, and Turner's voice didn't sound like he was conveying any good news. But then, he never did.

"Yes, Turner. How are you? How are you getting along?"

"Better."

Same old Turner, Anthony thought. Spare with his words.

"How can I help you?"

"Has anybody else called you recently?"

"No."

"I got two items in the mail today, and I wanted to thank you."

"What items?"

"Honorable Discharge papers."

"Yeah? Great, and?"

"A bronze star."

"Bronze?"

"Yes. For valor."

"Wow. That's fantastic! Man. I'm so proud of you!"

"Thanks. I'm guessing the others received the same."

"I hope so, but Myron?"

"Yes?"

"You only got what you deserved."

EPILOGUE

Anthony sat at the nominees' table with Carla, Mali, Bill Bradlee, Leonard Shanklar, Bill Walden, and Bradlee's secretary, Mariann Worley, and clapped as Seymour M. Hersh of *Dispatch News Service* received the Worth Bingham Prize in the international reporting category for his story on the tragedy of My Lai, Vietnam. Carla held Anthony's right hand, and Mali held his left.

Carla patted him on the knee as the recipient gave his acceptance speech. "Well, at least you were nominated," Carla said as she kissed him on the cheek.

Anthony smiled at his wife. "Seymour deserved it."

"No regrets, then?" Carla asked.

"Just one. I would like to have dedicated my speech to a few people."

"Other than The Seven?"

"Yep. The seven who made it, Sergeant Stinson, and the seven who didn't, Arne Nielson, the reporter I told you about, war correspondents in general, and all the soldiers who served, especially those who died."

"I thought you should have won, Anthony," Ben Bradlee whispered, "even though I might be a little biased."

Anthony laughed. "This will make me work harder, Ben. I haven't gotten there yet, but I've seen the top of the mountain."

"It's okay, Dad. They've got more awards where that one came from," Mali said so sternly that those around Anthony had to muffle their laughter.

Walden slipped Anthony a note. "Bolt was demoted to major. He's in the hospital with a severe stroke."

"He would have had one earlier if he had been in the same hell he put those soldiers."

"Anthony!" Carla whispered. "Be kind."

"I will, baby. I will."

J. Everett Prewitt is the author of the acclaimed and award winning novel, *Snake Walkers.* He received his Bachelor of Arts degree from Lincoln University in Pennsylvania and Master of Science degree from Cleveland State University. He received the Distinguished Alumni award from both schools. Everett was an army officer and served in Vietnam during the years 1968 and 1969. He currently resides in Cleveland, Ohio.

www.eprewitt.com

Jacket Photograph:	© Kevin Renes: Dreamstime.com
Jacket Rendition	Michael Hrvatin
Author Photograph:	Rodney Brown

CPSIA information can be obtained
at www.ICGtesting.com
Printed in the USA
LVOW12*1619180816

500934LV00009B/74/P